Bear
Bear, Elizabeth
The sea thy mistress

$25.99
ocn659236375
1st ed.   02/02/2011

The Sea Thy Mistress

Tor Books by Elizabeth Bear

A Companion to Wolves (with Sarah Monette)
All the Windwracked Stars
By the Mountain Bound

The Sea Thy Mistress

Elizabeth Bear

A Tom Doherty Associates Book
New York

THE SEA THY MISTRESS

Copyright © 2011 by Elizabeth Bear

A Tor Book
Published by Tom Doherty Associates, LLC
175 Fifth Avenue
New York, NY 10010

www.tor-forge.com

Tor® is a registered trademark of Tom Doherty Associates, LLC.

Library of Congress Cataloging-in-Publication Data

Bear, Elizabeth.
 The sea thy mistress / Elizabeth Bear.—1st ed.
  p. cm.
 "A Tom Doherty Associates book."
 Sequel to: All the windwracked stars.
 ISBN 978-0-7653-1884-8
 I. Title.
PS3602.E2475S43 2011
813'.6—dc22

                                    2010035746

First Edition: February 2011

Printed in the United States of America

0 9 8 7 6 5 4 3 2 1

For my Mom

BOOK ONE

Binding

34 A.R. (After Rekindling)
On the First Day of Spring

An old man with radiation scars surrounding the chromed half of his face limped down a salt-grass-covered dune. Metal armatures creaked under his clothing as he thumped across dry sand to wet, scuffing through the black and white line of the high-tide boundary, where the sharp albedo of cast-up teeth tangled in film-shiny ribbons of kelp. About his feet, small combers glittered in the light of a gibbous moon. Above, the sky was deepest indigo; the stars were breathtakingly bright.

The old man, whose name was Aethelred, fetched up against a large piece of sea wrack, perhaps the wooden keel of some long-ago ship, and made a little ceremony of seating himself. He relied heavily on his staff until his bad leg was settled, and then he sighed in relief and leaned back, stretching and spreading his robes around him.

He stared over the ocean in silence until the moon was halfway down the sky. Then he reached out his staff and tapped at the oscillating edge of the water as if rapping on a door.

He seemed to think about his words very hard. "What I came to say was, I was mad at you at the time, for Cahey's sake . . . but I had some time to think about it after you changed, and he . . . changed, you know. And I've got to say, I think now that was a real . . . a real grown-up thing you did back there. A real grown-up thing.

"So. I know it isn't what you hold with, but we're building you a church. Not because you need it, but because other folks will."

A breaker slightly larger than the others curled up at his feet, tapping the toes of his boots like a playful kitten.

"I know," he said, "but somebody had to write it down. The generation after me, and the one after that . . . You know, Muire. It was you wrote it down the last time."

He frowned at his hands, remembering reading her words, her own self-effacement from the history she'd created. He fell silent for a moment, alone with the waves that came and went and went and came and seemed to take no notice of him. "I guess you know about writing things down."

He sighed, resettled himself on his improvised driftwood bench. He took a big breath of clean salt air and let it out again with a whistle.

"See, there's kids who don't remember how it was before, how it was when the whole world was dying. People forget so quick. But it's not like the old knowledge is gone. The library is still there. The machines will still work. It's all just been misplaced for a time. And I thought, folks are scattering, and the right things would get forgotten and the wrong things might get remembered, and you know how it is. So I wanted folks to know what you did. I hope you can forgive me."

He listened, and heard no answer—or maybe he could have imagined one, but it was anyone's guess if it was a chuckle or just the rattle of water among stones.

"So I got with this moreau—they're not so bad, I guess: they helped keep order when things got weird after you . . . got translated, and if they've got some odd habits, well, so do I. His name is Borje; he says you kissed him in a stairwell once—you remember that?"

The waves rolled up the shore: the tide neither rose nor fell.

"Anyway, he's not much of a conversationalist. But he cares a lot about taking care of people. After you . . . left . . . nobody really had any idea what they should be doing. With the Technomancer dead and the crops growing again, some people tried to take advantage. The moreaux handled that, but Borje and I, we thought we should write down about the Desolation, so people would remember for next time." He shrugged. "People being what people are, it probably won't make any difference. But there you go."

The moon was setting over the ocean.

When Aethelred spoke again, there was a softer tone in his voice. "And we wrote about you, because we thought people should know what you gave up for them. That it might make a difference in the way they thought, if they knew somebody cared that much about them. And that's why we're building a church, because folks need a place to go. Even though I know you wouldn't like it. Sorry about that part. It won't be anything fancy, though; I promise. More like a library or something."

He struggled to his feet, leaning heavily on the staff to do it. He stepped away, and the ocean seemed to take no notice, and then he stopped and looked back over his shoulder at the scalloped water.

A long silence followed. The waves hissed against the sand. The night was broken by a wailing cry.

The old man jerked upright. His head swiveled from side to side as he shuffled a few hurried steps. The sound came again, keen and thoughtless as the cry of a gull, and this time he managed to locate the source: a dark huddle cast up on the moonlit beach, not too far away. Something glittered in the sand beside it.

Leaning on his staff, he made haste toward it, stumping along at a good clip with his staff.

It was a tangle of seaweed. It was hard to tell in the darkness, but he thought the tangle was moving slightly.

He could move fast enough, despite the limp, but when he bent down he was painfully stiff, leveraging himself with his staff. The weight of his reconstructed body made him ponderous, and were he careless his touch could be anything but delicate. Ever-so-cautiously, he dug through the bundle with his other hand. His fingers fastened on something damp and cool and resilient.

It kicked.

Faster now, he shoved the seaweed aside. A moment, and he had it: wet skin, flailing limbs, lips stretched open in a cry of outrage. He slid his meaty hand under the tiny newborn infant, scooping it up still wrapped in its swaddling of kelp. After leaning the staff in the crook of his other elbow, he slipped a massive pinkie finger into its gaping mouth with an expertise that would have surprised no one who knew him. The ergonomics of the situation meant both his hands were engaged, which for the time being meant as well that both he and the infant were trapped where they stood on the sand.

"Well, this is a fine predicament, young man," Aethelred muttered.

At last, the slackening of suction on his finger told him the baby slept. Aethelred balanced the child on one hand, laid his staff down, and picked up the sheathed, brass-hilted sword that rested nearby in the sand.

"Heh," he said. "I recognize that." He shoved the blade through the tapestry rope that bound his waist.

With the help of his reclaimed staff, the old man straightened. Sand and seaweed clung to the hem of his robes.

The baby blinked at the old man with wide, wondering eyes, eyes that filled with light like the glints shot through the indigo ocean, the indigo night. The old man had a premonition that this child's eyes would not fade to any mundane color as he grew.

"Oh, Muire." Aethelred held the infant close to his chest, protectively. She'd been the least and the last remaining of her divine sisterhood, and she had sacrificed everything she was or could have become to buy his world a second chance at life. And now this: a child. Her child, it must be. Hers, and Cathoair's. "Takes you folks longer than us, I suppose."

He turned his face aside so that the tears would not fall on the baby. *Salty,* he thought, inanely. He shook his eyes dry and looked out at the sea.

"Did you have to give this up, too? Oh, Muire, I'm so sorry."

Year Zero and After

Over three and a half decades, Cathoair had found his rhythm. In the beginning, after Muire sacrificed herself, he and the humanoid snow-leopard moreau Selene had tried to use ancient swords salvaged from the Technomancer's Tower to make more waelcyrge and einherjar. It hadn't worked, and though he and Selene were fond of each other, the association eventually wore thin.

After they parted company, he had mostly just walked. Walked and found things to do, at first in the lonely places and then, as the vanguard of human resettlement caught up with him, along the frontier. The resettlers found resources, long abandoned—the Desolation had been so complete as to leave sturdier structures standing as untouched by organic decay as if they had been preserved in a nitrogen environment—and found also the fruits of Muire's miracle, paid for with her life and independence.

Fire could not burn Cahey now, nor cold freeze him, nor the long night weary his bones—and so he fought fires and sat late on lambing watches, and carried out all the small possible tasks of making the world less hurtful to those he encountered.

Angels walked the world again, he said, though they were few in number. And you never knew where you might find one.

The lambs didn't surprise him—if Muire's self-immolation had brought them birds and trees and flowers, it only seemed natural that she, being Muire, would make certain the practicalities were handled. Nor did it surprise him that the humans he met behaved just as he expected humans to behave, from the very start. Some few impressed him with their common decency, their loyalty, their sense of purpose.

But the majority were no better than they should be, and Cathoair found that comforting. They were human, after all. Just people, and people were fragile.

He found he missed the permission to be fragile most of all.

He visited Freimarc with the first wave of immigrants, amazed by how different it was from Eiledon—a warm seaside town, its pastel adobe houses mostly empty under tile roofs— and helped to find a killer in a little farming village that grew up under the branches of an olive grove not far away. Selene came down to assist, and he found her presence comforting and disquieting in equal measure. She told him that she, Mingan and Aethelred were planning a shrine on the beach near Eiledon, but Cahey could not bring himself to participate. It was too much like forgiving Muire's choice, and though he would fight for her legacy, absolving her of abandoning him was more selflessness than he could manage.

And that was without even considering Mingan, Muire's brother, the ancient immortal who styled himself the Grey Wolf. And to whom Cathoair owed a debt of hatred that left his mouth sticky with fear and rage to so much as hear his enemy's name.

Cathoair had words with Selene over it, that she would even speak to Mingan. She simply gazed at him, impassive, luxuriant smoke and silver tail twitching at the tip, whiskers forward in a sort of mocking unspoken question, and shrugged and turned away. So he left her to the palm-stuck cobble streets of Freimarc on a balmy sun-soaked afternoon, and headed north again, walking over fields where the plows still turned up a new crop of bones after every winter.

Not to Eiledon, though. He hadn't returned to the city on the banks of the river Naglfar since he left Muire there for the last time, and that, too, was an oversight he had no intention of correcting. But there was a lot to do in the world, and he was well-suited to doing it.

36 A.R.
Autumn into Winter

Thirty-six years after Muire went into the sea, in one such fallow autumn field, Cahey found a girl who reminded him a little too much of who he'd been, once upon a time.

When they'd gotten tired of raping her, or maybe when she quit fighting enough to be interesting, they'd started in with the knives. They were still at it when Cahey—following a *swanning,* a kind of imposed intention he'd become familiar with since he became immortal—heard the screaming, and came from the road down an untended track at a run. He saw, through the dusk, the silhouettes, the moving shadows he could have seen as men and instead recognized only as the demons of his own memory.

Cathoair drew the sword Muire had given him, the blade he'd never drawn in anger. He slaughtered all five of them in about ten seconds, and only realized afterwards that he'd killed.

Against the purple dusk, three-hundred-year-old oaks with no business existing loomed in indigo silhouette. Alvitr burned in Cahey's hand, stark behind the strings of blood that flew from her when he snapped his wrist. He licked his lips, frowning at the blue-silver light that cast razor-real shadows behind the bodies at his feet. A shudder rattled him, clattered his teeth, heavy as his breathing.

With panicked concentration, he put the blade away.

His first murders in thirty-six years. He guessed he was out of practice.

Shaking, he went to the girl who lay on the wet earth beyond them, curled around a broken arm that could not by any imagining have been the worst pain in her body.

She was a redhead, although you almost couldn't tell under the blood and in the dark, and she had freckles and the stubbornest chin and nose he'd ever seen. She tried to fight him when he picked her up, and then passed out, which he figured was a blessing.

Well then, where to? he asked the knowledge in his head.

East, it *swanned* him. So east he went, and found there— hearth-cold, hours abandoned—a shaggy-turfed gray farmhouse with an unmilked goat bleating on her tether in the yard. A gray cat hissed in the dooryard and fled in the kitchen window when he approached.

Inside, he kindled a light, and a fire in the cold stove, and ladled water into a bucket from the barrel by the door to wash the blood from his damsel in distress and begin to assess her injuries.

Her eyes had been green. She still had one of them.

She wasn't dead, and she wasn't ready to die, either.

Three days later, she woke lucid and free of fever in her own homestead's bedroom, in a pretty wrought-iron bed she must have salvaged from Ailee. She was a patchwork of the neat black stitches with which Cathoair had sewn her up, her arms and face matching her own patchwork quilt, which Cahey had tucked her under.

She pushed herself up on her elbows, fell back against the pillows, and said, "Who the Hel are you?" Her voice cracked a little, coming out girlish and fragile as a thread.

He'd been watching her from a chair across the room. Even when she was delirious, she'd start to scream if he got too close, so he stayed away unless he was changing the dressings. Funny thing, that: Cahey didn't have any medical training, though he had some experience both with nursing the dying and with rough-and-ready fighter's first aid.

But Muire knew how to splint an arm and sew a wound, and after she gave him her soul-kiss, he knew how, too. She left a bit of herself inside him. Just as the Wolf had.

Except it wasn't the same thing at all.

"My name is Cathoair," he said, in his most placating tones. "Don't be scared: I rescued you."

She tried to sit up in the bed, and then she rolled to the side and puked all over the floor. Tried, anyway—she hadn't much in her but the broth he'd been feeding her, so what came up was frothy yellow bile.

He came over to hold her hair back, and she shied away so violently that he retreated across the room instead. She curled away from him, huddled under the blanket, and for a minute or two he wondered if he should withdraw. But if it had been him, he'd have wanted someone to stay there, even if he wasn't strong enough to face them yet.

After a little while, without poking her head out, she said, "Why?"

"I don't know why," he answered. "It's crazy shit, is what it is, and it isn't because of anything you did."

"No," she said. She sat up, the blankets still pulled to her chin. "Why didn't you let them kill me?" She touched the bandages over the socket of her right eye gingerly, wincing.

Cahey felt the sting behind his eyes, and had to keep his hands down when they wanted to creep up and press the ugly furrowed scar across his own cheek. She looked like she'd been pretty, not that it made any difference. Well, maybe it made things worse for her.

She said, "Why make me live like this?"

Cahey shook his head. "That's your choice to make, not mine. In the meantime, now that you're awake, I'll be in the other room if you want me." He stood and walked toward the door. "Just yell if you're hungry or need a lift to the toilet. I've played nurse before."

She didn't say a word. He had walked halfway out before he remembered and turned around.

"Hey, what's your name?"

She picked her head up off the pillow with a grimace of pain. "Aithne," she said. "Now leave me the Hel alone."

Aithne screamed in the night a lot, and then screamed at Cahey when he went in to her. Finally, he got so he'd just go in and let her hit him for a while. Or he'd open her bedroom door to let her know he'd heard her, and then go back and make believe he was sleeping on the couch. The bandages came off, and except for the eyepatch, he had to say he thought she was really better off than Aethelred. Her face was messed up, but at least half of it wasn't *metal*.

Six months or so later when, instead of waking up screaming, she quietly came out and took his hand and led him back to her bed, she never said a word. All she did that night was cry, and all he did was hold her, and wish he could manage to cry a little himself.

Not for her. She didn't need it. But for Muire, and for him. Except he was all cried out, by then, so Aithne had to do the crying for both of them.

Still, it felt nice to be close to somebody.

He didn't sleep, but after that, he stayed in her bed at night and pretended. It was no surprise when, at last, in the cold of winter, she seduced him. He'd been ready for it for weeks, and ready to give whatever she asked and be glad to offer it. The surprise, when it happened, was how badly *he* needed it.

She was the first woman he'd touched since he killed Astrid and Muire left him, and everything about Aithne's body was different from either of them, from the way she met his kisses to the sound of her breath caught in her throat.

37 A.R.
High Summer

Cahey was out in Aithne's yard digging a well, of all things, when Selene poked her whiskered face over the edge and stuck down her hand. "I have something to tell you." She never was much on polite small talk.

Cahey looked up at her and read the squint of her eyes, the worried creases along the bridge of her nose. He grabbed her wrist and let her haul him up, holding on to the shovel with the other hand. He wasn't a small man, and she managed it one-handed, her engineered claws that could slice stone only grazing his wrist like burrs.

Behind her head, he saw Aithne watching out of the kitchen window of her little house. From the way Selene's ears twitched, he could tell that she knew someone was looking.

She was lean and elegant, inhumanly proportioned in her black leather and chrome harness, the cloud-soft, cloud-colored pelt that covered her dotted with storm-gray rosettes. She purred low in her throat when she looked at him, an evidence of unfeigned affection that left a complicated pain in his breast.

"Lover?" she asked, as he shook the worst of the mud off.

He sucked his lip in and tried to meet her eye, but his gaze kept fastening on her toe-tips. "Occasionally."

"Inconvenient," she replied, her tail lashing. She crouched next to the heap of moist earth he'd spaded out of the ground. The layer with all the bones lay near the surface, and a few clay-stained reminders of the Desolation peeked from under the crumbling pile of deeper sediments. "There's something you need to see to over near Eiledon."

Cahey raised an eyebrow. He'd grown up in Eiledon, when Eiledon was all the world. He'd planned never to go back there. "What sort of something?"

"How does your girlfriend feel about children?"

"Excuse me?"

"Aethelred," she said, her face going strange, "seems to have custody of your son."

Cahey was never quite sure how he wound up doubled over the shovel, using the handle as a prop while the world heaved and swayed around him. He would have sat down hard without it, he thought, and melodrama be damned.

"My son?"

Selene let herself smile, a lip-curling mockery of the human gesture that revealed teeth like needle-sharp pegs, and cuffed Cahey gently alongside the head, suddenly all affectionate cat. "Your son. Muire's son. I've been tracking you for the last two years to tell you about it. You haven't been easy to find."

She hesitated, but Cahey didn't fill the silence, so she continued. "Apparently Serpents have long gestational periods. He's about three now. Aethelred is raising him. I suspected you might want to know."

"I have a son." Cahey looked down at his boots, his feet encrusted with the bright mud of the well. He had learned he was sterile when he was a teenager. If anything, he had figured he'd be like Aethelred, eventually, and take in strays. "What's his name?"

37 A.R.
Spring

$\mathcal{A}$ goddess led a red mare down a rainbow toward the sand, pausing halfway to shake out her hair. It was winter where Heythe had come from, and melting snow scattered from her cold blond locks when she shook them out. It melted and fell like rain, stippling the beach below.

She shed her coat, too, and dropped it carelessly, already walking again before it thumped softly at the edge of the surf. Her revealed throat glistened beneath a network of jewels threaded on golden wire—spinel, beryl, tourmaline, topaz, peridot, aquamarine, sapphire, diamond: everything that might shatter light in all the colors of the rainbow she walked down as if it were a swaying bridge of planks held taut in knotted rope.

The mare followed on a relaxed rein, head low on a soft neck as if she ambled across a pasture. There was nothing to indicate that she—or the goddess—had come fresh from battle, from tumult and massacre. When the mare's hooves scuffed the sand with solid thuds, she snorted and shook the flaxen mane across her ears.

Heythe scratched behind them while the rainbow bridge unraveled itself into the sky. The day was perfect spring and glorious, the sky above deeper and more pure than any of the gemstones of her necklace. And yet the goddess frowned.

"Well," she said, scuffing at luxuriant salt grass with the toe of a worn leather boot that was some two and a half millennia out of fashion. "*This* is not the apocalypse I was hoping for."

37 A.R.
High Summer

This day of the solstice is endless, which suits the Grey Wolf's purpose very well. No night falls in these latitudes for a long week each summer. Now, when the golden light of evening lies upon mountain and sea, the sun only touches the ocean, rolls along the rim of the world for an hour, and lifts again.

The wolf witnesses the spill of thick light from an elevation, as he had once before. But this time he sits cradled in the embrace of white wings, the width of a broad back beneath him. Kasimir, his mount—a baroque and extravagant creature, two-headed, plumed and antlered, hooved and taloned in the finest tradition of mythological chimeras—holds them deep in the cold sky above the flank of the green mountain, the breakers pounding its roots so far below they seem white lines of chalk smudged on a wrinkled gray paper sea.

The wolf tucks his cloak beneath his thighs, tight so it will not billow in the wind from the valraven's wings. Kasimir waits on like a hunting falcon, hovering steady and high—a feat no merely physical animal could muster. But Kasimir is the Grey Wolf's half brother, and as much a being of wild magic and divine intent as the wolf himself. Though Kasimir has not said as much, the wolf knows the pause is not merely to reacquaint themselves with long-forgotten territory. It gives the wolf a chance to marshal his composure under pretense of surveying the landscape, something Kasimir doubtless wants as well.

It has been a long time since they were here. And the last time—

A hurting smile pulls the wolf's lips against his teeth. It might be safest not to dwell on the events of so long ago. But then, it is those very events that have brought him back here, inexorably as the scent of a rotting corpse drawing scavengers. He must think on them.

Which means thinking on Heythe. Goddess, lover, monster, betrayer. The most terrible and subtle thing the wolf has met in a long and terrible life, and he has known a great many gods and monsters. Heythe the seeress, Heythe the world-killer.

Heythe, the returned.

Thinking on her is hard. It requires thinking on his own weakness, evil, and failure. But he tells himself that he is—at long last—prepared for that.

He'd better be.

He has no sense he's made a decision or telegraphed it to Kasimir, but as abruptly as a broken wing, they fall. The sea air reeks like electricity and the wind rips the wolf breathless. They plunge toward a stand of lush conifers threaded by slender birch, the wood cracked wide where the rising bones of the mountain shove through soil. A pewter ribbon of snowmelt slides across jagged granite, tumbles from a cliff edge, and plummets to vanish through the canopy, raising its own evening-gilded veil.

Kasimir's pinions snap wide, bent back like fingertips, and cupped wings clap air as they plunge between trees.

For all the violence of the descent, they land like scattered petals. The wolf smooths escaping locks back into his queue and fills his lungs.

On this breath as the last, he expects the scent of the sea. But rising from seven thousand feet below, it has no chance of cutting the overripe perfume of blossoms coating mountain air. Cloying, rotten, the scent should come attended by the kind of thick silence cut only by the drone of insects.

A waiting silence, like the first morning of the world.

But the water rings down the cliff, filling the air in the alpine meadow with spray. Wet jewels speckle Kasimir's necks, collect in the strands of his manes. He furls his wings.

Rustling feathers settled, he steps forward, lowering both porcelain-white heads to drink. Cloven forehooves splash into the waterfall-fed pool as the wolf slings one thin gray-clad leg over the stallion's withers and slides down, boots thudding into the muddy bank. He crouches beside the stallion, watching Kasimir's long white-velvet throats work with each swallow, the way his whiskers move with his lips.

The stallion does not look up, or acknowledge the wolf's attention. The wolf, with an amused snort, stands. He unclips his sheathed sword from his belt and hangs Svanvitr on the stallion's harness. He lays a hand on his mount's shoulder. "I'll be a moment, Kasimir."

The stallion raises one head—the antlered one—and allows water to drip from his finely sculpted muzzle onto the wolf's wool-cloaked shoulder and silver-brindled braid. But Kasimir says nothing, and so the wolf turns.

As he hesitates on the edge of the churning pool, the val-raven speaks finally.

Mingan. Are you certain of the wisdom of unleashing this?

The wolf stops in his tracks, turning back to meet Kasimir's gaze. "No. But I am certain of its necessity. And if anyone can control her, Cathoair can."

Given his wyrd, the wolf adds silently. *Given how much of Muire and me he bears within him. Given his history, he has as much to feed her on as anyone.*

Kasimir tosses his antlered head.

The wolf glances at the sky, the blue transparent with altitude. A contrail crawls across it. He shakes his head with rueful admiration, his queue snaking against his shoulders.

Historian, he thinks, feeling rich for a moment with gratitude.

The valraven snorts. His horned head finishes with the water and moves to crop the grass. The wolf watches for a moment, reluctant to go, but at last he turns aside to gather a fistful of deadfall from beneath the birches and poplars bordering the meadow. His queue bobs against his back as the wolf strides around the pond toward the cliff that backs it.

He glances over his shoulder at the placid valraven and sighs silently. *Like a dog.* His fingers curl at his belt groping after Svanvitr's knotted brass pommel before he reminds himself that he's left her with Kasimir.

Covering the sticks of wood with his cloak, he squares his shoulders and steps into the icy water.

The pool deepens quickly. In three strides, he's hip-deep, glacial melt swirling and sucking about his thighs. Roiling water hides the deep-worn pit he knows lies before the waterfall, but he skirts it with well-placed footfalls until the edge of the torrent hammers his bowed head, stings his nape, trickles down his temples to blind squinted eyes.

He plunges through the waterfall and with his free hand heaves his body up onto the ledge behind. For a moment, he kneels behind the curtain of watery light, chest heaving, steam already rising from his skin. Then he stands, gloved palm gliding on sandy rock, and shakes the droplets from his lashes and his hair.

A rocky irregular gulf stretches back into utter darkness, the floor crossed by a trickle of water no broader than his palm. The mouth of the cavern is bathed in shattered light refracted through the cascade. What might lie deeper is hidden.

The wolf kneels on the sandy floor while the echoes astound his ears. With a finger he sketches a rune in the sand. He touches the driest stick from his bundle to the mark—*kenaz,* the torch— and blows across it, stirring the sand, so that it kindles. When thin flames flicker up, he tents the other wood over the fire so it will dry and catch.

While the blaze grows, the wolf strips off his gloves and pulls them through his belt. Soon the cave is bright to his dark-adapted eyes.

He reaches into the flame bare-fingered and pinches off a shard. Holding that fire high in his fist, a few more sticks in his other hand, he stands.

He dampens the blue-white glow from his own gray eyes as he starts down the passageway. He'll risk no starlight where he is going, nothing to awaken his quarry prematurely. The cavern is narrow and braided, seeming to branch only to rejoin, but the wolf is sure of his path. Millennia cannot dim this memory. He picks his way over sandy floors and ducks crabwise through too-low passages; it is an unlovely cavern, in the granite stone, not one elegant with limestone cascades and battlements.

It is a weapon you awaken.

I know, he answers. *Was it not I who sealed her away?*

He descends for a long while before he reaches the ragged chamber marking the bottom of the climb. The cavern is bare, ledges and jumbled boulders making the floor and walls. He pauses for a breath of damp air before laying the sticks he carried down on a block of stone. He places his flame against the kindling. When it is lit, he stands again and picks his way to an object in the center of the room.

Firelight reveals a rectangular stone block as large as a dinner table.

The wolf circles, considering its rune-carved surface from behind a thin angle of frown. Cracks around the perimeter outline the lid of a rectangular granite box. The cracks, sealed with sap, are too narrow to admit a prybar. Lines of ancient writing run across them without a break. There is no obvious way to remove the lid.

The wolf tugs on his gloves, deliberately, one finger at a time. He stretches his hands into the leather, then lays one gloved palm on the block of stone, tracing the deep inscription gouged there in runes older than he. He reads them aloud, very softly, mouthing all their dreadful cautions.

Then he raises his left hand over his head, makes a fist, and brings it down on the center of the lid in a single blow.

A snap like a thunderclap echoes through the underground and the stones creak in protest, dusting the wolf's head with grit. The lid cracks across and through, sagging at the center as it leans into the hollow space within. The upper edge projects some fraction of an inch above the surface of the table now, and the wolf walks back to its head. He stretches his left hand in its glove, face expressionless, hearing the crunch as broken bones settle. He pauses a moment so they will knit before grasping the now-protruding edge of the lid, pulling each piece aside and discarding it by turns. He winces more from the grinding of stone on stone than from the blow that pulped his hand.

He looks down into a bower that is also a coffin.

The figure within—uninjured by the violence he has done her sarcophagus—flutters in her darkness. She lies like a child tumbled in sleep, unbreathing, one arm pillowing an inhuman head, lightly shut eyes seeming half as wide as her face, owl-soft obsidian wings clutched tight around her like a blanket. The other hand is outflung, knotty spiderlike fingers tipped with razorblade claws that gleam in the dull reflected light.

She is a thing of sinew and bone, skin velveted by the growth of fine short fur so dense it has a nap. Scars and gouges mark the inside of the foot-thick pieces of the discarded lid. The air that rises from her confinement is warm, stale, and a breath of it makes the wolf's head spin. She smells of the dust of old warm houses full of old worn things.

I do not approve.

Your complaint is registered.

"Imogen," the wolf says. "Imogen. Sister. There will be starlight when the sun sets. It is time to awaken, beloved."

A moment passes. The feathers of the wing furled near her mouth are still, until they stir with her first taken breath. There is a pause before she breathes out, and then they stir again. The warmth of her breath rises, stirs the fine hairs on his cheek above where the beard is shaven.

He bends down to whisper. "You will go from this place, sister, and find the einherjar known as Cathoair. He will be your keeper now; obey him as you would your brother."

He kisses her cheek before he straightens away.

The Grey Wolf turns in the firelit darkness and leaves her.

Farther south, where the sun sets even in summer, the wolf watches from concealment. Despite distance, his vision is precise in every particular. What holds his attention is an adult and a child strolling along a beach at high tide. A thoughtful surf rolls alongside as they pick through strange runes and sentences written in lines of kelp and driftwood tossed on the sand.

The taller of the two seems a man in years, if barely, lean and muscular, dark shoulders gleaming in the afternoon light. Grains of quartz and flecks of mica glitter pale against the rosewood skin of his feet and calves. A sword both like and unlike Svanvitr swings from the belt of his short canvas pants, the hilt sparkling metronomically in the descending sun.

The wolf identifies the blade with a thin-lipped smile.

The other figure, a toddler, outlines his father's path in a meandering orbit. He plays tag with the waves, splashing in and out of the sea without care.

The man pays no heed to the boy's game with the ocean. Instead he keeps his own path—following him in an unwavering line along the foam-flecked waterline, never quite crossing over into the sea—until they come to the foot of a high, sandy bluff. There, the man scoops up the child one-handed, balancing him with unconscious strength as they scramble toward a white building perched on the hilltop, overlooking the tossing sea.

The wolf, unobserved—as is his nature—turns away, descends the bluff, and when he knows Cathoair cannot see him calls down his winged, white and patient steed. As the wolf mounts, Kasimir stomps a hoof impatiently.

You could just warn him.

Because he would heed my warning, Bright One?

He would heed Selene's. And because it would be more decent than this skullduggery.

Heythe must not learn of my survival. Not until it is too late. Not until we have won.

You're afraid of her, the valraven says, spreading his wings in the sun, but hesitating. The wolf feels Kasimir's muscles tense against the insides of his thighs and settles himself for the leap, but it does not come. He waits for Kasimir to call him coward, as he deserves, but instead the stallion leaves it for the wolf to condemn himself.

"Aren't you?" the wolf says, aloud for the dignity of the dead. And there are so many dead behind him—his dead, and the dead of the wicked goddess. "Aren't you afraid?"

Cathoair relished the living weight of his son in his arms. Carrying the boy up the narrow trail to the chapel, he cursed himself for an idiot. *Three years you could have had with him,* he thought, *if only you had known. Fool.*

He chuckled. *But there's nothing new there. Besides, if you had been here, Aithne wouldn't be alive, would she?* And she had been worth saving. He hoped she found some young man who would treat her like a queen forever. A queen with scars, and a tongue like an adder's.

Climbing, he smiled, and pretended to himself that the thought didn't sting.

Aethelred, the chapel-keeper, had paved the trail with sea-smoothed stones; this at least saved them from having to fight the sand and scree. It was still a scramble, and the sword Alvitr threatened to trip him every third step.

He gained the summit at last, pulling himself up the last few steps with a grabbed handful of the salt grass that grew thick along the ridge. Resettling his son, Cahey turned to look over the ocean. Light flickered across it like the sparkles on a mirrorball. Down the coast, the arched rib cage of some great sea-creature lay bleached ivory on the sand, echoing the shape of the little chapel.

Cahey glanced down at the boy in his arms. Somewhere along the jouncing trip up the hill, Cathmar had dozed off.

Cahey shook his head ruefully and turned back toward the chapel, walking faster now. *Fool,* he told himself again, *three years lost that you can never have back. Idiot, moron, einherjar.*

Synonyms, Aethelred would say.

Aethelred was right a lot of the time.

Cahey crossed the flagstones paving the hilltop. Pausing at the chapel door, suddenly self-conscious as a boy at his date's front gate, he tried to smooth his wind-snagged hair. Another einherjar—the *only* other einherjar—still wore his hair in the single braid of long-ago custom. The kink in Cahey's hair demanded a modified style. Though he'd always liked a ponytail, he'd grown it for decades, and now he kept it in small braids wound back into a single larger one, for the sake of tradition. If he admitted it, for the sake of Muire. Or the memory of her. Something like that.

It had all come undone in his climb, and now one of the smaller braids was starting to unwind, too.

The breeze gusted, whipping a ringlet across his mouth and catching strands on his rough, unfaded scar. He reached distractedly with his free hand to brush them away. They eluded him, the braid unraveling further, tangling his fingers and wrist.

The tug brought him back from the edge of distraction. He felt the light spill down his face like tears, a response to something that would not show itself, and turned his gaze back out at the ocean.

He raised an eyebrow at the sea. "I suppose you think that's pretty funny. Don't you."

The waves tossed and hissed, far below. He nodded and bit back a flare of anger—irrational, and all the deeper for it. The remains of the braid stayed tucked, this time, and—like Aithne under her patched covers—he wasn't sure if the silence was what he wanted, or what he feared.

"I miss you, too," he said before he turned away and opened the door.

He half-expected his son to wake crying as they walked out of the warm afternoon sunlight into the dim chapel. It was, however, more brightly lit than Cahey had anticipated: whatever white stone formed the cantilevered ceiling was translucent, and the single large rectangular room was bathed in shadowless brilliance.

Cathmar sighed and snuggled closer to his father's chest, but didn't wake.

Cahey stood silently for a moment, allowing the quiet of the chapel to soothe him. He wondered if Aethelred had borrowed the design from somewhere, or if one of the refugees from Eiledon who had helped to build it had been an architect.

The center of the chapel stood empty. Long benches were set back a meter or two from each of the walls, each one different, lovingly crafted of reused iron and stone. Panels made of salvaged metal and glass covered three of the four walls: some sheets that must once have been sliding doors or office windows, accented by fragments in a dozen colors, framed and decorated with wire and other bits of copper, brass and steel.

The books hanging in their racks behind those glass doors numbered in the hundreds.

Someday, Cahey thought, *I really do have to learn to read.* His son yawned and stretched in his arms.

The fourth wall faced the ocean, and held the only window. Three statues stood on a dais in front of it: one pale; one dark; and the one in the center gleaming bronze, backlit by the afternoon.

He avoided looking at that one. Rather, he stood in front of the one carved in pale alabaster with gray swirls running through it like lines of smoke. A woman with the face of a snow leopard, or perhaps a snow leopard with the body of a woman, she crouched as if ready to spring: one hand splayed on the warm rock before her, the other extended and holding up a sword.

A real sword, not a carven one. A sword with a blade of dark crystal, and a hilt like the brass hilt of the blade that hung at Cahey's hip.

"Hey," he said to his yawning son. "Look. It's your auntie Selene. Do you see her?"

Cathmar blinked storm-gray eyes. "Not Auntie Selene," he said, lisping her name.

Cahey laughed. "No, not really Selene. Just a statue." He carried the child past the statue in the center again, and over to the one that stood on her right hand.

The angel's lips pressed together in a frown. The ocean rolled at the bottom of the bluff, hissing against the beach. A woman's lighthearted voice spoke in his recollection, plain as if in his ear. *I'd like you to model for me sometime.*

In the end, he hadn't needed to. She'd done it from memory. Flawlessly.

He closed his eyes for a moment, shutting out the gleam of afternoon sunlight on veined black marble. Then he opened them again and forced himself to regard his own image.

She had captured him standing, but in motion. He balanced with more weight on the left foot than the right, head uplifted and cocked to one side as if a moment from whirling in place. The sword, in this case, was held low in one hand, continuing the incipient movement of the torso.

The statue was impressionistic. He could not say it was idealized, and it was rough-hewn in places as if she had not been able to bear the polishing. But the movement and proportion were striking, and the face was unmistakable. *Is that how she saw me? Is that what she loved?*

He saw a caress in every chisel mark, passion in every stroke of the mallet. Somehow, it was worse, not to be able to deny that she had loved him in return.

He turned his face away.

"Da," said his son, one hand extended toward the statue.

Cahey wiped his nose on the back of his hand and forced a

smile. "Yep. That's me, kiddo." *Aethelred showed it to him, of course, and he thinks the statue is his father.*

Idiot. Moron. Einherjar.

He turned toward the final statue. "C'mon. I have a story to tell you." He paused and then laughed a strange, choking little laugh. "I'll tell you all the racy parts first, while you're still too young to understand what I'm talking about."

Cahey held his son up to the third and final statue. "That's your mom," he said. "Before she was the ocean, she looked like that."

The sculpture brought less painful memories than he'd expected. She'd been wearing her hair much shorter by the time they met, and she'd never been one to fuss with jewelry or clothes, so the formal robes on the statue made her seem almost foreign.

Cathmar reached out fat toddler fingers and tugged the statue's outstretched hand. Cahey winced and covered the boy's hand with his own. The chapel brightened, starlight washing the shadows from the statue's bowed face. Cahey did not have to raise his hand to his face to feel for moisture. He knew by the sting of his eyes where the light spilled from.

He carried his son outside. The sun was settling, scraping orange light across the wavetops, and Cahey paused to draw Cathmar's attention. They waited until the spill of color across the horizon had dimmed to shallow gold before descending the bluff in chill twilight shadows. The high points held the light longer.

The world was blue, the ocean invisible under mist, by the

time they crossed the sand and the rocky strand to Aethelred's
little stone cottage up among the dunes and the salt grass.
Aethelred was locking the blue wooden door when they got
there.

Cahey wondered if he'd been waiting for them to come
down the hill. Beach plum branches scratched at the walls,
bowering a low sod roof dripping with summer flowers. Five-
petaled roses the same flushed pink as seashell insides grew low
at the foundations, making Cahey hide a smile. He had never
imagined the scarred old man as a gardener. Or as a priest, for
that matter.

Aethelred turned around and handed Cahey the key.

The einherjar studied Aethelred's bright eyes and ruined
face. "Where are you going?"

Aethelred shrugged and chuckled, swinging his staff and
shouldering a pack that had lain half-hidden among the roses.
"I've still got time to see a little of this new world before I die."

"Cathmar?" As if attracted by his name, the baby wriggled
in Cathoair's arms.

"Your kid," Aethelred said, reaching out and smoothing the
child's hair. "You raise him. Keep the house. There's no food in
it, but that won't trouble either of you. Solar panels work, and
the 'screen's in good shape: you can even raise the city from
here. Go ahead and sell the bed. I'll call once in while. You've
done enough wandering these last thirty-odd years; twenty in
one place won't kill you."

"I . . ." Cahey took a step back. "I don't know how to be a
father."

"Bullshit, kid." When Cahey flinched, Aethelred continued
in a harsh tone. "You know how *not* to be a father."

Cahey stood there with his mouth half-open, feeling the sandy pathway rock under his feet.

Aethelred modulated his tone toward kindness. "Just don't do anything that yours did, and you'll be all right."

"Aethelred. I can't. I can't be . . ." *a father to him.*

Why didn't Muire tell me? Why did I have to find out from Selene?

Because you never would have walked away from her if you knew she was pregnant, and she wanted you to go. "What if I can't control myself? What if I shake him, hit him?"

Aethelred put a giant, worn hand on the einherjar's shoulder. Cahey watched his own reflection in the mirrored side of Aethelred's face, his familiar features unchanging as they reflected from Aethelred's half-sagging ones.

So old. Cahey, who had been twenty now for almost forty years, suddenly understood why Muire had always seemed so pensive when she looked him in the eye. Back when *he* was mortal, too.

"Cahey," Aethelred said. "He's Muire's little boy. What would you ever do to hurt him?"

Aethelred clapped a callused palm to the young-seeming man's cheek and smiled. "Take the time. Raise your son. You've done enough for a while; the world will wait for you. Borje will keep an eye on the chapel." Then he turned away and walked off down the beach, whistling, leaving Cahey forlorn by a locked door with a toddler in one hand and a set of keys in the other.

Never get angry, Cahey reminded himself. *Never get scared.*

He felt like he should say something. But what was there

to say? Aethelred would have answers for all his arguments before he, himself, even thought of them.

The einherjar stood for a long moment, watching Aethelred go. Then he looked down at the child and shrugged. "Well, kid. I guess it's you and me against the world."

He put the key in the lock. It clicked when he turned it—well-oiled, of course. He opened the door and they went inside.

37 A.R.
Summer

Darkness. Deep darkness, and a musical sound. The Imogen lies half on her side, and feels where the blood has pooled in limbs unmoved for centuries. Awareness returns slowly.

What she hears is not music. It's water. Trickling. Echoing in a rocky and convoluted space that builds itself out of sound in her mind.

When she opens her eyes, she sees that the darkness is leavened by a dull glow. A red light, or the black-red below red. She sees by the reflected heat of her own body, and by that light she sees also that the space that drinks that heat is cold.

Not brutally cold. Not dangerously cold—well, dangerous for frailer things, enough cold to make a warm animal breath mist in the humidity but not freeze to rime. But the Imogen has never met cold that could discomfort her, in neither this world nor the dead one.

She smells her brother in the dark, but the scent is old. Days gone, and soaked into the stone. She is alone. She has been a long time awakening.

Something twists inside her. The lenses of her eyes flex, alter, stretch wide. Her eyes enlarge, the sockets growing to encompass them. Now she sees clearly, as if in broad and detailed afternoon.

She rises up from a pallet of hard stone and steps out of her coffin, feeling the restless flex of pinions along her spine. The wings strain out, broad vanes made visible by the heat of blood within, and strike against the hard, low stones overhead.

There was a fire here, but it has burned to char. Fire, coals, smoke. The smoke must have gone somewhere. *Mustn't it?* The scent of burning hangs on the air, coupled with an odor of bitter musk.

The smell of the brother.

She scoops a handful of charcoal and ash, brings them near her face. There is no heat left in them. The rock is wet, the ash saturated. When she wipes her hand on her thigh, pale caked streaks remain behind.

The sensitive hairs on her skin trace the ruffle of air movement. Upward, outward.

With the force of instinct, she knows what she must do.

Upward. Outward.

Or die.

She understands *die.* She does not prefer it.

The winding corridor twists and forks and forks again. But she feels the shape the echoes describe, smells the smoke, smells the darkness. Smells the path the brother took, and the cold remains of his second fire, and the meadow and the flowers beyond.

The Imogen moves into the air. It holds her, pushes back. Her feathers cup it, find resistance, row her forward on wingbeats silent as an owl's.

Echoes splinter off the falling water, but there is brightness beyond. The Imogen beats hard for speed, pinions feathering sand and stone, then folds her wings tight and arrows through the fall.

The water strikes her like a rockfall, snapping her down feet in the instant it takes her to pass. Then she is through, dazzled by unspeakable brilliance, slapping her hands across her eyes as her wing tips skim the water. On a still pool, each touch would leave spreading ripples, but this turbid water eats up the evidence of her passage as if she had never been.

Too brilliant, the dark. But when she peeks between her fingers, her eyes have adapted. The silent trees await her, verdant against a sky silver with night. The sun has barely dipped below the rim of the world. One side of the sky is royal-blue, the other gray as dawn. It is possible to see the face of the lady moon, pale in the washed-out twilight, once the Imogen's adaptations coax away the painful brightness. Two bachelor moons—damaged satellites—trail her forlornly, but the moon is platinum and they are brass.

She will not have them. One of the little ones is most pitifully scarred. Around them, in the dark half of the sky, the Imogen can discern a salting of stars.

It is their light that has awakened her.

On the bank of the pool she settles, pausing to trace with her fingertips the hoofprints that were not made by any deer.

The Imogen rises, and follows the stream on down. It tumbles from pool to pool, the lower ones more still and limpid. She crouches beside one, where the light of the sky filters between black-green pine boughs to fall over her shoulder. It is not still water, but it smooths beneath her shadow, making a dark, silvered surface.

In that shadow she sees the thing from which she takes her name, or what passes for her name, if a name she must have.

The form in the mirror. *Imogen.*

Dark as sorrow, skin like black velvet. When has she seen velvet? How does she know the sleekness of its touch?

Skin like black velvet: dull, soft, plush across the naked body, which is muscular and long, small-breasted, taut-tendoned. Black wings, lusterless in the twilight, soft as an owl's. Eyes lucent, amber held up to the sun, the pupils changing shape as she peers into the inexplicable silent water. *What are all these things in my mind?*

She has never seen herself before. *Have I?* Has she? She must, because this is familiar. Familiar even as it changes, her face reshaping under her own probing touch.

I am like nothing in all the world. I am a trickster's daughter.

It sounds right. A trickster's daughter. But then, what is that? What is *trickster?* What is *daughter?* What is *brother* and *shadow* and *mirror,* for that matter?

She knows the answers without knowing how she knows them. She thinks she has forgotten much, in her long slumber, but the knowledge comes with no sensation of loss. It is enough that she also knows—as she knows everything, with interior conviction—what she must do, where she must go.

It has always been so, the wisdom bred in her, the wyrd written on her bones. She is the Imogen, and she has always done as she was made to do: fed her hunger on a master or at her master's command, and gone hungry between. Hungry always, as is her nature, and always unsatisfied.

She must go. She feels the pull, the command, the echo inside her. Her brother—her master—has spoken, and bid her find a new master and cast herself in his service.

The Imogen does not wish to do as she is bid.

Almost without warning, the wings unfurl, the tendons stretch, and she is skybound—for the first time? Once again? Moonshadows fall about her like tattered rags, and the waterfall begins to splash again.

She rises.

38 A.R.
Spring Solstice

Footsore in mendicant's sandals, Aethelred leaned on his staff. It was his second since he'd set out from the cottage some nine months before, and now he used it as a prop to rest each foot by turn, like a mule cocking one leg up to sleep standing.

He'd gotten to meet a few mules since Rekindling, though the Dweller Within knew where they came from. Well, now that he thought of it, the Dweller probably did know, at that. As she no doubt knew everything. More or less. The trick was getting her to do something more informative than casting up mysterious babies.

Aethelred liked mules, with their long floppy ears and solid common sense that brooked no tomfoolery. He wondered, somewhat idly, if there were any mule moreaux.

He raised his hand and scratched around the rim of the chromed side of his face. The bright spring sun felt like a pressing iron applied to his face, and the old burns still itched. He could feel the heat in them, soaked deep into living tissue where it would never come out. It warmed his fingertips where he pressed them to ridged scars.

Aethelred shook his head, rolling heavy shoulders eased by

the warmth of that same sunlight that scorched his face. He'd walked a long way to find this place. There was no point in hesitating now. The dirt track under his feet led past a little shingle farmhouse slumped, broken-backed, into a shaggy green hillside. Weathered cedar shakes caught the light that angled between fluffy clouds, silver over gray like the wings of a moth. The roadcut ran black through moist earth on the sunrise side of the house. Aethelred could make out the tea-stained gleam of broken bone in the dark, living soil.

A little north of the Ailee resettlement, just as Cahey had said. Not that the kid would have told him if he'd known Aethelred planned on coming here. And Selene's elemental loyalty would never stretch to telling Aethelred where she'd tracked Cahey down if she thought he didn't want Aethelred to know.

Aethelred shrugged. Some people, righteous as they were, didn't possess much sense.

I'm getting too old for so damned much walking.

He kept on down the lane.

He was here to see about a girl.

She was outside, hanging sheets up on a line, her copper-colored hair catching plasticky glints off the day. The image didn't remind the old preacher of his childhood: there hadn't been much in the way of sunlight or clean sheets hung out to dry in Eiledon. Before times changed, anyway, and the soil and the sea came back to life.

He grinned to himself. Things were different now.

He didn't make a lot of noise coming up the lane to the gate, but she turned around anyway, pushing escaping hair back off the eyepatch that punctuated an ugly, haggled scar. Her hand dropped to the pistol at her belt, so he thumped his staff on the ground. She hesitated. He rewarded her with a cheery wave.

"Hello the house!" he called out. "Got a drink for a mendicant man?"

She dusted her other hand on her trousers, leaving a loamy smear on canvas. He saw her watching his face to see what he made of the scars.

They were pretty bad. Not as bad as Aethelred's, but he wasn't a pretty redheaded girl of oh-about-twenty-two. And he still had both eyes. Shame about hers.

Her brow creased—with concern, not concentration. When she finally nodded, it carried an air of resignation.

"Come around back," she said, not taking her hand off the pistol. "We've got a well."

We. He glanced around. A small gray cat coiled through the woodpile and a chicken scratched in the hardpacked yard. Aethelred hadn't yet gotten over marveling at the existence of so many plants and animals. There sure hadn't been any before. As miracles ran, he allowed, Muire had done pretty good.

Aethelred didn't think that anybody lived here but this young woman—too young to remember Eiledon, and the life there bounded on all sides by the Desolation. But it was all right with him if she wanted to lie a little for safety's sake.

He wasn't an angel, after all.

After he'd drunk from the dipper he turned and handed it back. She hung it up on the yellow wooden wellcover while he studied her profile. She was damn pretty, really, if you didn't mind the eyepatch and the fading cut lines on her arms and face. Interesting nose and an interested expression. Freckles on slightly sunburned skin, and all that red hair braided back away from her face, except where it was draggled with sweat and getting away from her. Not hiding behind it. That took courage, too.

Provisionally, Aethelred thought Cahey was an idiot. Well, he *knew* Cahey was an idiot; he'd as good as raised the kid. But after a life spent tending bar and lifting Burdens, Aethelred fancied himself a pretty good snap judge of character. And he hadn't thought Cahey was enough of an idiot to walk away from a girl like this one.

He said, "I hope you don't mind if I ask you a question."

She stiffened a little, but didn't look ready to snap. Aethelred took it for permission. Something about her, the lift of her chin when she felt herself challenged, reminded him of someone he used to care for. It was not until she snapped her head aside to toss her braid back that he identified who, however, and understood abruptly why Cahey would have found her both irresistible and unbearable.

She moved like Astrid, who'd died in a useless accident for which Cathoair had never forgiven himself.

Aethelred took a breath, crunching his shoulders down to look as small and inoffensive as he knew how. "I'm called Aethelred," he said. "And I wonder if your name might be Aithne?"

She frowned slowly, as if she had to think about each individual minute muscular contraction that made up the expression and choose consciously to allow it. Her hand dropped to the pistol again. She looked as if she could use it.

She gave him a chilly, motivated grin. "You'd better have a good excuse to know that name."

"A young man told it to me. Dark skin, black hair. Strik-ing eyes and a ponytail. Bad scar here—" Aethelred touched his cheek. "Missing some teeth from it. Name of Cahey. Sounded like he thought fondly of you."

Her face relaxed a step, but her shooting hand didn't shift. "Where'd you see him?"

"Last near Eiledon." Aethelred rearranged his face in his best "you can tell me; I'm a bartender" smile.

She lifted an eyebrow. "You're *that* Aethelred." She nod-ded. "Come inside, then. He's not coming back, is he?"

"Not right away," Aethelred said, following her to the sag-ging gray farmhouse.

She gave him an odd sort of look over her shoulder as she held the scarred, salvaged storm door for him to catch. She pro-duced a key, opened the inside door, and stepped up over the threshold into the shade of a clean, weary-looking kitchen. "I wasn't expecting to hear from him. I imagined he'd be pretty busy with his son for a while."

"I imagine he will," Aethelred said. The storm door shut be-hind him with a click. He stepped out of the way so she could shut the interior door as well. She locked it, which seemed only good sense. "We're old friends, though. I knew him when he was half your age, or a little older. So I thought I'd check up on you, as a friend of a friend."

"Ah." She might have let him into her house, but she wasn't unstrapping the sidearm. "He didn't exactly ask you to stop by, did he?"

Aethelred smiled with the corner of his mouth. "No, not exactly. But he did speak highly of you. And we are very old friends."

"Mm." A noncommittal noise, the way she made it. Her weight shifted to her heels, but she didn't fold her arms. "So what the hell do you want from me, Aethelred who meddles uninvited in the affairs of friends? Everybody has a motive."

"I came to help," he said. "That's all. Assuming you need any."

The question must have cost her something, because she gave him her shoulder while she thought about it. Not the blind side—that would have been too much trust. But the turn of her profile was enough to hide her expression as she crossed to the sink. She dipped water from a pot beside the stove and primed the green cast-iron pump, then began to work the handle. Aethelred watched her biceps and triceps knot as she gave it three hard pulls, metal rattling against metal, before the water gushed forth.

He wondered where the blacksmith lived. Ailee, or closer? The pump and the stove hadn't been cast and forged here, not unless she had a foundry out back behind the chicken coop. They looked like post-Rekindling manufacture, so they must have been carted out from town. That implied positive things about the local economy.

The smell of water—clean, a little metallic—filled the kitchen, following the sound of a flood ringing into metal. Aethelred hitched his elbows on the counter or what passed for it—a crudely knocked-together table painted yellow and blue—and leaned back to watch. Aithne dipped cold water into a kettle, hooked a stove lid aside with the other hand, and set the kettle on the hob to boil. When she turned back, her arms were folded over her chest.

"How do I know I can trust you?"

The crux of it. He knew why she'd let him in the house, and he knew the only words that would hold the key. He said, "Cahey does."

Her nod was curt, her stare assessing. He felt her considering the scars, the walking stick, the creak of his exoskeleton when he shifted his weight back onto his feet. "Can you work?"

"I can chop wood and haul water."

"You'd have to sleep on the floor."

Aethelred patted his pack. "I have blankets," he said. "I'll sleep in the yard."

Borje the chapel-keeper knew he loomed. He thought of himself as capable, and not nearly as dumb as he looked, but he also knew his size and strength led others to mis-estimate him. Hauling a load of rags and polish up to the chapel was his idea of a pleasant afternoon, and the wind tickling the salt grass, the sunlight glittering off the ocean far below, consoled and energized him.

He didn't run across pilgrims often, and most of the ones he did meet shied from his massive, scarred shoulders. His shaggy minotaur's head and spreading horns tended to give others pause. If that was not enough to intimidate, there were the stone-hard cloven pincers that formed what passed for his hands.

Borje was moreau, a warrior servant created by the Technomancer from the body of a beast in the days when Eiledon was falling. But Borje had been kissed by an angel in a back stairwell forty years before, and so he was also a Believer, and free.

On a half-sunny day just before summer truly began, he met the pilgrim who did not seem afraid. She led her star-faced, evenly colored mare up the back side of the bluff as Borje crested the hill.

He stopped so that he would not startle the animal. She was the first horse that he had seen since he really *was* a bull, the four-legged sort, and his nostrils flared to collect her scent. The woman's hair was pale and shining and her skin was as fair as that of the angel whose kiss had freed him from servitude so many years ago.

The mare smelled of barn and hay and fresh-turned earth. The woman smelled of herbs hung to dry. She led her snorting mount up the path toward Borje, stopping a few meters away. The mare tested her reins, scuffing the ground with her left fore-hoof, eyeing the bull uncertainly.

Borje tilted his horns at the woman cautiously. "Welcome to the chapel," he said. "Have you come to pray?"

She ran her left hand through her long, smooth locks. Her cloak and trousers seemed gray to Borje, and her knotted blouse might have been white at the beginning of her road. She carried no weapons that he could see, although there might have been a pistol in her pocket.

"I've come to meditate," she said. "What is the name of this place? I saw it from the Eiledon road."

"It hasn't a name," Borje answered, stepping off the path so that she and her horse could continue. He fell into step on her right, watching the mare out of the corner of one wide-set eye to make sure she didn't try anything foolish. "But some call it the Chapel of the Books."

"Books?" She glanced over at him, looking interested. Her eyes sparkled. He thought she might be pretty, as human women went. His heavy ears flickered to scoop up more of her sooth-ing tone.

"Many books. They belonged to the Angel-who-went-into-the-Sea. Have you heard the story?"

She nodded. "Several times." She stroked the nose of her mare as they came up to the little chapel. "I've heard rumors another angel dwells here still. Is that so?"

Borje angled his head to regard her directly with his left eye. Just because you knew things didn't mean you had to share them with every passing stranger.

"Oh," he said, "there are a lot of little cottages and villages hereabouts. Hermits and fishers and farmers and other reset-tlers. But angels? I couldn't tell you anything about that."

She dropped the reins on the damp sandy ground. "Stay here, Elder," she said, patting the horse on the shoulder. The mare whickered and lipped the woman's shoulder, then low-ered her head to nose among the salt grass for anything that might be good.

The blond woman squared her shoulders and threw her head back, allowing her eyes to drift half-closed as she tested the scent of the sea breeze. The collar of her blouse gapped a little, and the bull saw something like a run of tears sparkle against the white skin of her throat.

She turned abruptly back to Borje and thrust out her right hand. He juggled rags and polish, reaching out hesitantly to touch his bifurcated hoof to her palm. "You're the chapel-keeper? Is there a priest?"

The bull shook his head. "I'm Borje. We don't preach here. But people come to look at the statues, and the sea. I can tell you the story if you'd like that." He hesitated. "Although you said you'd heard it."

"I'd like to hear it again," she said, turning her face away from him to watch the seabirds wheel overhead. Nearby, from the edge of the bluff, a raven fell into the wind. "I'm called Heythe these days, when I'm called anything at all. I've come from a long way off, you see."

"Then welcome to my door, Heythe. What's brought you this far?"

She smiled a smile that filled him with warmth and the will to please. "I travel," she said. "I trade in stories. And in other things."

$\mathcal{A}$ethelred hefted the knife in his hand, flexing his fingers around its worn black handle as if that could ease their ache. The blade was old, pre-Desolation, and held an edge like glass, but even so it had been sharpened so many times that the remaining width was thinner than his pinkie finger. Piles of strawberries loomed on the blue and yellow table before him, hulled on the right, not-yet-hulled on the left. The cutting board between his hands was gory with their juices.

All that, and he couldn't smell them over the reek of boiling vinegar. Flushed and dripping cloudy sweat from the draggled ends of escaping locks, Aithne bent down by the stove, poking up the fire so it would leap through the stove-holes. She'd laid a board over the sink, and on it were arrayed two dozen mismatched pieces of glassware, each containing a ration of sliced green tomatoes, peppercorns, sugar, salt, cloves, and coriander.

Aethelred picked up another strawberry, thinking about putting up food for winter and for trade. And thinking of the far-flung trade that had sprung up with such urgent immediacy, once people were free to move about the world again.

When he was a younger man, he would have been unable
to imagine a world in which such a thing was possible, never
mind needful. Now he performed the functions of survival
without thinking, with the skill of long practice. And with a
certain contentment. Useful work was a blessing.

"Aithne," he said, when she stood up and hooked the stove
door shut with her poker. She reached for her pot holders, glancing over her shoulder on her good side to let Aethelred know
she'd heard him.

He weighed a strawberry in his hand, laid the forefinger of
the other hand along the knifeblade, and hulled the berry with
a practiced twist. "Have you thought about getting out in the
world for a while?"

"Come over here and handle the funnel, would you?"

Aethelred put down his knife and came around the table,
gathering equipment along the way. He set the sterilized funnel
in the first jar, careful to touch it only with the sterilized pliers,
and stepped out of the way. Aithne wore a sweat-and-food-
stained blouse with the sleeves ripped out. When she gripped
the stockpot and hefted it, long muscles cabled along her arms.

She poured, and Aethelred moved the funnel, and each jar
filled in turn. From the side, he could see her lower lip sucked between her teeth in concentration, the way her eye watered from
the vinegar steam, the way she measured the distances with her
body because she couldn't accurately judge them by perspective.

"Getting out in the world?" she said, as she set the almost-
empty pot down and tossed the pot holders aside. Sterilized lids
rattled and slid as she snagged the container holding them, and
began to sort through with tongs. "I think running this house
is enough work for anyone."

"Stagnant work," Aethelred said. "Churning water. Have you thought about going somewhere?"

She shrugged. "Pull that other pot over the heat, will you? It needs a rolling boil. Where is there to go?"

He picked up her discarded pot holders and did as she had asked. When the second pot was squarely on the fire, he dropped the pliers and the funnel back inside. "Forward," he said. "You know, there are other people out there who need help the way you needed help when Cahey came to you."

She set the last mismatched lid on the last mismatched jar and frowned at her work, tilting her head to make sure she'd dealt the *right* mates together. Still using the tongs, she swapped two, and then sorted out the rings. "You think I owe the world something, preacher-man?"

"No," he said, stepping back to give her room. "I think you owe yourself something. Something beyond staying alive."

"Sometimes staying alive is all you can manage." She didn't look up from her work.

"Sometimes it is," he agreed. "And when it's not, anymore?"

She didn't answer. She just bent down behind her escaping hair and started tightening rings.

38 A.R.
Summer

Heythe bends at the waist beside a clear stream, up to her knees in water, sunlight caught golden along the pale curve of her muscled flank. She washes her hair, not knowing a wolf stalks her. He has been watching for years now, not always but often, finding and following as she moves from place to place and small, seemingly innocuous task to task. Somehow, though, her path brings her among the moreaux more often than not, and when she shares stories and conversation with them her questions always seem to—sooner or later—touch on what they know of the Angel-who-went-into-the-Sea.

Muire, the Historian, who has become what Heythe sought so long to destroy.

Lather floats from her as she plunges her hair to rinse it, white lashings on a brown surface borne away under the arching branches of trees. When she straightens, swinging yellow locks, sun glittering in the strands of the intricate necklace that is the only thing she wears, the water flies from her like a cascade of diamonds.

She stretches, goosefleshed, hands on her hips and her shoulders already pinkening, while the wolf watches from the shadows halfway into another world, and hopes Heythe cannot see him.

He's never had any real sense of her capabilities except that they are greater than his own and constantly surprising. What he *does* know is that she defeated the assembled might of the children of the Light—or, more precisely, that she caused them to trick themselves into defeat. That she used his own weakness to help bring about that destruction. That nothing is beyond or beneath her. That it was a trivial exercise for her to step forward more than two thousand years in time, to when the Dweller Within should have been dead of the blow she dealt him with Mingan's unwitting help—or that she had had the wherewithal to make it seem trivial, at least.

He knows also that it must have been a shock to her to find her victim replaced by one strong and hale, without crippling injury. But she is Heythe, and she will take this setback in stride, and move forward in her extermination of everything the wolf finds bright and brave in the world.

Most tellingly, he knows he cannot hope to defeat her if she knows he exists to oppose her. She is stronger and more subtle than he—his methods in his youth were never subtle, but over the centuries he has learned otherwise. If he is to lay her down for once and all, he must do so as the unseen hand in a velvet glove. He must apply her own techniques.

The poetry of it pleases him.

He'd kill her for vengeance, for vengeance is enough. But even more than vengeance, he'll kill her for love.

Not the love she once deluded him into thinking she bore for him. Not that. But other loves entirely, even if the wolf's own ancient treachery has rendered them no more clean than what was between him and Heythe. Loves that he can at least still honor in the defense, though he has poisoned them.

This boots thee not, he growls to himself, cloak furled tight to his shoulders against an otherworldly chill he cannot feel as pain, as much as he might sometimes wish to. This, too, Heythe has done to him. It is not his way, to dwell in the past, to second-guess while his thoughts whine and circle. But in the witch's presence—even if she does not remark him—he does. She makes him more man than wolf, as always, and as always he is undone by it.

You are brave, says the great, calm presence at the heart of him. **Most wounded as you have been would not return to the fray.**

Because it is such courage to linger here, on the edge of reality, and watch a woman wash her hair.

It is courage to approach a thing that can destroy us, Kasimir says. **The more so when we have already felt its sting.**

The wolf snorts. Beyond his shadowed gateway, Heythe picks her way up the stream bank, wet feet slipping in mud. She passes close, so close the wolf could reach from the oak-shadow he hides inside and clutch her wrist. Her scent is a visceral memory, a twist inside him of lust and hatred and self-loathing so bright and sharp that for a moment he feels nothing else. The growl caught low in his throat surprises him; it's a moment before he can silence the sound.

If Heythe cannot see him, chances are she cannot hear him, either. But it was not exactly his own growl. Or rather, it was, for though he wears the shape and clothes and words of a man now, two wolves live still within him. One is a gray wood-ghost, a canny old loner, lost to his pack, a sorrowing shadow of the darkling forest. But the other, fire-eyed, seared within by a heat that rises up his throat and burns below the collar that chokes him every time he swallows, is the Suneater, a monster out of myth and mystery, a beast driven mad by pain and despair until murder is its only passion.

The Grey Wolf watches Heythe pick her sun-dried clothes off the twigs of a bush, where she spread them after washing them among the stones, and feels the Suneater stir within. He tastes the mad wolf's fury; he remembers the savor of steaming blood, rent bowels, torn flesh. He imagines tasting it again.

He will not fail this time. He will not stop until Heythe is dead.

With a curl of the Grey Wolf's lips, the Suneater smiles. And a growl near-silent, like the deep grinding of glaciers, rumbles in his chest again.

38AR.
Summer

The village of Newport lay three miles down the beach from
Cahey's cottage—an easy hour's walk, with time to let Cathmar
down out of the shoulder harness along the way so he could run
through the sand between the bones. Cahey also had a heavier
sack filled with repaired fishing nets slung over his other shoulder.
It banged his hip in counterpoint to his stride as he ambled along,
the strap cutting his trapezius.

Cahey set out at sunset, meaning to reach the village when
the fishing boats were putting in. His first glimpse of the village
came as he rounded the point. It sat inside the curve of the land
where the coast hooked around a deepwater harbor, a single long
pier stretching out like a hand greeting the sea.

Newport proper sat up the bluff, accessible by a switch-
backed road. New construction, houses cobbled together with
salvage and ancient, pre-Desolation materials. Good sawn tim-
bers were reserved for boats. Diode lanterns gleamed along the
path up, and shone down the length of the pier, illuminating
the bustle of unloading fishing craft. The landward end of the
floating pier was clotted with rickety market stalls.

Cahey ignored them. He slipped through the crowd, head

ducked, the little boy on his back engrossed in tugging his braids this way and that, staring over his shoulders at the crowd. It was familiar-strange walking among people, feeling the boards of the floating pier shift under his feet and theirs also. The old skills of moving in the city came back fast.

The boat he wanted berthed at the far end of Newport pier, the hull painted marigold and picked out in leaf-green and gold letters: *The Merry Fetch*. He caught the eye of the *Fetch*'s brown captain by the bottom of the gangplank and walked up to her, unslinging the bag of nets as he did.

"Merry," he greeted the captain. She grinned up at him, and thrust out a thick arm for the nets.

"We got a holdful, Cahey," she said. "Not too much time to chat. Your payment in dried fish to the usual address?"

"Yes," he answered. Cathmar bounced on his back, kicking his heels against Cahey's hip bones. He winced to make Merry laugh. "Anything else that needs mending?"

She shook her head. "Lucky trip. Look . . ." Her eyes traveled up and down his body. He wondered if it was a blatant pass or a livestock appraisal. His face might be cut up, but his body was pretty enough. And if it wasn't that, he knew he looked fit for hard labor.

"You look like you can handle yourself. Why don't you come out with us, next trip? Earn more than dried fish."

Cahey laughed and bounced to make Cathmar giggle. He knew she could see the bright eyes of the little boy peering around his shoulder. "I'm a dad," he said. "I stay onshore where it's safe."

It wasn't a lie. Just two facts, and she was free to make connections between them.

She chuckled. "All right. The rate you mend nets at, I suppose you do all right. What the hell do you do with that much fish, anyway?"

"Mostly, I bring it up to the city and donate it to charity," he answered. "But don't tell anybody that. It's our secret."

She sucked on her lips, obviously disbelieving him. "All right," she said, pushing an ebony-black tangle out of her face. Her hair might have started the day braided, but it hadn't stayed that way. He wondered if she was just too vain to crop it. "But remember my offer. *Merry Fetch* can use good hands."

He smiled and nodded, turning away. "I'll do that. If I ever find myself wanting to go to sea."

38 A.R.
Autumn

*A*ithne straightened, pushing both fists into the small of her back. She flipped the curls that had escaped her braid out of her face and sighed, glancing around her former kitchen one last time. The stained wooden cupboards and the pantry door stood open, early-morning sunlight spilling in the window over the sink. She swallowed the smile that hovered around the corners of her mouth. She wasn't sorry to be leaving.

Still. A moment's image came to her of a lean, shirtless man doing dishes while a gray cat watched with interest from the edge of the sink. She thought about the sunlight catching dark red highlights off his skin, and the smile returned. A spike of regret killed it.

And if he noticed you were anything but a charity case, he might have been worth fighting for.

She kicked her pack lightly with a booted toe. "All right, old man, that's the last of it. Is there anything else you want to see if we can trade for, or are you happy with what we've got?"

Aethelred weighed a traveling pack in his left hand. "I can take more than this," he said.

"You're three times my age." She reached down and caught

hers up. It was heavy, but it would get lighter as she ate her way through it. She pointed with her other hand, indicating worried blue eyes peering out of the greenery atop a wounded old hutch in the corner. "Besides, you talked me into this road trip to save the world. So you're carrying the cat."

"Does the cat have a name?" he asked, dragging a stool over to the hutch.

Aithne shook her head. "Like a damn cat will come when you call it?"

She watched his massive, thick-fingered hands coax the little animal out from under the philodendron. "Well, men have names. So I suppose that's got nothing to do with it."

Aithne grinned. "The voice of experience?"

He turned around and handed her the cat before hopping off the little stool. He landed hard, betraying his great weight. She imagined she heard the mechanisms whine under his skin.

"There," he said. "You get to pack the cat."

42 A.R.
Winter

The wolf folds his arms inside the shadows and watches man and boy along the salt-grass dune, racing a kite against the swooping gulls. A twinge closes his throat; he looks away. There are more gulls in every direction, and the wind that blows across the worlds brings the wolf the scent of sharp sea and dry salt.

He steps through shadows to a sheltered corner, out of sight of Cathoair and Cathmar. The dunes march long and iterative in every direction; if he climbed higher, he would be silhouetted, but eventually come upon a road.

Someone is not here, has not been here, who should be. It frightens the wolf, who is becoming accustomed—again—to the slow march of fear in a life he had, for a while, rid of it.

"Imogen," he says. *Kasimir, can you hear her?*

No, the stallion says. **I think I speak into her, but she does not answer.**

"Imogen," says the wolf, aloud again.

The Imogen does not answer.

42 A.R.
Midwinter

At least Freimarc is warmer than Eiledon, Selene thought, pacing deliberately down the boardwalk at the waterfront in the curling mists of predawn. The weathered old buildings were different, too: the Free City crouched on the coast of a long, curving gulf that brought warmer water north. Eiledon would be lousy with snow by now. Freimarc's peeling pastel stucco houses and low-roofed commercial buildings were still snarled with vines and climbing roses between roads stuck about with crooked palm trees, although the blooms were past until spring.

Selene had never liked the snow. She glanced down a rocky black beach at the broad, placid gulf and smiled. In the angled winter sunlight, clumps of seaweed bobbed with the tide.

Freimarc angled up steeply away from the water, ranks of colorful dwellings roof-tiled in red, yellow and blue ascending a series of hills. Many lay vacant still, the uninhabited ones having become overgrown. It didn't rain much here, but the warm gulf sent nightly fog-banks and morning gloom rolling across the hills to saturate gardens and hanging plants—enough moisture to sustain lush subtropical growth. On the south side of the hills, against a south-facing wall, lemons could be coaxed to grow, and gardens even of uninhabited houses were thick as well with oranges, olives, almonds and apricots—though the latter were out of season now.

Resettlers had come here in droves, for the climate, for the technological resources still in fair repair—for Freimarc had been one of the last surviving cities of the Desolation—and for the easy access to a fine harbor. In the world after Rekindling, these things were precious. While Eiledon's university still produced the only engineers and technomancers, some were now emigrating to Freimarc, and a few hoverboards and taxis cruised the city's skies again. In its tropical lushness, fruit-sellers might gather produce in the urban orchards and peddle it along the road to travelers or to householders who had exceeded the production of their own small plantations.

Selene did not eat fruit, her system being adapted to flesh and organ meat. Still, she enjoyed the aroma of winter citrus dewed with mist, which carried down the hills on warming currents of air as the rising sun began to burn the hilltops clean. It combined with the clean salt scent of the sea.

Someone had been collecting bones and shells from the beach, and all along the edge of the boardwalk they made a latticed wall—or more of a heap—stretching down to the sand below.

Selene paused, arms folded, to contemplate the beach and the rolling tide, until her ears swiveled at a shout. She turned away from the water, boardwalk not so much as creaking under her padded feet. Ahead, she saw a scuffle. Teenage gangsters and a middle-aged blond woman with a net marketing bag full of those very lemons and oranges. The fur on the back of Selene's neck rose. Her gray-ringed tail lashed.

Banded ceramic and leather armor creaked as Selene grinned behind her whiskers and sprinted toward the fight, not bothering to draw her sword Solbiort or uncoil her whip.

The young men saw her coming. They didn't stand their ground. Selene had something of a reputation in Freimarc by then; moreaux still weren't common in this city, though they traveled to the limits of the Eiledain diaspora. Though the Technomancer who had created them was no more, Selene and her brethren were peacekeepers still.

She helped the woman to her feet. While Selene crouched to collect spilled blood oranges, the woman thanked her profusely. The snow leopard glanced up, looking into startlingly blue eyes framed by a twist of honey-colored hair shot through with ash.

"Thank you," the woman said. She reached out to offer Selene her hand, and Selene refused politely, showing her glittering claws by way of explanation. It was one thing if she scratched one of her brother einherjar by accident: they would heal.

Humans were fragile.

Those eyes really were distressingly blue. Selene glanced away, found herself looking at a glittering necklace peeking out from behind the woman's collar. "You should keep that covered," Selene said, gesturing to it. "It's probably why they bothered you."

"Oh," she said, and put her hand on her throat. "You're right. I'll be more careful from now on."

There was something in the woman's tone that continued to haunt Selene long after she returned to the little flat she sometimes shared with a friend. It was a bright and simple space, tile-floored, the furniture simple wooden benches and chairs and a desk constructed of a salvaged door balanced across a cabinet and two stools. There was no bed, for Selene did not sleep, but she'd painted the walls warm shades of umber and red echoed by the blankets folded for comfort on the benches, and five of the seven walls of the crooked two-room space were lined with waist-height racks that held books—a few bound volumes, a few etched tablets, and far more traditional scrolls—salvaged from all over the ruins of the world. The curtains were red and gold wool that kept the sun back in the summer and the cold out in the winter, though the shutters beyond them were currently closed anyway because glass, even salvaged, was still dear.

Selene sat down in front of her viscreen to check the news and message Cahey and his son. Recollection distracted her while she typed a casual greeting and a brief, newsy mail.

Humans' motivations were often mysterious to her. More mysterious than they knew, than—she suspected—they could ever be to one another. Her years in law enforcement, her experience as a Black Silk, one of the commanders of the Technomancer's militia, had taught her that humans were complex and contradictory in ways no animal—and certainly no moreau—could predict. But the woman hadn't seemed as frightened by her misadventure as Selene would expect, and she'd had an air about her when Selene refused her hand that could have been embarrassment over being rebuffed, or could have been something else. Thwarted malice, calculation carefully concealed.

Selene made a note to remember the woman's face, and cursed herself for not getting a name. A failure of instinct and professionalism. But there weren't that many people in the world. She'd keep an eye out, that was all, and chances were they'd meet again.

Her 'screen beeped, a message back from Cathmar, typed awkwardly with an eight-year-old's spelling. Strange how an eight-year-old angel was still an eight-year-old first and only second an angel.

Selene's ears pricked in pleasure. She began keying her reply, but her typing was interrupted by the swing of the garden door and a lean dark-clad shape silhouetted against the morning.

Adapted to the dim room, Selene's pupils narrowed to pinpricks before she could see without pain. But she knew by scent and the sound of his breathing who came, and so she stood to greet him. And folded the 'screen closed over her unsent message so he would not see, and be distressed.

"Mingan." She crossed the room to him on padded footsteps, and paused at arm's length. "Were you lurking in the garden all this time?"

He shut the door behind him. "I came from the shadows," he said, as if she would not have been able to tell by the dank cold rising from his cloak and the smell of ashes that complicated the everyday animal musk of him. But what he said next made her ears and whiskers twitch: "I followed thee. It is well thou didst touch not the woman with the necklace; she is not what she seems."

"Cryptic," Selene said. "But that's what I've come to expect. Are you cold? Would you like tea?"

"I swelter," Mingan snarled. One-handed, he grasped his cloak by the collar, flicked the catch, and cast the heavy fabric aside. It was his fourth or fifth since she'd known him. This one had a collar lined in squirrel fur, silver-gray against the char-gray of the wool where it puddled on the floor. "That woman—"

"Something seemed off about her," Selene admitted, giving way before him so he could advance into the room. She touched the handle of her whip, reflexively, and the hilt of her sword as well. "You *followed* me?"

He shrugged. "Or her. She is an old and dangerous enemy. Forgive me if I say not too much more on the topic: it is a painful one. But best if thou avoidst her in future, for she would not scruple to use thee against me, if ever she knew our association. Now, thou art her target for thou art waelcyrge, which is a small and idle thing. If she knew more, though, her interest might be . . . personal. And I do not know that I could protect thee from that."

He glanced aside, at her closed 'screen, and neither asked nor made a gesture toward it. Nevertheless, Selene felt a chill raise her hackles. Mingan was not a fearful creature, but his caution carried more behind it than the words implied. He was frightened, and Selene was not sure she'd ever seen him frightened before.

He continued, "Best also if thou should not speak my name or offer word of my existence for a time. To anyone."

"You could," she offered gently, "just tell me what's going on."

He cocked his head at her. "Thee before any other," he said. "But no. Not yet."

44 A.R.
Autumn

Ten-year-old Cathmar sprawled on the blue and red rug beside the fire, idly scratching at his slate with a stylus. He tapped the butt of the implement against his color pad, changing it to burgundy, and started sketching rows of little roundheaded stick people holding hands.

He didn't feel the cold any more than other einherjar, which his father found reassuring, but both of them enjoyed playing with fire. Cahey watched Cathmar idly over the top rod of the book the einherjar was supposed to be studying. Teaching his son to read had given Cahey the excuse to learn as well.

He set his book aside.

The boy looked away from his slate, staring into the fire pensively. Flickers of light reflected in his dark gray eyes, painted his mahogany skin with traces of orange and gold. The boy reached into the granite fireplace and poked his fingers into the flames, playing at pinching bits off and then putting them back.

He's a beautiful boy, Cahey thought. *He takes after his mother.*

She would have seen it differently, of course.

Cathmar turned his head to regard his father. "Dad?" The

edge of a frown crossed the boy's face, a world shadow eclipsing the moon.

Cahey nodded, rolling his shoulders and twisting his neck. The old pain was gone with his transformation, but the habits of easing it remained. He leaned forward in his bentwood chair.

Cathmar took a deep breath and spoke very fast. "Why did my mother leave us?"

Cahey rocked back in his chair. "She had . . ." He paused and bit back his bitterness, waited until it would not color his voice. Cathmar deserved to think well of his mother. "She had something she had to do. You know that. You know why she had to go."

The boy shrugged, rolling over on his back like a puppy, propped up on gangling elbows. "Yeah, but . . . couldn't she have waited? Until I was grown-up? Did she have to go right away?"

Cahey rubbed a thumbnail against an eyebrow, thinking. "I don't know."

That's not an honest answer, is it? Angels don't lie, remember? It was the voice of his own conscience, but for a moment he pretended it had a woman's tone.

He cleared his throat and added, "Well, no, I guess I do know. I think she felt she had to make her decision fast, before more people died. And I . . ."

She didn't tell me about you. She must have known. She must have hidden it on purpose.

Cathmar pushed himself up farther. Cahey looked at the boy's unmarked face, and his fingers worried at his own scar. *When I was his age . . .*

Cathmar would never have to know about those things, though. "I suspect . . . I know . . . I chased her away."

The boy sat up completely, crossing long legs on the red and blue rug. He was—oddly—both tall for his age and young-seeming. His brow furrowed, then smoothed. A moment later, and he came back with a childish non sequitur. "Hey, I want to go over to Kailley's house in the village later. Is that okay?"

He so badly wants to be a normal boy, Cahey thought. *And I so badly want him to be something else. I wonder if it were kinder if he weren't?* Cahey nodded, relieved that his son had dropped the other line of questioning. "Sure."

Cathmar nodded and went back to his game with the fire. But a little while later, when Cahey had raised the book again and was winding slowly through the chapters, pretending to read while he watched his son over the rod, Cathmar looked up again.

"Why?"

"Why can you go to Kailley's?"

"No," he said. "Why did you chase Mom away?"

Cahey fell silent for a long time, and then shrugged. He spoke in a level tone to get the words around the pain in his throat. "It wasn't on purpose. I was young. I had no idea what she wanted from me. I'm not sure I could have given it to her then if I tried. I hurt her, by accident, and she left me. It wasn't long after that that she changed. Became what she is now, because she had to. Because she didn't think she had a choice. We were desperate, Cath"—and maybe you weren't supposed to admit things like that to a kid. Maybe you were supposed to let them believe in adult omnipotence, but that really wasn't Cahey's style—"and then there was no going back. Or maybe she left me because she knew she had to go into the sea."

He thought back to his first day with his son. The memory took Cahey away completely for a moment, and when the einherjar leaned forward in his chair again he realized he'd lost the thread of the conversation. "I'm sorry; I was thinking. What did you say?"

Cathmar pursed his lips in a gesture his mother would have found familiar. "I asked . . . how you hurt her."

Oh, Hel. Not what I want to be talking to a ten-year-old about.

Cahey pinched the bridge of his nose. "She came from a different world than I did. She . . . when she was young, her people paired up in a way that I didn't understand. Husband and wife, will and action. Almost as if they became one person. She had grown beyond that, over the centuries, become something bigger, something complete. But she still expected to be . . . one half of a whole. And I—well—I had seen the other side of that, growing up."

The angel took a breath. "I wasn't einherjar yet, then. I'd seen how marriage could be a trap, and how it could destroy both sides. So I never chose just one person. I had a partner, Astrid, my best friend, but we weren't tied to each other that way. And then there was your mother. And then there was Selene."

"Aunt Selene?"

Cahey blew air out through his nose. "Yes."

The boy bit his finger, rolled back over, and poked at his slate a few more times.

"And your mother—I think she thought I was somebody she used to care about once, reborn, and it bothered her."

The boy—lean, growing tall, wearing his hair cropped close

to the scalp, in contrast to his father's—looked suddenly curious. "Are you?"

Cahey shrugged. "I don't suppose it matters."

"What happened to Astrid?"

I knew he was going to ask that.

"She was mortal," the angel said quietly. "I killed her. By accident. There were a lot of people dying, then."

48 A.R.
Winter

The night before he and Cathmar were to go into Eiledon, Cahey sat before the fire sewing shoes. He wasn't yet as much of a cobbler as he'd like, but he was improving over last year. Soon, he thought, he'd be better than passable.

This, however, would do for now.

By the time dawn had begun graying the horizon behind the dunes, several small pairs of shoes joined food, coats and other things on a handcart in the cobbled yard. Cathmar, tugging a hat over oiled curls, appeared in the doorway. A pack dragged his shoulders back, the belt cinched above his hips. The hat and coat were camouflage, nothing more, but Cahey was glad to see Cathmar wore them. Early on, after he'd changed but before Muire bought a Rekindling, he'd flaunted his difference, walked barefoot in snow and made a spectacle of himself. But now that she was gone it seemed right to obscure himself.

He was not, after all, so special.

Cathmar tugged the door closed and locked it, pocketing the key with concealed pride. In his turn, Cahey concealed amusement. Cathmar was thirteen, and Cahey had only just turned the key-ring over to him. A sign of incipient adulthood, which the boy gloried in. That made Cahey's anticipation of what came next all the more enjoyable.

Cahey tugged a long bundle out of the handcart and handed it to Cathmar as Cathmar came up beside him. Cathmar took it, unquestioning, and weighed it across his palm. His hand stroked blue silk and silver silk cordage, and when he looked up again he frowned. "This is elaborate."

Something rare, in the simplicity of their lives. "It's a gift," Cahey said. "Open it."

Cathmar slipped the knot with his teeth, unwinding the tasseled cord. He slung it over his shoulder while he worked on the silk, which was fine enough that Cahey could see the gray pale brightness of morning twilight through each draped layer. He knew the moment when, the wrappings still half-on, Cathmar knew what the present was, because he glanced up at Cahey through his eyelashes, tilting his head incredulously.

"It was your mother's," Cahey said. "Draw it out."

Now silk fell in indigo coils. Cathmar stood among them, sheath clutched in one hand, the other closed on the wire-wrapped hilt of a sword. He tugged, gently, and the sword slid into his hand with a sound like flicked crystal.

He held it, weighing it on his palm, and Cahey heard him take a deep breath and keep it in. Deep in the obsidian blade, a pale blue spark ignited, raced the length of the fuller, and filled the sword with Light.

That held breath hissed out again. Cathmar asked, "What's her name?"

"Nathr," Cahey said. "It means—"

"'Adder.'" Cathmar nodded. "Why now?"

"It's time," Cahey answered, uncertain how to tell his son

that he just knew, with a *swanning* certainty set bone-deep. "She was always meant for you. See? She knows your hand."

Cathmar stared at the sword. Then, as if he'd been doing it all his life, he slid the blade back into her sheath and hooked the sheath on his belt, where the sword would hang beside his thigh. "Come on," he said. "Let's get some charity done."

Within its walls, Eiledon hunched on both banks of a wide, slow, mud-colored river. From his vantage point on a hilltop, Cathmar watched a caravan roll up the road toward it, and a flying taxi glittering in the sun as it described an arc over the city. The walls were brave with banners, and the same stiff breeze they floated on blew the river water cascading from the floating island of the University into rainbow arcs, veils like silk scarves in all seven colors. The river Naglfar seemed not to notice the perpendicular bend in its path as it leapt the empty gulf that bisected its broken bed, flowing directly upward hundreds of feet, crossing the University campus, and then plunging down again to wear a rocky cauldron deep into the bedrock under the city. Many—if not all—Eiledain must live within the sound of its thunder, though from this distant vantage Cathmar could hear only a faint rumble and so it seemed dreamlike, unreal.

From this height, Eiledon behind its veils seemed like a city made of patchworks of several other cities. A squat medieval town with close-leaned roofs and walls of stone and timber huddled at the feet of soaring arcologies, their glass and metal towers maintained by the technomancers and engineers still trained at that unearthed University. Stone and brick masonry high-rises and factories lined up martially along the riverfront, and Cathmar could make out the erratic leaning roofs and walls of a shantytown in the shadow of the University.

Though it was yet early, the valley road below was crowded. In addition to the caravan with its drakes and dogs and outriders, there were mule-carts, hovers and horsemen, solar trolleys ticking along at their incremental, inexorable pace. And people on foot, dozens into hundreds, arriving for the winter carnival.

The day was still new when Cathmar and his father arrived amid the crush of people seeking entrance at the gates. The bottleneck ate up a few moments, but the gate guards with their automatic weapons weren't searching anyone today and Cathoair was a known face. The two of them were passed inside without questions.

The walls were ancient, once crumbling and tumbledown but now patched with construction less than fifty years old. Those walls described the same arc as the shimmering curtain of light—the Defile—that circumscribed the city. Cathmar might have flinched from the green incandescence, but he had passed through it before with his father and knew it would not harm him.

Inside, he spent a few happy moments listening to his bootheels click on the cobblestones of the paved city streets, while beside him his father hauled the handcart, wheels rattling. Cathmar bounced on the balls of his feet and swung his arms.

Finally. Something *different* for a change.

Helios the moreau, black-maned and golden-eyed, met them just inside the Wolf Gate, an irony not wasted on Cahey. They were expected, and approximately four hundred pounds of former Black Silk saw them through the winter carnival crowds jamming the streets without misadventure. The lion topped Cahey by a head, and was easily twice as wide; people just seemed to melt away in front of him. They had no trouble bringing the cart through at all.

"Thank you," Cahey said.

"Easier when you loom," Helios answered. "It's harder to claim they didn't see you coming. And if they really *don't* see you coming"—his grin bared chipped yellow canines as thick as Cahey's fingers—"they're awfully apologetic."

The chuckle was a profound bass chuffing, deep enough to make the space inside Cahey's lungs feel strange.

Inside, Helios guarded them through the Wolf Gate neighborhood as far as the Riverside Market, where Borje the bull met them and admitted them through a makeshift barrier into the carnival grounds. All around the market square the creaking machinery of thrill rides whirred; the voices of candy-sellers and barkers boomed. Cahey pretended serenity, but really it all made him want to put his back to a wall.

Borje was the only moreau Cahey had ever seen bigger than Helios, and as Helios laid his massive, furred fingers against the back of Borje's bifurcated hoof Cahey wondered that the transformation they had both endured seemed to have wiped out any trace of natural suspicion between predator and prey.

"This it?" Borje asked, while Helios took a step back to make room for Cahey.

"The whole wagon," Cahey said. He dropped a hand on Cathmar's shoulder when Cath came up beside him, and felt the young man straighten.

Someone was watching him. Cahey always knew. In this situation, that was no surprise: two big moreaux and a couple of humans standing by a handcart drew attention. But he turned left and right, as if stretching, to see if he could catch a glimpse. No luck.

Borje folded black-bronze arms, hide shining over forearm muscle. "This isn't the biggest wagon this year."

Cahey grinned. His hand went up reflexively, to cover the missing teeth, and he forced it back down again. Ridiculous vanity. "Good."

Ten years before, that had not been the case, but now what passed for Eiledon's affluent—and even more so, the working poor—turned out with what they could give. Cahey was endlessly surprised by the basic generosity of people, when they were given half a chance and a decent example. He should probably consider himself fortunate that their rottenness, as easily and frequently provoked, never came as a shock.

"Dad—," Cathmar said, whatever he'd been about to say interrupted as Helios spun around and roared, "Hold it right there!"

Cahey whirled, pushing Cathmar behind him. Cathmar went, but Cahey didn't expect him to stay there. Maybe it would buy him enough time to deal with the threat while Cathmar was making up his mind—

But there was no threat to deal with. Helios was already finished with it.

It wasn't that Cahey had forgotten about Black Silk, precisely—what they were, how inhumanly fast and impossibly strong. It was just that it had been a long time since Cahey himself had become something equivalent to those elite among the moreaux. So when he saw that Helios had a black-haired kid about Cathmar's age pinned against the side of the cart by one twisted arm it took Cahey a moment to lock his surging adrenaline back down, to calm himself and accept that somebody else just as competent had already handled the problem.

Helios' mane shook forward around his snarling face, the tawny shoulders dark in fragile morning sunlight. Breath steamed in jets from flaring nostrils as the lion leaned over the kid, rumbling.

"Helios," Cahey said. "Don't break him."

"Just putting the fear of me in him," Helios said, taking a half step back on padded feet. He hauled the kid up, and the kid staggered with him, sprawling feet kicking a tumble of shoes and boxes of biscuits that had fallen out from under the tarp on the handcart.

Helios gave his captive a little rattle—little by Helios' standards. It lifted the kid off his feet, and he squealed. "You're stealing from a charity, kid."

Cahey frowned at the thief's worn shoes, too-short trousers, ungloved hands. He tilted his head back and looked at Helios. Helios huffed and stared up at Borje.

Borje nodded. He gestured with a hoof and Helios let the boy find his feet again. "You follow us," Borje said. "You'll get fed, new shoes. We'll get you a sweater. You run, you get nothing. Maybe the kitty here"—Helios curled his lip at Borje—"will run after you. They do that, you know."

The kid's complexion was too dark to show blanching, but Cahey saw him sway on his feet. Hunger or fear, it didn't matter. He leaned away from Helios' grip, staring down at the stones, hiding his face behind a snarl of forelock.

Cahey said, "What's your name?"

Cathmar touched his father's elbow. "He's a thief," he said, behind his hand. "Are you going to reward that?"

Cahey touched Cathmar's shoulder and murmured, "I'm going to prevent it. Wait, please."

Cathmar grimaced, but subsided.

"Young man," Cahey said—stepping forward, letting a little of the Light show in his eyes—"tell me your name."

The boy's eyes lifted. The side of his face was bruised, and so was his free wrist. He licked split lips. When he opened them, Cahey thought at first it would be to curse. But he swallowed, looked down again, and muttered, "Kirwin."

"Just one name?" In the old days, that would have meant he was lower-caste, not truly considered human. The Technomancer might be gone, but the prejudices lingered.

Silently, the boy nodded.

"Me, too," Cahey said, folding his arms. "Mine's Cathoair."

48 A.R.
Winter

Merry wasn't on the pier that day: a storm was tossing the harbor, and all but one of Newport's six fisher-captains were in the little pub that opened its doors on the landward side, presenting a stolid, broad-shouldered bulk to the ocean. Cahey found her hunkered over a bowl of steaming tea that smelled also of whisky.

She smiled when he came into the cramped, dark pub, Cathmar a step behind, and she straightened on her bench. "Come over," she said. "Sit; I'll buy you a drink."

Cahey shook his head. "I'm afraid I'm a very easy drunk," he said. "Best if we stick to tea." He pulled out the opposite bench for Cathmar before sliding in himself. The captain signaled the server for them while they got settled.

Merry glanced over at the boy. "Cath, you've gotten real big. You must be eating whatever Borje does." She chuckled when Cath blushed, blood tinting mahogany skin. "You boys aren't reconsidering taking up sailing, are you? I've been thinking that fishing is no life for a middle-aged woman. I might be looking for someone to pilot my boat for me."

"I stay off the sea," Cahey said.

Cathmar shook his head quietly. "I'm not much of a sailor."

Merry shrugged. "You tie a good knot. I've seen enough on the nets to know. I could teach you the rest."

Cahey looked over at his son. Cathmar seemed to be considering it, and shook his head. "I think I can do more good here," he said. "Or in Eiledon."

The tea came, and Cahey sipped it. It was weak. "I did come to talk to you about something, though."

Merry raised an eyebrow. "Oh?"

He nodded, and smoothed a thumb along the perfectly polished wooden table, the center inlaid with blue tile. "I've been thinking. You've wanted me on board your ship for years now, and we both know I'm never going to do that. Why don't I help you find somebody—somebody young, you can train yourself—and you'll be helping a kid out of the city and into something like a life."

"It's not an easy life," she said, holding her drink to her lips, allowing the fumes to rise up her nose. She sighed and took a sip, set it aside.

"I'm sure I could find somebody. A good kid. And fishing's a better life than hooking. Or stealing."

She laughed. "Cahey, you don't have to save everybody on the planet."

He finished his tea. "Actually," he said, "I do. One at a time. It's my job."

He felt her studying his face, suddenly struck quiet. "You've got a kid in mind already."

"Yeah." He shook his head. "Kid's got a history. I'll warn you."

"Yeah, well. I've got a history, too. Show me somebody

alive who doesn't." She shrugged, shook her head, swirled her drink. At long last, she nodded. "I'll think about it," she said.

"That'll have to be enough."

Merry didn't look away. The weathered creases in her olive-brown skin got a little deeper. "You're a religious man, aren't you, Cahey?"

"You could say that," he admitted. "Why do you ask?"

"You're really different from the old priest who used to live in your house, is all. He wanted everybody to Believe. Not that he was as bad as some, mind you, and that moreau Borje is all right. But you—you just do stuff for people, whenever you can. Why is that?"

It was a pretty good question, and he gave it the favor of a long, thoughtful consideration before he answered. Cathmar bounced ever so slightly on the old wooden bench beside him. "Somebody set a good example for me, a while back. I'm trying to live up to her, is all."

She chewed that over for a bit before she nodded. Then she jerked her head to the side and grinned. "Go on, get. Your kid is bored. Send your little lost lamb along to me, I'll see what I can make of her. Him? Him."

Early-summer sun tugged at the short coils of Cathmar's hair, provoking him to restlessness. The rays angled in under the wide overhang of the cottage's blue tile roof, and he ducked his head to keep it out of his eyes, trying to make his voice carefully casual. "I was thinking," he said, tying another knot in the fishing net draped over his thighs, "that I could go up to the city tomorrow. If I left early, I could be home by dark."

His father, closer to the woodshed, struck the edge of a log with his axe, sending split pieces flying. He turned his head and raised an eyebrow at the boy, studying him, sucking on his lower lip. Cathmar concentrated on keeping his face casual.

"Huh," Cahey said. He laid the axe aside. "Home by dark?"

The boy nodded, feeling sudden unreasonable hope. He had not expected to be allowed to go alone. Not for a year or two yet. Maybe longer.

"What do you want to do there?"

"Go to market," Cathmar said. "Hear some music. See . . ."

"Somebody other than your sweaty old man?" Cahey dragged the back of his right hand ostentatiously across his forehead, grinning. He wasn't sweating. He bent down to pick up the wood, thinking about it for a long time, and Cathmar could almost see him adding up years in his head.

Cathmar held his breath. Finally, his father picked up the scattered sticks of wood. He considered them for a moment before throwing them at the woodpile one at a time. He said, "Take the small 'screen; call if you need me. Bring trade for a taxi home, just in case. Don't go anyplace you don't know your way. All right?"

Cathmar jumped up and ran to hug him.

It was the only city Cathmar had ever seen, but he knew from the weave that it was a very large city indeed.

He started down the hill.

Eiledon. A much more interesting place than home.

Odors and sounds tickled his fancy as he made his way down Boulevard toward the market. Even early in the day, it was crowded with people: women, men and a few moreaux. The latter favored him with brief acknowledgments as they passed—the flick of ears, the direction of their whiskers. Moreaux, technomantic constructs that they were, lived until they were killed. Eiledon was still home to many old enough to remember having served with Aunt Selene, old enough to remember Cathmar's mother and father.

Not a one of them pointed Cathmar out to any of the humans in the market. It might not have been safe, after all, to draw attention to him. Humans could not be trusted as moreaux could. And the moreaux were bred secret-keepers.

Nathr had become such a constant presence on his hip that Cathmar felt off-balance without her now, and Cathoair always went armed. Cathmar's father said the swords were part and parcel of being einherjar; they came with the duty of it, and were a protection and a tool. *Tool* was probably the right word, because Cathmar knew his father didn't hold Alvitr in esteem or affection, as the Vikings and jarls in old stories held their swords, but he did take meticulous care of the blade. *"Your mother gave it to me,"* he'd say, as if that trumped all other considerations.

And in this, Cathmar mimicked him.

But Cathmar wasn't accustomed to being among so many armed people, alone. At first, it seemed everyone he passed openly wore firearms and knives, and it made him wary, like a constant reminder of the edge of the precipice. He didn't see another sword, though, and before too long the presence of the weapons settled into the background noise it was when he came here with his dad.

The streets were not so busy today as when they usually came. A little thought led Cathmar to conclude that this was because usually they came on carnivals, festivals, or high market days when folks streamed in from all over the countryside for an outing.

Cathmar didn't need to eat, and his father wouldn't let them waste food that could go to people who couldn't survive without it, so the first thing he did was trade some of his salt for a berry pie. He devoured it in a side street.

Musicians drew his attention next. Cahey couldn't sing, either, although he enjoyed trying occasionally, and Cathmar knew from Selene that Muire had teased him about it. Cathmar himself had a crystal-clear tenor. It had never broken, but one day six months previous he had woken up and it had been two octaves deeper than before.

He stood on a street corner for over an hour while the sun

rose high enough to slant between the towers and touch the street, first listening to a violinist and then to a flautist ply their trade. He gave them little bags of gritty pewter-colored seasalt, too: it was easy enough to make.

Finally, tiring of the market as the day grew warmer, Cathmar wandered toward parts of the city where his father had never taken him—west into the old city, crowded as it was along the south bank of the river.

The streets were narrower here, a labyrinth that seemed intended for foot traffic rather than vehicles. Cobbles worn smooth with the passage of years formed the pavement, and the buildings—dressed stone, hung with gargoyles and decorated with stone trellises—almost touched overhead. Cathmar reached up to brush his fingertips against the rusted metal of a wrought-iron staircase clinging to the face of one.

He didn't see the men until they were alongside him, and one laid a mock-friendly hand on his shoulder. The man stank of gin and something harsher, and there was food smeared in his untrimmed beard.

"Boy," the man said, "are you looking for somebody?" He leaned down slightly to peer into Cathmar's eyes, breath reeking. The boy jerked his arm back out of the man's grasp and started to reach for the hilt of his sword.

Someone else grabbed him from behind. "Oh now," said a deeper and less drunken voice, breath hot on the back of Cathmar's neck.

"Let me go. . . ." His voice did not come out on the strong and confident note he had anticipated. He was tall for his age, but both these men were bigger.

Something twisted in his stomach as he remembered a

number of times his father had halted in the middle of a story with a phrase much like "but you don't need to know about that."

The first man came forward to block his escape as the second one pulled Cathmar back into an alley. "We'd hate to have to hurt you, little one. Don't fight us, do what we say, and you'll be home safe with Momma soon."

The boy yanked his mother's sword from her sheath, ducked, and drove himself head-first into the man in front of him. Pain marked his upper arms as he dragged them out of the grip of his second attacker. Cathmar knocked the first man down, surprising them with strength beyond that of a normal adolescent boy, and slashed the first one's thigh with Nathr, swinging wildly, forgetting everything his father and his aunt had ever taught him about fighting.

The second one made a grab for his arm again and Cathmar's sleeve ripped from shoulder to elbow, spinning him half around before he tore himself loose. He caught a glimpse of a third man behind the second and brandished the sword, blade meeting only air.

Somebody yelled, "Kid, *this way*!" A young voice, a girl's voice.

He took a chance and bolted toward it.

The girl caught his arm when he pelted past her, running beside him, long legs matching him stride for stride. She was blond, he saw out of the corner of his eye, blond and tall and wearing a green tunic and sturdy brown boots.

He didn't see much else of her as she clung to his ripped sleeve, shouting directions in whispers. "Come on; come on!" she demanded, pulling him down one side street after another.

Behind him, for a long while, he could hear at least two sets of running feet.

I'm going to have to come up with some sort of explanation for the sleeve, he thought inanely. *I can never tell Dad about this; he'd kill me.*

He still had the sword in his hand, and when the girl pulled him into a doorway he took the opportunity to shove Nathr back into her sheath. His rescuer flattened him against the portal with her body. "Breathe quiet," she said.

The appointed task wasn't made any easier by the pressure of her small breasts against his chest when she leaned into him. He concentrated on the sound of her breath: deep, even, unwinded by ten minutes' hard run hurtling garbage and skidding around corners. He tried not to think about the way she smelled. Like flowers and rainstorms. But more so.

She was taller than he was, perhaps a year or two older. Hair the color of wildflower honey was drawn back in an elaborate braid threaded with golden ribbons. Her eyes sparkled, bright blue, set off by the green of her tunic. *Don't think about the way she smells. Or you're going to embarrass yourself in a moment.*

"Oh," she said quietly. "You're brave *and* cute."

He bit his tongue.

"And," she continued, a moment later, "you like me." She cocked her head to one side, listening for any sound of pursuit. "How old are you?"

"Fifteen," he said, feeling like an idiot.

"Good," she said. "Come with me." She smiled at him, and he followed her almost without thought.

She led him down another labyrinth of side streets and

stood watch while he slithered through a cobwebbed basement window she showed him. There was a hop down to the cement floor inside, but it wasn't far.

The legs between the boots and the hem of her tunic were long and muscled like a dancer's. He had a lovely view of them in the moments after he turned back to help her and before she finished wriggling through the window.

He suddenly couldn't breathe, but he managed to catch her by the waist and soften her fall.

She tilted her head at him, tossing her braid back over her shoulder. "I'm so much trouble," she said. "You have no idea who you're dealing with."

"What's your name?" he asked.

"Mardoll," she said. "What's yours?"

"Cathmar."

She raised an eyebrow. "Unusual name. You're an angel, aren't you?"

He rocked back on his heels, stammering. She kept her grip around his neck. He was acutely conscious of the slight dank smell of the basement and the light trickling through the high, filthy windows. Most of the room was shadowed.

"Your sword," she said. "The statues of the angels have swords like that. Crystal."

"Oh." He couldn't think of anything else to add.

"It's okay," she said. "You don't have to tell me anything."

He was looking into her sea-blue eyes. He didn't want to take his hands off the soft, strong curve of her waist. He suddenly realized more sympathy for his father than ever before.

She swept in and kissed him once. Her mouth seemed to have an intelligence of its own, teeth nibbling his lip like hungry fishes until he relaxed and let the searing slickness of her tongue flicker into his mouth. Her fingers knotted in his short hair, holding his head immobile while she explored his mouth with her own.

He leaned into the kiss, barely remembering to breathe, head full of the scent of dried herbs and thunderstorms.

She stepped back, smoothing his rumpled shirt over his chest with both hands. "Cathmar," she said. "Good name. Come back and see me when you have time, all right? I'm always around. You'll be safe here until they get bored and quit looking for you."

She turned away, took two steps toward the darkness, and turned back over her shoulder. Light from the high narrow windows glimmered off her amber braid as she bent her head and blew him a kiss.

"Mardoll," she said. "Don't forget." And before he could say another word, she ran back into the darkness. Her footsteps thumped on stairs and she was gone.

Four months later, Cathmar stood again in the raucous market, turning a length of brightly dyed cloth over in his hands, trying to decide if it actually could be brighter than Mardoll's eyes. It *was* brighter than the late-autumn sky overhead.

He hadn't seen her since her daring rescue, which led him to drift fretfully to wondering how to locate her, and from there to daydreaming about the curve of her thighs.

"Pretty," she said in his ear, and he jumped into the air.

Sputtering, he dropped the cloth and turned to face her. "Hi," he said, on the second try.

"Hi," she said. She reached out and stroked a finger down the warp of the blue cloth, crumpled on top of a pile of other scarves in a dozen silken shades. "That's a nice color. Is it for your girlfriend?"

"I don't have a girlfriend," he blurted, and then felt himself blush. "I mean, I was just looking."

She gave him the corner of her smile from behind a wing of amber hair. Her eyes *were* brighter. "Oh. Are you doing anything today?"

He shook his head. "Not right now, anyway."

The smile broadened out, dawn overtaking the morning sky. "Excellent," she said. "Let's go play."

Play, it turned out, involved all sorts of places he wasn't supposed to go. She was wearing a shorter tunic this time, with a little circular skirt under it that brushed the top of her knee. The skirt was the same golden color as the fine, soft hairs that glowed when the sunlight hit her calf at an angle.

She kept turning around to make sure he was keeping up, but she never quite let him get within touching distance. Her path led them down twisty side streets and out into a courtyard that ran into a little rough-hewn footbridge crossing the river.

She stopped on the raw brown and gray stones in the middle of the bridge and spun, hair flying out about her in a storm. Cathmar stopped a few meters away and watched until she caught his hands and spun him, too, laughing.

He got dizzy before she did and staggered away to cling to a railing worked in patterns of serpents or vines, watching the brown water roll by below.

"Naglfar," Mardoll said into his ear, suddenly close and smelling of roses, this time. "Named for the ship that bears the dead across the sea."

He turned to her, and she leaned in, ran her tongue—moist, ardent—around the rim of his ear. He gasped, and she danced back out of range again, even as he reached for her.

She was laughing as he gave chase through the narrow streets. They plunged down a flight of stairs into the shadow of the University and found themselves among squat shadowed buildings, shanties crumbling with disuse. It was a ghost town within the confines of a bustling city, and Cathmar wished she'd slow down enough for him to look around.

She drew up short on the top of a little slope, a place where the dimpled underside of the University had left a scallop of earth behind. He came up next to her, was about to reach for her, but she caught his eye and jerked her head down toward the lower part of the city, pointing. "This used to be called the Well," she said. "This part that is always in shadow."

Something possessed him. "Do you know where Bridger runs into Maple?" he asked.

She nodded. "I live down here. Right on the edge, where the sun gets through the waterfall," she said, which seemed strange to him. It was supposed to be mostly deserted, now that people could come and go from the city at will. But if she didn't have family, and she was on her own, she might squat here where no one cared.

He said, "I want to see that."

She shrugged and linked her arm with his, leading him down the hill into the shadowed, strangely square valley.

It wasn't far. From his father's stories, Cathmar almost could have named the building without checking the intersection, although it was abandoned and the door to the basement stair had been bricked up so long ago that the mortar was crumbling. The sign had been torn down, and the basement and first-floor windows were boarded over.

"My father grew up here," he said.

She grinned. "Wanna go inside?"

He looked at her, eyes wide. "Can we? I mean . . ."

The grin grew wider. "A-ban-don'd," she pronounced. "C'mon; I bet there's an escape around the back."

There was, and that stirred the memory of another story. He gave her a lift so she could reach the ladder, and then he chinned himself up to it. The whole thing was built of salvaged metal, pre-Desolation welds the strongest part of a twisted and rickety structure, and Cathmar at first was reluctant to trust his weight to it. But Mardoll seemed fearless, clearing two and three steps at a lunge, and Cathmar was damned if he was going to be left behind. Boy and girl clambered up the stairs, giggling.

One. Two. Three.

"This one," Cathmar said. Mardoll spun in place on the fire escape and kicked the board out of the window.

His eye holographed her at that moment, body extended, eyes clenched as she channeled the power from her hips and shoulders down her right leg—the image of lithe young strength. The board burst into splinters with a report that echoed off the walls of the nearest buildings, almost close enough to touch from the escape.

The way the board shattered told him that either the wood was rotten or she was phenomenally strong.

He was nearly sixteen, and his father had never stinted on explaining the sort of things that go on with one's body. *The map is not the territory,* he thought, as desire awoke, shivery and ice-hot, at the base of his spine.

They climbed in the window and made their way out to the hallway. The smell of dust hung on the dim air. Cathmar counted doors from the stairs. *Second room on the right.* He opened the unlocked door.

It was empty, but he could pick out furniture scars on the tiled floor. There was a connecting door on his left, and he opened it. Suddenly, he remembered that Mardoll was following him. He turned and held the door for her, admiring her profile as he allowed her to precede him.

"This was my father's room," he said as she shut the door behind her.

"Small," she said, walking over to the window. This far from the escape, it wasn't boarded, and the light snagged her hair like catching on gold.

Cathmar heard his father's voice in his ear.

He took a step closer to the girl in the empty room. It was even smaller than he had pictured it: more a closet than a room. The floor was hard tile, and the smell was cold and vacant. *His bed was a mattress under the window. This is where they stayed together, for a little while. It's not where she left him, though. That was across town.* Cathmar wondered if he could find that building, too—with its courtyard and its tall windows facing the river. That one might still be inhabited. Or, he should say, might be inhabited again.

"This is where my mom and dad were. When they were together."

Mardoll turned around and smiled. "Really?" she asked. "That sounds like a tradition, somehow."

He took a single breath that tasted slippery and jagged all at once. *She means that. She means me. I had no idea girls were like this. . . .*

She came to him and caught his face in her slender ivory hands. "Do you want me?" she asked him.

Mute, he nodded.

Flickering like a candleflame, she laughed and spun away. She stood in front of the dust-golden window, framed in its light, and spread her arms wide. A moment, and in one fluid movement she grasped her tunic, raised her arms over her head, and threw it aside.

Light gleamed off her necklace and her hair. Without seeming to stoop, she kicked the yellow skirt off and stood in front of him wearing only her jewelry and her boots.

He thought he'd never seen anything in the world as magical as the sun's rays limning the edges of her body.

"Well, Cath," she said, holding out her arms, "what on earth are you waiting for?"

50 A.R.
On the First Day of Spring

D ad," Cathmar said, glancing up from his book. "Remember a long time ago, you were telling me about Mom?" The question came out sounding less casual than he had intended.

Cahey, potting a tomato plant at the kitchen table, looked over at his teenage son, sprawled in the bentwood chair by the door. "Many times." Spring had come early this year, but it was still too cold to put the seedlings in the ground.

Cathmar bit his lip, leaning his head against the gray field-stone wall behind the chair next to the door. The rough stone snagged his hair. "Do you remember telling me that she thought you were somebody else reincarnated?"

"What brought this on?"

The kid shrugged. "Just something I read." *Because Mardoll asked me where angels came from. And I couldn't find an answer in the book.*

He watched as his father pressed his thumbs down into the dirt, seating the slender bud more firmly. The old man never seemed to get tired of plants, and dirt. And seagulls. Crap all over the blue tile roof or not.

Finally, Cahey nodded. "I think so, yeah. An einherjar she

loved when she was young. Named Strifbjorn. Alvitr was his sword." He pointed a muddy finger at the pair of brass-hilted swords hanging beside the door. The one on the left belonged to Cahey.

The one on the right was plainer in design, and it had belonged to Cathmar's mother.

"And what about Aunt Selene?"

Cahey rolled his shoulders and stretched. "I suppose it's likely her blade belonged to someone else first, too, and your mother thought it was significant enough to mention." He picked up his tomato plant to take it outside.

Cathmar was silent for a long moment. He tapped his finger on the cloth of his book. Something nagged at him, triggered by Mardoll's innocent question about angels. By the unhappy thought of her brief mortality.

"Dad . . ." There was no easy way to broach it.

Cahey stopped midstride and looked at him, a smile tilting one side of his mouth. Cathmar recognized the expression: it was what he looked like in the familiar statue up the hill. *That was how he looked at Mom,* Cathmar realized.

So if he loved her, why did she leave him?

And then a thought he didn't like at all: *So maybe that smile doesn't mean "I love you" after all.*

". . . how old were you when you had your first girlfriend?"

Cahey's brow creased in puzzlement for a moment before he gave his son a wide, knowing grin. "Oh," he said, as if it were a sudden realization. "You're sixteen."

"For two months now."

Cathmar instantly regretted his tone, but Cahey shook it off. "Astrid," he said, thumbs curling over the clay sides of the pot and sinking into the rich black soil. "I could get . . . very boring about Astrid." He grinned, but Cathmar thought there was something sharp hidden in it. "Girlfriend's not exactly what I would call her, though, Cath. We were committed, I guess, if that's the right word. But we never tried to own each other. I mean . . . well. She knew a lot of things I didn't. I . . ." He paused, and the expression on his face was tangled.

"Yes?"

"Well." Cahey took a breath, far away. "She was my first. The first one that counted, anyway. The first girl who kissed me. What do you want to know?"

"I just . . ." Cathmar paused. "I wanted an excuse to tell you about somebody."

Cahey's left eyebrow rose a centimeter. "I wondered if there might be a girl."

"A girl I don't deserve," Cathmar said.

His father laughed. "The trick to keeping 'em," he said, "is to act like you don't deserve them whether you think you do or not."

Cathmar raised an eyebrow in unconscious echo of his father. "That's all it takes?"

"It's more than you might think."

Cathmar thought about that for a moment and changed the subject. "Astrid?"

"Ah. Astrid. Well. I was . . . a skinny street kid, looking for a place to hide from some older boys. I ran down a flight of stairs that I thought led to somebody's basement.

"It was a bar. There was a match going on. They were just sparring. But this girl . . ." His voice trailed off in memory. Cahey took a breath, brought himself back to the present.

"Cath. She wasn't pretty; she wasn't girly. She just was. She totally was; do you know what I mean?"

Cathmar nodded thoughtfully. Even when Cahey talked about Cathmar's mother, there wasn't this edge of intensity to his voice. Watching his face, Cathmar noticed how dark his father's eyes became. *It wasn't just that he cared about her,* Cathmar thought. *It's something else. He owes her something? Or he just hates himself, still, because of what happened?*

"After they were done, she wiped the sweat off her face on a fluffy white towel and walked over to me. I was standing in the corner by the door, hoping nobody would see me, and she walked right over and dragged me out into the light."

Cathmar found himself chewing on the side of his finger. "And?"

"She saw the bruises on my face," Cahey said shortly. "She picked me up by the scruff of my neck and she spent . . . months, years . . . teaching me to fight instead of running. She. Light, Cath. I'd been through a lot, you know?"

Cathmar shook his head. Some things you knew; some you guessed. But it still didn't seem right to admit them.

Cahey chuckled darkly. "Anyway, I guess it was a few years later that she decided she liked me for something more than a starving kitten. I was . . . fourteen? Fourteen. I thought she walked on water. She very nearly did." He looked at Cathmar with sudden clarity. "We were partners for something like seven or eight years, all told, and . . . lovers for five. So don't think you're too young to find a good one. What's her name?"

"Mardoll," Cathmar said, unable to hold back his grin any longer. Trying was stinging his mouth too much. His face got hot, and he hid it behind his book, staring at the old translation—relating to the Last Day and the death of the first einherjar and waelcyrge—without reading it. His father didn't say anything, but Cathmar felt him watching for a long moment before he continued toward Cathmar and the door.

There were two unclaimed swords up the hill, he realized, and there had been—once upon a time—hundreds of einherjar and waelcyrge. He stared at the page for a moment, and looked back up, coming back around to the original question. "So if it's all about reincarnation . . . what happened to all the rest of us?"

"I don't think it's all about reincarnation. Maybe I'm wrong. Maybe it is. If I was somebody else before, I don't think it matters now. I'm not him."

"What happened to the rest of the swords? There were a lot, weren't there?"

Cathoair rolled his shoulders. "We gave them back to the sea. Muire's mount said that was what we were supposed to do."

Without a knock, the front door opened. Cathmar, sitting beside it, jumped in surprise.

The pot slipped out of Cahey's fingers and shattered on the hearth. He moved toward the door, hands coming up, ready to swing.

Morning light silhouetted a furry, tailed female form, clad in leather and ceramic armor and wearing a sword.

"Hello," she said.

"Speak of the Devil," Cahey said. His foot smeared dirt. He stared down at it, brow wrinkling, as if unable to understand why his fingers had failed him. Wordlessly, Selene handed down the broom from its hook beside the door.

"Aunt Selene!" Cathmar dropped his book and hurled himself into the moreau's arms, provoking a loud and startled purr.

"You're big!" she said a moment later, holding him back at arm's length. "He's big," she said to Cahey, turning her head.

"It's been a while," Cahey replied, bending down to clean spilled dirt. "We missed you. Come in; I'll make tea."

She laughed. "Tea. It's a hard habit to come out of, isn't it?" She dropped her pack by the door and leaned her sword up next to it.

"We have human visitors often," Cathmar said, shutting the door behind her as if to make sure she wouldn't get away. She scanned the red and blue living room in an approving manner that made Cathmar aware of how cozy and warm it was, and how clean. "Dad makes fishing nets and helps them farm. We go to the village and sometimes into the city."

Selene nodded, as if she already knew all that but was too polite to say. "Tea would be fine," she said.

Cahey busied himself in the kitchen while Cathmar helped the snow leopard out of her armor. Her familiar fur felt like hanks of silk, soft as milkweed tufts. The muscles underneath rippled, and he found himself looking at her in a new manner that he was not entirely comfortable with. Her body was slender, deep-chested, nothing like a human woman's at all. Cathmar tried to picture her as a girl, and saw only the cat.

He wondered what had drawn his father to her. He wondered how two creatures so differently constructed could have imagined themselves lovers. He pushed the thought away when it became too distressing.

Later, Selene coiled on the hearth-rug, combing her fur before the fire. She was talking. ". . . Freimarc has been quiet. I think the cities are emptying out again. People found them comforting at first, but now they're dispersing more widely. There's still trade and some industry, though, there and in Eiledon."

Cahey was toying with an empty tea bowl. "I think so, too. When Cath is old enough, I suppose I'll be on the road again myself."

Cathmar paused in pouring himself more tea, listening. Wondering if there was a subtle hint concealed in the words. *Does he want me gone so he can get back to his life? I think that sea captain in Newport likes him. I wonder if he wants to go off with her and sail, and not be stuck here raising a son.*

Selene folded her comb away into her pack and nodded. "I think that would be good. I'm not sure what I'm going to do next. Keep playing law enforcement, I suppose." She picked up her bowl and held it out to Cathmar. "More tea?"

"Don't mind if you do," Cahey said, and handed her the pot.

Her eyes crinkled with pleasure. As she refilled her bowl, she said, "It's a special occasion. I brought some goodies."

Cahey's face pinched, but he nodded. "It's only fitting."

"Special occasion?" Cathmar asked, because it didn't seem as if anybody was likely to volunteer the information.

"Fifty years," Selene said, while Cahey overstirred his tea. "It's been half a century since your mother went into the sea, Cathmar."

Cahey looked up, touching his mouth absently, as if it hurt him. "She gave us back all this," he said. "Seagulls, kittens, salt grass and fish, and people able to live outside of bubbles and have babies if they want them, butterflies and beach plums. You name it, it's all hers."

Selene touched his arm, reaching across the distance between them to lay the back of her fingers on flesh. "You're not still mad at her?"

"She could have told us. Beforehand. Included us in her choice."

"You're not," Selene reiterated, "still mad at her."

Cahey shrugged. "I got over it eventually. But you know how I found out she was dead?"

"Transformed."

He shrugged, gaze unfocused, as if he were staring through the walls. "I found out because I saw a bird. I'd like to tell you it was something special, a red one. A cardinal. But it was a city pigeon. Dirty white, with sooty splotches. First bird I'd ever seen."

Selene pulled her hand back. He looked down. "When I figured out what it meant—for a long time, I was very sorry I hadn't wrung the neck of that little white bird."

"Cahey!" She laughed, cupping both hands around her tea, but looked away. *"Male."*

She said it so disgustedly that both Cathmar and his father had to laugh. But then Cahey touched her hand, in his own turn, and said, "Where did you go after she . . . sacrificed herself, then? You never told me. Was it straight to Freimarc?"

She said, "You left, too."

He got up, as if to refill the teapot, but didn't lift it from the table. "After we split up, I mostly just walked. Walked and found things to do. Here and there. I picked a number of cats out of trees. Cats." He shook his head in disbelief. "Out of trees."

"Meow," she answered, steepling her fingers. "So when are you going to find a woman again, Cathoair?"

He raised a hand, teasing, as if to ward off a blow. She put the teapot in it. "All right," he said. "All right then." Moving toward the hot plate, he continued, "There hasn't been time. And besides—"

"There was time for the redhead."

He rinsed the pot out and set it on the sideboard. Water rang into the kettle as he filled it. "That was—she was working on dying when I found her. Would you have had me leave her in the weeds?"

Selene sat back and crossed her arms. Cathmar just made himself small in his chair, hoping his father wouldn't remember he was there and stop talking.

Cahey said, "You were building the chapel—"

"Not just me," she said.

Cahey nodded, but it looked like a dismissal. "I couldn't. I—" His breath caught, as if his throat were too narrow for the words to squeeze through. He said, "I know I more or less lost touch with all of you while you were doing that. I'm sorry."

"You didn't want any part of it," she said, tail-tip lightly tapping the leg of her chair. "I get it. You were talking about the girl."

He set the kettle on the burner and stayed facing it, hands flat on the counter on either side. "Cats in trees," he said. "There wasn't much left of her by the time I got there."

"Brigands," Selene said. "I met her, remember?"

"She wanted to die. I remember what that was like. When the whole world wanted to die. But she *wasn't* dead, and her body had its own ideas about if it was ready to give up. I backtrailed her to her house, a little north of Ailee, and cleaned her up and sewed her up and put her to bed. Pretty bed, wrought-iron. She must have salvaged it. I can picture her, too, dragging it home one piece at a time from Hel knows where. It would be like her." Cahey measured tea into the pot, not bothering to warm it first, the way you were supposed to.

He said, "When she woke up in it, she cursed me out like a sailor for saving her life."

"So you stayed."

"For a year or so. Until she was strong again. And you came to get me." The kettle whistled. He lifted it off the heat. "And then I met Cath, and I was busy for a while."

Morning found Cathmar shrugging into his pack by the front door and clipping his sword, Nathr, to his belt. "I'm going into the city," he said.

Selene, who had apparently been meditating on the knotted hearth-rug, rolled over and looked up at him. "I'll come with," she said. "Let's visit Borje along the way."

Cahey came in from the kitchen with the latest of many pots of tea. "This may involve a visit to a girl," he said, as Cathmar felt a slow, deep blush warm his skin.

"Like father, like son," Selene said. "Cats excel at vanishing. Fear not." She winked at the boy, who blushed deeper.

He hoped she didn't see him cringe at the comparison.

His father stepped back into the kitchen as Cathmar called out to him, changing the subject. "Do we need anything, Dad?"

"Tea!"

Selene chuckled, a throaty purring sound when she made it. "I'll pick up a bottle of whisky. It's time you and I had a good sit-down talk." She pointed from her own chest toward Cahey's vanishing back.

"I don't drink anymore," he said from the kitchen.

Her tail flickered. "Tonight you do. Today," she said. "Fifty years."

He turned and came back into the room. "I know," he said. "We had this conversation already."

50 A.R.
On the Second Day of Spring

F_ifty years,_ Selene thought, holding aside young branches of the beech trees that crowded the Eiledon road.

Cathmar tromped along behind her through the black spring mud, not the least bit tired yet, stepping over roots and rocks and bits of old bones. The only new einherjar in fifty years.

They'd tried.

Light knew they'd tried.

She'd even attempted to get pregnant, which had worked about as well as she had expected. And then there had been Cathmar. It must have been Muire who made them, they had concluded, and if she wanted more like them she was just going to have to do it herself.

Selene shook her head in irritation, as if shaking water from her whiskers, and glanced back over her shoulder at Cathmar, passing him a slender branch, showing him her feline smile that might almost have been a snarl.

He knew the look, though, and grinned back at her. They walked in silence for a little while longer.

Fifty years.

Selene mused, nodding to herself. She stole another glance at Cathmar out of the corner of her eye: the image of his father, but with his mother's focused gaze.

Intent. Watchful. Introspective.

Precious.

Irreplaceable.

Selene turned back to the trail. She couldn't complain, really. She had a partner—she squelched an almost-human grin—and she had a friend, and she had a nephew, of sorts, to help raise.

Still, there was a lot that needed doing. Angelic doing.

And four pairs of hands wasn't much, to carry a world.

Deep, black, sticky mud sucked at Aithne's boot. She worked it free carefully and looked up at Aethelred, still waiting at the end of the drier part of the road. The verge was prickled with brown grass and a few very early wildflowers. Alongside the low place—which Aithne was determining was little better than a hog wallow—weeping willows grew.

"This is not the way," she said. "We could cut across country."

Aethelred shrugged and held his staff out for her to grab onto and haul herself out of the mud. "How's the verge?" he asked.

"Slimy," she answered. "We could go around."

Whatever Aethelred was about to answer was cut off by an animal scream and a woman shouting. "Bearer of Burdens," he said. "Through the mud. Somebody in trouble."

Aithne hauled herself up the staff, nearly leaving her boots in the mud. She threw her pack up into the willows, out of sight. Aethelred's, bulging with unhappy cat, she hung more carefully.

The two of them left the road and slogged across the moor toward the sound. Once they got around the screen of trees, they clearly saw the shape of a large red animal—a horse, from images Aithne had seen in books and on 'screen—who seemed to be struggling in a mire. A blond woman was leaning on the reins, trying to haul the animal free, but it was beyond her strength.

Aithne hurried to help, Aethelred a few steps behind her. The mud, off the road, was nasty—but nothing like the sucking bog Aithne had been trying to find her way through. Aithne thought the horse would be able to get out, but she was panicking and the woman wasn't big enough to haul her out by main strength.

Aithne slipped down the little slope into the boggy section and cursed. The blond woman looked at her, blue eyes bright in a mud-smeared face. "If you're here to rob me," the woman said, "I've got nothing but the mare. And I'll kill you if you try to take her away from me."

"I'm Aithne," Aithne said. "This is Aethelred. Need a hand with her?"

A long appraisal before the woman nodded. "Here, take the reins and pull. I'll get in beside her and see if I can't move her hooves forward."

The mare calmed somewhat with the blonde's hands on her. Aithne stood in front of her, guiding the reins, talking to her much as she would have talked to her cat. Aethelred grabbed the saddle girth on the opposite side and hauled mightily, using his weight and powerful arms to almost lift the mare out of the muck.

The mare took a hobbling step forward, the blonde helping her place her feet. The mare's eyes were white-rimmed and rolling and she kept tossing her head, almost yanking the reins out of Aithne's hands. Black mud caked the mare's slender legs and dark red hide, but the blond woman kept talking to her, gentling her, and they walked her out of the mud slowly and with care.

They were all mud to the waist and bruises to the neck by the time they had her free, and Aithne bent over to rest her hands on her knees. The other woman thumped her on the back. "I don't know how to thank you," she said.

"Call it our good deed for the day," Aethelred replied, getting his wind back.

Aithne chuckled in the general direction of the mud under her feet. "What's your name?"

The blond woman nodded. "I'm called Gullveig," she said, offering Aithne a hand. Aithne took it and straightened up, feeling an odd tingle in her fingertips when she did. *Light-headed,* she thought. "I'm glad to have met both of you. Are you headed for Eiledon? Maybe we could travel together."

Aethelred shook his head. "We're for Freimarc right now. But maybe we'll see you next time we're out Eiledon way."

"Excellent," the woman said. Then she flung an impulsive hug around Aethelred, waved, and led the unhappy mare back toward the road.

"Well," Aethelred said when she was out of earshot, "that was a little surreal."

The wolf is the most patient of predators, and he's had millennia to practice his patience with regard to this prey. Assuming that Heythe is, in any meaningful sense, the prey and not the predator. He stalks her, certainly, but it's not as if Heythe would be beyond letting herself be stalked, if it suited her purpose.

Were I not a coward, I would meet her face-to-face, and put an end to this.

If you were a coward, you would not fight her at all, Kasimir says, a warm and comforting weight imagined as if at the wolf's shoulder. **It is not unreasonable to battle someone stronger by stealth. Especially when you do not know what she is doing.**

Making contact, the wolf says. *Touching them. Weaving her snares around them. Making enchantments and snares.*

The way she always does.

The door closed behind Cathmar and Selene. Cahey watched them go from a window, and when they were out of sight he rolled his head on his long neck as if to loosen it.

Fifty years gone. He sighed, and went into the bedroom to strip and change. There was no bed in there, of course, but it made a handy place to keep his clothes.

Fifty years today. One thing that hadn't changed about him over the years was his need for the physical. Leaving the little cottage, following the track down to the beach, Cahey ran.

Down the sunlit beach, along the drum-tight sand at the water's edge, he threw himself into the movement. In his other existence he'd fought for a living, and then he had fought for his life: he'd worked hard to make his body a strong and perfect machine. As well, the physical effort of exercise had been one of two things he'd found that could come between himself and his pain.

The other had been losing himself in his lovers, and he'd done enough of that, before Muire.

Then Muire changed. Became something that existed to transform misery into joy, to suffer every ill the heart was heir to. Cahey, once he understood what she had sacrificed, had traveled from settlement to settlement, working in each for a season or three, putting his inhuman strength and endurance into the hard, bloody, brutal, blessedly mind-deadening task of rebuilding a world from the bedrock up.

With every furrow he plowed, every roof he raised, he thought of making someone's life better, of lessening their pain. He thought of one less crumb of suffering Muire would have to absorb, transmute, make clean.

He never considered what his own pain might mean to her.

There were friends, too, where he thought he could make joy, where his inevitable leaving would heal rather than harm. He'd been einherjar and scarred, but he'd also been young and strong and an excellent listener.

And there had been redheaded Aithne, living alone in a forgotten old house just a little north of Ailee.

He'd stayed with her longer than anywhere. Eventually his hand laid on her shoulder no longer shocked her into a unicorn-like startle and flight. By then, she'd started to be annoyed—he thought—by what she saw as his hovering.

She was unicorn-like in that, too—a creature of spirit and wilderness. The memory of coarse red hair and a pistol never far from her sinewy hand brought a wistful smile.

His body bore him along.

There had been no one since, in the thirteen years he'd spent in the house by the sea, raising his son.

And though he still spoke to the ocean sometimes, he'd also never once so much as dipped his hand in her.

Fifty years.

Cahey ran.

He loped easily along the sand, long legs eating up first one mile and then another. It seemed a long while before he noticed a red-clad figure in the distance, walking toward the beach from the waves. Something about her silhouette caught him with memory: the sun gleaming in golden highlights off ash-blond hair, the slenderness of her frame, the angularity of bare shoulders.

He broke stride as he drew closer. She stood calf-deep in the surf: it whipped her red-velvet divided skirt back and forth with the ebb and flow of the waves. His heart came up in his throat, hammering, almost burning him with a sudden, incandescent heat. Her face was still indistinct with distance when he broke back into a run, a hard run this time, toward her.

She didn't hurry. He had plenty of time to record her image as she strolled up out of the surf. She was dressed as he'd never seen her before, in the crushed velvet skirt, ankle-length, and a laced bodice in crimson silk embroidered with snarling golden dragons. Ceremonial dress.

A bridal dress.

The sunlight caught her face as she stopped walking and watched him come.

He crossed the border from strand to sea without hesitation and swept her up into his arms, laughing and weeping simultaneously. He spun her around, calf-deep in the ocean, spray flying up around them like hurled fistfuls of diamonds, and set her back down where her footsteps would have been if the breakers had not taken them. He thrust her out to arm's length to study her, and then pulled her to him again, knowing he copied the gestures of a romantic drama and doing it anyway. Her eyes seemed more blue than the pewter he had remembered, but he supposed that was only natural.

"Muire," he said, "your dress . . ."

He meant to question her, to kiss her, to praise and berate her in equal parts. But before he said anything more, her mouth was moving against his collarbone, sliding along his skin in almost exactly the way he remembered. She dragged him down into her arms, into the surf, and the water was like fingers on his skin. The waves closed over them, and he didn't resist.

Her clothes and his were shredded by the force of the water. She pressed her body against him, eel-slick, and a blue-white phosphorescence crackled over his skin. The sand and the surf scoured his body as streamers of Light tangled and unknotted and retangled around them, the ends tattering and sparkling like confetti shredding through the breakers.

He wanted to linger over her skin, her mouth; he wanted to draw her up out of the thundering water and make love to her on the shore. He wanted to lie with her head on his shoulder, after, and watch the gulls she'd bought with her soul wheel overhead. And then he wanted to walk back up the beach when night fell and introduce her to her son.

She was having none of it. The sea was in his mouth, in his eyes, blinding and deafening him. Sea-nymph, undine, she was cold and hard and slick in his arms, and then she was taking him before he knew it. Fever-hot, demanding, she was slicker still inside. The breakers crushed him in her arms, beating, bruising him. Her body went taut against him and he would have kissed her but she tangled the sea and her fingers in his hair and turned her face aside.

I cannot, she said in his heart.

I thought I had a goddess in my arms before, he thought. He remembered very little after that.

Cathmar's girl was nowhere to be found in Eiledon, though Selene spent the better part of the day following him to her squat and a series of other favorite haunts after he failed to raise her on her 'screen. He feigned unconcern, but after all these years Selene was good enough at reading the apes to know it for a construct.

Cathoair was not in the house when they returned, and the hearth had gone cold. Selene and Cathmar came looking for him after moonrise. They found him sprawled naked on the beach as if sleeping, cast up by the waves.

There wasn't a bed in the house, but Selene made him a nest of cushions and blankets in front of the fire. He shivered badly. Cathmar had carried him home in his arms, and he and Selene had stood Cathoair in the shower until the crusted rime of salt and seaweed had flaked off his skin. The salt smell and sticky-crumbly texture reminded Selene of clotted blood. Then she tucked him into his makeshift pallet and came back with the bottle of whisky she'd traded for.

Cathmar walked out into the night, and Selene let him go. *Triage. Worst wounded first.*

"Were you trying to kill yourself?" she asked matter-of-factly. She saw Cathoair try to decide if it was an accusation or not. She could still read him very well.

"No," he said, pulling the fuzzy blankets tighter around his shoulders, still shivering. He coughed, wiped spittle tainted with sand-and-seawater on the back of his hand. "I saw Muire."

"You saw the Wyrm?"

He shook his head, and another coughing fit took him. Selene poured whisky into a blue china bowl and then held it for him, steadying his head. After the coughing subsided, he seemed strong enough to hold the bowl himself, and she let him.

"I saw *her*. She . . . made love to me." He choked on a laugh, washed it down with another sip of whisky.

Selene felt her upper lip try to tense into a snarl. She smoothed it away and lay down beside the einherjar, warming his cold skin with her furry body, overcoming her feline desire for space. She laid a hand flat on his belly, careful to keep her diamond-sharp claws retracted. Her entire body was an engineered weapon, and she never forgot it. She could disembowel him in a moment of distraction.

"She could have killed you."

"I didn't care."

"Did she?"

He paused, ran the hand that wasn't holding the bowl down Selene's storm-colored mane. The hand trembled. "I think so. I think she was being careful, actually." His voice was edgy as glass, and it went through her just as a shard of glass might have. "She was . . . a goddess. Life. The ocean."

"Was she . . . Muire?"

He sighed and finished what was in his bowl. "Yes and no.

Nearly. She was . . ." He laughed. "She was dressed as a bride. An old-fashioned bride. All in red, with a skirt split for riding. She was . . . I think I just wasn't strong enough, is all. She was trying to be gentle."

Thirteen years the Imogen resists, before she can resist no longer. Thirteen years she resists the hunger, the command, the desire. She has never challenged these imperatives before, but she was a long time in the dark. It has given her things the Wolf her brother never expected or intended.

It has given her a sense of herself.

Twelve winters, and at last the spring.

She can endure the desire no longer. The Imogen seeks. Following the scent, following the longing that daggers in her. The need, the seeking.

It's a little house by the ocean with a blue tile roof, amid a tangle of roses. She stands in the moonlight watching. There is an angel inside who has a need. The need calls out to her.

He is sleeping when the woman who is also a cat leaves him at last, goes out after the boy who went walking down by the shore. The Imogen saw him go, but did not follow. She has been watching.

For many sunsets, she has been waiting. Resisting.

He is inside, propped up on pillows before the fire. He sleeps, and his need is a beacon.

The Imogen lays her hand against the chinked stone wall of the cottage, sliding through it. A moment in the cracks between the stones, and she stands inside. In the cloying warmth and soft brightness, she smells him.

He is hurting. She is hungry.

Short steps bring her to his bedside. She kneels, quivering from ears to feathertips. This is the one she was intended for. This is the one she was awakened for.

She bends over him, presses her lips to his throat, feeling his pulse against her tongue.

He stirs.

His skin is soft and thick. She tastes salt, copper, and blood through it. There is passion and old pain, new pain.

Sleeping, he whispers a name.

He is dark and not fair. *But still einherjar. Worthy? Deep? We shall see.*

She lies down beside him as she saw the woman or the cat do, furling her wings back into her body, making herself small. She breathes his scent, sandalwood and loam. A taste of blood fills her mouth. Thick, bittersweet with longing and pain.

His need shapes the change.

The Imogen allows the change to take her.

Selene walked down the weedy path from the blue-roofed cottage to the sea, ears flat, tail twitching. Her eyes dilated, drinking in the moonlight, revealing the panorama of the ocean, the cliff, the chapel in shades of silver and gray.

Muire, she thought, *why now? Why did you have to do this to him now?*

The sea, of course, made no answer.

Selene wrinkled her nose against the strength of the smell: clean salt and sea wrack, and the ranker odor of the tide pools.

It didn't take long to catch the boy, for all he had been hurrying when he left the house. He spread a thousand-yard stare across the moonlit ocean and didn't turn when she came up to him.

"What's wrong with him?" Cathmar asked, before she could say anything.

Selene shrugged. "It's a hard thing, losing somebody."

"I never even got to know her, and I don't act like that."

"Precisely."

The boy turned on her, angry starlight gleaming in the back of his eyes. "And I suppose you know so damn much about losing people."

"You're damn right I do," she said quietly. "And I don't know nearly as much about it as your father does. Cut him some slack, Cath. He's doing his best."

The boy snorted.

Selene flicked one ear forward, then back: a warning signal. "Look," she said, "why don't you go back up to the house. Your dad is sleeping. Keep an eye on him."

"We don't sleep," Cathmar answered.

"We do when we're hurt," she said. "He almost drowned. Have a little pity. At least until you have some idea of what he's lost."

A pause stretched between them, until the teenager turned on his heel and stalked back up the beach.

Selene shook her head, watching his squared shoulders out of sight. When he had gone, she turned back to the sea. "You and I," she said, "are about to have a long, unpleasant talk."

The waves lapped placidly along the shore.

"Oh, don't give me that shit," the waelcyrge snarled, ears flat back against her head. "Are you going to let him heal and get on with his life and serve you as best he can, or are you going to keep jerking his chain every half-hundred years or so?"

The sea gave no answer. Resentment puffed the snow leopard's tail. She was nearly snarling when she mastered herself and spoke again. "Look, bitch. You gave him up. You broke his damn heart. If you were half the goddess you claim to be, you'd stick by your decision and let him move on. Today . . . was unacceptable. Do you understand me? Unacceptable. You could have killed him. You nearly did kill him, and you broke his heart all over again. I won't stand for it."

A shimmer slid over the moonlit ocean and the waves lapped higher, touching Selene's feet. The moreau held her ground. She felt herself boiling, and she was heedless in her wrath.

If she was going to snarl, she wanted somebody she could see to snarl back at. "Moonlight, earth and ocean," she said, at last. "Muire, I invoke you."

A shimmering shape formed over the water. Selene had half-expected a Wyrm, a Serpent broad as the morning, but the figure that walked up out of the waves to meet her was a woman—a woman wrought of Light—slender and fine-boned, nondescript of feature but proud of bearing.

SUMMONED, I COME, said the voice inside Selene, a voice she had reason to know well. WHY HAVE YOU MADE ME NO NEW ANGELS?

Selene took a half step back away from the tide. "What?"

Phosphorescent ripples slid across the sea and back again.

LITTLE SISTER, YOU BEAR A BURDEN ALONE THAT YOU COULD SHARE MORE WIDELY. WHY HAVE YOU AND CAHEY NOT MADE ME ANY NEW WAELCYRGE, ANY EINHERJAR?

"I don't understand. We . . . tried. It didn't work."

IT TAKES TWO PARENTS, the goddess explained patiently, MALE AND FEMALE, TO CREATE A CHILD.

Selene felt her jaw drop a half-notch as understanding filled her. Muire and Mingan had both given Cahey the kiss. Cahey and Muire had both kissed Selene. Only Muire had ever given the kiss to Borje, the chapel-keeper, and Borje had never been anything except a freed moreau.

FIND THEM; CHOOSE THEM, Muire continued relentlessly. KISS THEM AND BRING THEM DOWN TO THE SEA. I HAVE MANY SWORDS TO GIVE, IF THEY ARE WORTHY. DO YOU UNDERSTAND?

Selene nodded, and gathered her thoughts. "Muire. You're changing the subject. Today. Cahey. What you did to him . . ."

SELENE. The image over the water graced her with a wintry, heartbreaking smile. WOULD THAT I COULD. BUT IF IT HAD BEEN ME, LITTLE SISTER, HE WOULD NOT HAVE COME BACK TO YOU ALIVE.

Selene caught her breath in her throat and then whirled, charging back up the shore toward the house with a predator's sprint.

Cathmar opened the front door and saw the woman in bed with his father.

Well, *bed* wasn't exactly the right term.

Nor was *woman*.

They seemed friendly enough, however.

Cathmar's pack was still propped against the wall by the front door, and he grabbed it and Nathr before spinning back around and closing the door quietly behind himself. *Wouldn't want to disturb anybody, after all.*

He glanced down toward the beach. Aunt Selene must be out of sight behind a dune. Just as well. He thought he'd just walk back on up to the city. *I have friends there. I can stay a day or two. Who the Hel was that, in there?*

He started hiking up the path, trying to push the roiling emotions in his chest down hard. *He saw Mom today. And he's still in there with somebody else. Somebody I've never seen.*

Cathmar had gone perhaps a half-mile when someone stepped out of the darkness and fell into stride beside him.

He stopped, turned, put his hand on his sword. He took a step back, recognizing the description.

"Mingan," he breathed.

The gray cloaked figure stopped as well. He tilted a hatchet-carved face at the boy and smiled with just the corners of eyes that gleamed with silver Light.

"You recognize me," Mingan said. The voice was harsh, but somehow gentle. "I've been looking forward to this meeting, Cathmar."

Cathmar took another step back. "You know who I am?"

The Grey Wolf permitted himself a small chuckle. "Of course," he said. "You see, although you don't carry my name, I am your father as well."

The door was ajar, and Selene came through it low and rolled into a fighting crouch. She didn't know what she expected to see.

It wasn't Cathmar's pack gone, Cahey still curled sleeping by the fire, and a slender, dark-haired woman squatting, warming her hands before the flames.

Selene put one hand on the handle of her whip. The woman's scent raced down Selene's spine like a curve of lightning, and a growl rose up the moreau's tight throat.

My territory, the sound said. *Mine.*

The woman stood slowly, turned, and opened her hands further to show that they were empty. Selene allowed her balance to flow to one side, preparatory to uncoiling in a killing leap. She thought she could hit the interloper chest-high and carry her back into the flames. Fire, Selene hoped, would hurt only one of them.

The interloper said nothing for a moment while they studied each other. Selene assessed a compact powerful body clad in dark trousers, boots and a uniform-like jacket piped in mustard color. The woman's hair shone dark, curly, shot through with strands of silver at odds with the youth in her tawny-skinned face. She allowed it to fall to her shoulders in a style no warrior would affect. Her eyes . . .

Selene drew back from the regard of those eyes.

Lucent as amber, they caught the firelight and glowed.

"The boy left," the woman said, dropping her outstretched hands. "He was distressed."

"What did you do to him?" Selene eased her crouch, but kept her hand on her whip.

"I touched him not." She glanced down at Cahey, who seemed to Selene to be sleeping more peacefully now. The woman's voice was pleasant, deferential. "I believe he saw me feeding."

"Feeding?" A hiss, and a snarl. Selene glanced down at Cahey, saw the dark bruise blossoming on the side of his throat, just above the collarbone.

"I am the trickster's daughter. The Imogen. You have heard of me?"

"No."

"I am here for this one." She knelt down beside Cahey and laid the back of her hand against his forehead, glancing down with an affectionate half-smile.

Selene took the last step forward and crouched as well, placing a taloned hand on the other woman's upper arm. She allowed her thumb-claw to press through the Imogen's jacket—whatever an Imogen might be—and felt flesh part under her grip and a bead of blood start. "What do you mean, *feeding?*"

"The hunger," the Imogen said. "It is very strong. It is safest if I feed often. And he is deep: he can sustain me." She licked her lips. "If I am careful, for a very long time."

Selene stood, yanking the other woman to her feet. More blood oozed from under Selene's claws. It wasn't enough to make her happy. Yet.

The Imogen glanced down at Selene's hand. "That is painful," she said, calmly.

"You will explain to me," Selene replied carefully, the tip of her tail describing a slow and fatal arc, "*exactly* what you mean by *feeding.*"

"Oh, that," the Imogen said, her smile never changing. That deferential tone: Selene remembered having heard it in her own voice once, and it sickened her. "I only take a little, not enough to harm him. His *sceadhu* . . . ah, shadow? I think you would say in modern tongue his soul? Only a taste, and only the parts that give him pain."

Selene's fist clenched on the Imogen's arm, a grip that must have been piercingly hurtful. She felt the claws of her finger and thumb meet through the flesh, and her palm was sticky with blood.

The Imogen never flinched. She looked back down at the einherjar who lay on the floor between them, and let her smile grow another fraction. His brow was untroubled; his breathing was even. "Does he not sleep more quietly now?"

It was true.

"Come away from there," Selene said through tight jaws. She didn't want to fight this madwoman, supernatural creature or whatever she was. Not here, not with her friend helpless on the floor between them and the son of her heart alone somewhere in the night. She took a step back, and another, pulling the Imogen with her.

The woman—the creature—came reluctantly but did not struggle, stepping over Cahey's still body. She turned and gave him another glance as she followed Selene across the room, blood rolling in slow drips from her dangling fingers.

"But . . . ," she said in protest as Selene led her toward the door, "he is better now, you see. I have drawn away the worst of the pain. Does he not sleep more quietly?"

Outside, in the darkness among the dunes, Cathmar looked into the Grey Wolf's phosphorescent eyes and took a step back. "What is that supposed to mean?"

Mingan allowed the edge of a smile to curl the corner of his mouth before flickering away. "Cathoair can teach you many things," he said. "But he cannot teach what I can."

"Which is?"

"How to wield power. How to pass through the shadows. How to walk through the world and leave no trace."

"What do you mean, you are my father? I can't have two fathers." The boy kept a hand on the hilt of his sword, although he knew if would be useless. Suddenly, he remembered his father telling him, "Be polite."

"Sir," he finished.

The smile came back, a touch broader this time. "I loved your . . . mother as well," the Grey Wolf said, and Cathmar caught the little hesitation but did not understand it. "And both she and your father carried a little of me inside them when they made you. That makes you my child, too."

"Why haven't you come to see me before, then?" Cathmar realized that he should be frightened, but he couldn't find it in himself. Instead, he was fascinated by the Grey Wolf's steady regard. Incongruously, he thought of Mardoll.

"Cathoair does not approve of me," the Grey Wolf said. "Come; walk beside me. We have much to talk on. And you should meet your mother's steed, as well."

The light was muddy, but it was nonetheless light. Cahey blinked against it and turned away.

Fire.

His neck hurt.

Soft, urgent voices were arguing near the door. He felt under the covers for the hilt of his sword before remembering that he had not taken it with him. He pushed himself into a half-sit.

"Selene?"

She had another woman by the upper arm, and blood was dripping onto the floor. Both of them turned to look at him. Selene said, "You need to lie down, Cahey."

"Who's that?" Light smeared across his vision, and he sagged back against the cushions. "Where's Cathmar?"

"Outside," Selene answered. "This is Imogen. We were just about to go look for him."

Imogen—Cahey blinked again, trying to focus—almost seemed to be leaning against Selene's grasp, as if she intended to rip her arm right through the other's talons and walk over to him. Selene gave Imogen's arm a warning tug and released it.

Immediately, the blood stopped dripping.

"Come on," Selene said to the other woman. "Come with me. We still have a lot of talking to do."

The steed—a valraven, the Grey Wolf said—was the biggest living thing Cathmar had ever seen. It shone like split chalk in the moonlight, both heads regarding him with unsettling wise eyes.

Your mother would be proud of you.

The voice in his head came as a shock. Cathmar didn't quite step back, however, and Mingan rested a light hand on his shoulder.

"I didn't know you could talk," he said.

The stallion snorted and tossed his manes. Mingan chuckled. "How else would he tell me what to do?"

Cathmar turned his head to look up at the dangerously lean old man, unsure if he was joking. Examining Mingan's face, Cathmar still could not decide.

"What's your name?" he tried again. "I'm Cathmar."

Greetings, Cathmar. My name is a secret only one may know. But you may call me what you like. If I am able, I will answer.

He liked the sound of that. "I could call you Angel, then."

That is what I am.

Cathmar heard voices coming down the dune behind him, and turned to look.

Selene. And a dark-haired woman.

Selene called down the dune. "Cathmar!" Her eyes swept over the Grey Wolf and his steed. "Mingan. And Bright One. Greetings." Cathmar detected warmth in her tone, and wondered.

"Aunt Selene," Cathmar said. "Who's that with you?"

Selene glanced over at the dark-haired woman. "Her name is Imogen," she said. "She claims she's a friend."

Mingan came forward to meet them before they made it to the base of the hill. Cathmar could see his mouth shaping words—faintly—as he bent toward Selene's ear, moonlight glittering on a silver ring piercing his left ear and another one binding the top of his long queue. Cathmar, not having the moreau's senses, could not hear what was said.

She gave Mingan a quick, startled glance, and her ears flicked back. Then she nodded curtly. "We'll talk about it later," she said.

"Imogen," Mingan said, smiling at the strangely passive individual, "you and Cathmar should walk back to the house now, I warrant. Cathmar . . ." He came forward to clasp the boy's hand. "You and I, we shall meet again."

BOOK TWO

Branding

50 A.R.
On the Second Day of Spring

By the time Selene came back up to the house, Cahey was on his feet, dressed and folding the blankets.

"Where's Cathmar?" she asked. "And Imogen?"

Cahey shrugged. The play of emotions across his face flattened her whiskers. "Imogen . . . left. Cathmar went down to the beach."

Selene sighed. *Like herding cats.* Humorous irony, strictly internal, brought her ears flickering forward. Cats didn't believe in sharing the joke.

She said, "We need to talk."

He nodded. He touched his throat: a welt that showed purple-black against his skin was already rising to the surface. He turned his head and looked out the window, down at the beach. The moon was setting beyond the ocean, a pair of satellites sparkling in her wake. "We do. Where did she come from?"

Selene shook her head. "She's some sort of creature that associated with einherjar in the old days, I think. She feeds off us. A symbiote of sorts."

"What did she do to me? I feel clearheaded. Not like I did after I saw Muire." Cahey glanced back at Selene, almost shyly.

She wrinkled her nose at him, a catlike ingratiation. She smiled, a human gesture she'd taught herself years before. "Cahey . . . I don't think that was Muire."

His face stilled. *Never a good sign.* He turned to regard her directly.

"Who else could it have been?" Utterly level and reasonable, his voice, lifting the fur on her neck.

"I don't know." She knew this path of old: they were heading for a fight, and it was going to be a legendary one. "I summoned Muire, Cahey. I asked her."

"Summoned her? By the moonlight?"

Selene nodded, ears and whiskers flattening. Her tail-tip twitched although she tried to school it to stillness. It gave her away, always, even if she could hold her ears forward. Ape faces were much better at inscrutability. But they were social beasts, pack animals. They needed to be able to bluff, and they were good at it.

Selene's only bluff was the one that made her look bigger.

He didn't speak, just stared at her, stricken. She wondered if it was the idea of Muire being summoned that bothered him, or that Selene dared to do what he did not.

She sighed. "Go talk to her," she said softly. "Let her talk to you."

She watched the muscle in his cheek twitch while he chewed his lip. He turned and took two steps away. "I'm going to make tea," he said. "Do you want some? Should we go look for Cathmar?"

She bit her lip. "Cahey. Fold up the denial and *listen* to me, for once in your blasted life?"

He stopped in the kitchen doorway, spun on his heel, and

squared his shoulders. "I know the mother of my child when I see her." In *that* tone of voice.

Hel. Selene shook her head. "No. Not in this case. No, you don't."

She saw him take a deep breath. He weighed his words out one at a time, heavy cold pebbles. "You're jealous." Incredulous. "She came to *me,* and *you're* jealous."

She looked around for something to throw, but nothing seemed handy, so she hissed like a teapot instead. "Do I look *jealous?* Does this look like jealous to you?" Her tail slapped back and forth like a metronome. She was puffing up with rage, follicular contraction prickling up her spine and along every limb. When her vision tunneled, he could look like prey.

He nodded. "Yes. It does."

Two steps forward, and she stared him down. *Why is it,* the last calm corner of her mind wondered, *that he can still slide under my skin like a knifeblade?*

She knew the answer, though. *Arrogant asshole.*

She turned around, recrossed the room, opened the door, and stepped outside. The cool shock of the night air on her face cooled her temper, and she hissed once more. Then she stalked down the beach after the arrogant asshole's son.

He wasn't hard to find; he was sitting on top of a big boulder pitching pebbles into the sea. She scrambled up beside him and sat.

The waves sizzled on the sand until the silence that hung between them grew companionable rather than tense. The moon's belly dipped into the dark, moving water. Curls of phosphorescence moved across the surface like fire through an opal.

"Tide's coming in," Cathmar said at last.

"It is," she answered.

"He yelled at you, too, I take it?"

She nodded, knowing he would see her pale shadow move against the night.

Cathmar blew air out his nose and threw his head back as if to roll the stress out of his neck in unconscious mimicry of his father. The familiar gesture scratched red claws across Selene's heart. She curved her long, flexible body and looked over her shoulder, where dawn streaked the eastern sky.

"Why is he like that?"

"Why does he have to be such a human being, you mean?"

The boy nodded, but she saw the corner of his mouth curve as he recognized the irony of his own emotions. She hadn't expected him to display that maturity, and she found her search for a response complicated by her emotions.

It was a cruel thing the Technomancer had done, wedding the instincts of a cat to the social needs of an ape. But despite the pain it caused her, Selene was not certain she would change her makeup now if she could.

Or that might just be the ape talking.

Cathmar said, "He's not a human being. I'm not a human being. It's not fair. Why can't he just act like an einherjar, if he is one?"

There was the adolescent self-absorption she'd expected. Selene thought about that one while sky lightened and the cool breeze ruffled her fur. She almost said, *Whatever he acts like, that's how an einherjar acts.* But Cathmar deserved a real answer, and Cahey deserved better than to be dismissed so lightly.

"He wants something, Cath, that he can't ever have again.

And he's not reasonable about it, is all. Like most people wouldn't be."

She waited for Cathmar to say, *But he's not people.*

Instead, he shook his head. "At least you got to know her." The words hissed through a constricted throat. Selene ached to drape her arm around him, but from the rigidity of his shoulders he wouldn't welcome the breakdown her comfort would bring.

She closed her eyes, turning her ears to listen more closely, but all he did was breathe. There was a right answer here, and a wrong one, and she knew she had to find the one that would make things better, at least a little.

"You're right," she said. "We were lucky. And I am sorry for your loss."

When she blinked open again, he was looking directly at the side of her face, examining her profile.

She turned around and met his eyes. Feeling as if she dared greatly, she reached out and ran her fingers through his plush short cap of curls, careful not to brush the skin with razory claws.

"Your dad will be all right," she said. "Someday he'll grieve. It might not be a long time yet, but it'll happen eventually."

"Him," Cathmar said. "What about me?"

"You're already grieving," Selene said. She let her whiskers stroke his cheek.

50 A.R.
Spring and Summer

Ice.

Silence.

The rising sun reflects off the glaciers and the time-riven mountainsides, stark and holy: a world writ with a palette knife.

Darkness and the dawn.

It's better here.

Sun rises. Light touches the Imogen's wing tips, forehead, chin: is absolved by starless blackness. Curve of her throat, curve of her breasts, line of her belly, hips, sex, thighs, toes . . . rolling down the mountain to the valley, rolling up the shadow.

Every day she watches this, her only motion the slow blink of her eyes, the incremental rotation of her head to follow the sun setting behind.

She sees a world. It looks like the whole world. Empty. Voiceless. Shining.

And she is. Nearly. Comfortable. Nearly free. Of the clamor. The needs and the desires. Shaping her, bending her, making her anew.

Distant, but from here she can almost hear it:

Silence.

The wind wants nothing of her. It curls through her wings, ruffles her fur and feathers. The snowpack creaks under her talons. She raises her arms to the wind.

There is a moment—a shadow of a moment—when she *is* something. Something other than the trickster's daughter. Something other than the Imogen. Something discrete.

That existence, or the dream of it, brushes her mind, flutters past her heart in the darkness, tracing phosphorescence across the shadow.

I could stay here forever. I would like to stay here forever. I, I, I.
If not for the hunger that drives her forth.

50 A.R.
On the Fortieth Day of Spring

Sweat blurring his eyes, Cathmar sank into a fighting crouch and tried to feel his elusive center. Nathr rested in his slick right hand, left hand extended with fingers flexed, ready to grab. He turned slowly, boots scraping on pavement as he watched his opponent pace back and forth along a segment of arc, just a blade's length away.

The Grey Wolf placed each narrow foot among the litter as a cat might, thoughtful but not hesitant, Svanvitr held in a low and deceptively casual guard across his abdomen. He stopped, suddenly, watching Cathmar from the edge of his eyes, and then ducked his head and *smiled*.

Cathmar, trying to keep the soot-stained brick wall on Mingan's swordhand, nevertheless almost took a half step back under the weight of that wicked grin. The reflex unbalanced him, and Mingan moved in that half-moment, a smudge of cloak obscuring his outline as he slipped forward and then back without ever seeming to shift a foot. Cathmar recoiled, too late, a thin red line swelling blood down his cheek.

His left shoulder bounced off the bounding wall. "Damn, Uncle!"

Mingan stepped back, the smile falling from his face. "It's all of a part," he said. "Every gesture, every glance. Part of the dance. Show no pain, show no fear in combat. No doubt. The enemy's concern is your most powerful weapon."

Cathmar wiped blood from his face and healed the cut with a thought. "People who are scared make mistakes."

Mingan nodded. "As do the ones who are overcertain of victory. Never forget it. Choose your ground always. Prefer an unready enemy over an entrenched one, and never fear to strike the first blow. If that option is not open, then stay your hand until the enemy falters. The strongest warriors are like smoke—they stifle; they baffle; they choke and confuse. Often the flames are not even needed."

Tapping the tip of Nathr's blade on the pavement of the narrow courtyard, Cathmar frowned. "That sounds more like strategy than sword fighting."

"There is a difference?" Mingan moved as if he had never disengaged. Svanvitr lanced forward, would have pricked Cathmar over the heart, but Cathmar slid aside and brought Nathr up. Forte clashed on forte with a chime like flicked crystal, and Cathmar beat the blade aside, almost nicking the Grey Wolf's arm on the return stroke.

"Better!" Mingan crowed, throwing his head back in delight. "You lay in wait. Most excellent."

Cathmar grinned. "I can learn!"

"Indeed." Mingan watched him for a moment, then renewed the assault. For long moments there was silence and the ring of blade on blade, until Cathmar risked a foolish lunge and Mingan laid his shoulder open and stopped with Svanvitr's blade a centimeter from Cathmar's throat.

"Damn!" Cathmar lowered his blade, wincing.

Mingan stepped back and saluted. "More care when you commit," he said. "Enough for today?"

"Enough." Cathmar shook his head in frustration. "I'll never be as good as you are."

"In three thousand years, you shall be better," Mingan answered, wolf-grin widening on his lips. "You have your father's reach and quickness, his strength of arm. It will serve you. Now heal yourself, and think what you will do when we meet again."

Cathmar glanced up from wiping Nathr's blade on the hem of his shirt, although it was not blooded. He bit back the urge to deny the comparison to his father, and said instead, "Mingan. Why are you so kind to me, when you and he hate each other so?"

The Wolf, attending to his own blade, did not at first answer. When he looked up, he looked away from Cathmar, so Cathmar wondered.

"I hate him not," Mingan answered. "But there is history too complex to tell, and your father knows not the half of it." Sheathing his sword, he fell silent.

Cathmar took a step toward the old warrior, startled pain bright in his chest. "Uncle. I didn't mean to make you sad." He raised his left hand as if to lay it on Mingan's shoulder, hesitated before his fingers touched the cloth of his cloak. "I'm sorry."

"There is no reason for sorrow," Mingan said, unmoving. "One incurs debts in life, Cathmar—sometimes by choice, sometimes all unknowing. Your father. I owe him for something, for several things. That is all."

"Oh." The silence stretched thin and taut, and Cathmar

couldn't bear it. He laid his hovering hand on Mingan's arm. "What sort of a debt?"

The Grey Wolf made a soft sound, a sound that might have been a snarl or might have been a whimper, and turned on his heel, meeting Cathmar's eyes. Cathmar almost flinched before Mingan's stony regard, but—mindful of lessons learned and the ache in his arm—held himself steady.

He had to strain to hear Mingan's voice when the Grey Wolf finally spoke. The Grey Wolf's tone was strange, his words archaic and the rhythms formal. "There is no debt I do not owe him. And no price I would begrudge, an it be needed. Ask no more, Cathmar. I would as lief not burden thee with the details of my sorrow. Suffice to say, whatever wrath he bears me, I have earned it, I ween."

50 A.R.
On the Twentieth Day of Summer

Cathmar reached up, tracing Mardoll's pale jaw. She curled in her sleep, burrowing against his shoulder. He brushed tawny-bright waves of hair away from her face, outlined the seashell curve of her ear with his fingertips.

She stretched, yawned, catlike smiled. "Hi."

"Hey. I should be going soon. Dad's still not overly keen on me staying out all night."

"I'll bring you home on my mare. So you can stay longer."

"You have a horse?" He smiled. "Where do you keep her? I've never seen a horse."

Long white arm across his bare chest, pulling him closer. Her bed smelled of rose petals and poisonberry. She said she was eighteen, living alone. "Her name is Elder. Maybe you should come stay here with me."

He rolled toward her, buried his hands in the abundance of her hair. Out of its braid, it was coarse and heavy, not silken. "Do you mean that?" Brushing the hair aside, kissed her throat. "What do you need me for?"

"Silly boy," she purred, arching her elegant body against him, "don't you know when a woman's in love with you?"

Her fingernails marked his back in bittersweet counter-point. She drew him closer.

A little time passed. "I'd like to," he said. "But . . . Dad. He'll pitch a fit."

"About you leaving?"

"Yeah." He felt himself frowning. Conflicting emotions tangled in his breast. *Dad won't think I'm ready.* And a moment of honesty. *I don't think I'm ready. But how can I disappoint her?*

"Sun's not down yet?"

He shook his head.

"Does he know about me?"

Cathmar felt himself flush. . . . *in love with me?* "He's heard your name," he admitted.

Her lips curved against his face. He shook his head, her hair shifting on his cheek. He pulled her hair across his face and said, "I don't know. He's been acting . . . strange. He might not mind so much."

Cahey glanced out the six-paned window at the setting sun. Alone in the house, he was beginning to wonder where Cathmar had gotten off to. *He would have told me if he was going up to the city.*

Wouldn't he? Cahey shook his head, remembering sixteen going on seventeen. Leaning against the windowsill, he smiled and then frowned, touching his scar. Remembering a black-haired girl two years older than he had been, remembering leaving home. *Don't be so certain of that.*

Unlike Cathmar, he hadn't had a safe home to go to. He wondered if that mattered so much, when you were sixteen going on seventeen. Sometimes he ached to tell Cathmar the truth, that he had lost a parent, too, that he understood. But he didn't, really. Cahey had lost a parent—both parents—because he killed them, not because they left him. He imagined it was a whole different kind of pain.

He'd tried to help Cathmar heal, but in the long run Cahey had to admit that he didn't know how. He pulled his fingers away from the roughness of his scar. Maybe there wasn't any healing. Maybe there was just getting used to the hurt.

He didn't turn when he sensed the presence behind him. "I wish," he said softly, "that you would use the door like normal people."

The Imogen came toward him, across the small, spare living room. "Your wish is my duty," she said in a voice furred like the velvet of her hide. "In the future, I shall."

Then he did face her. She came to him sometimes as woman, sometimes as demoness. Only when he was alone, more often as Cathmar's explorations grew wider. *I wonder how she knows? Does she watch?*

Through the spring and into the summer, something—compassion, loneliness, need, when he could admit it to himself—moved him to entertain her presence.

When she came.

Her owl-soft wings brushed the ceiling, primaries bending slightly as they touched the rug and the tile behind her heels.

"Hungry?" he asked, frowning.

She nodded, eyes shining like agates set before candle-flames. "May I?"

He let his gaze slide up and down her greyhound-lean frame. Inhuman. Demonic, even. "What are you, Imogen?"

She came a step closer. "Hungry," she said.

"Who are you?"

"Whoever you want me to be." She flickered, shifted, seemed to shrink and expand at once. He had a brief sensation of heat on his skin, like sunlight, and watched in fascination as she stretched and shrank like a melting candle.

She cocked her head to the side, tossing curls over her shoulder. Her skin still gave the appearance of velvet, although it was dull gold now, and the fur had vanished. The face she adopted was interesting—pixielike, strong-chinned, it reminded him of someone. He wasn't sure who.

"What do *you* want?"

"To fulfill your wishes."

He froze in place. "I asked what *you* want."

She did not answer for a moment, and then she said, "I am a trickster's daughter, Lord. I am permitted no desires of my own, beyond: to feed, to serve, to persist. Those are my purposes."

He swallowed, watching her. "Slavery."

She shook her head, hair like a moonlit river tossing around her ears. "Slavery is for people. I have no soul of my own."

"So you don't think you're a person?" *I remember hearing that before, if not in those words. Selene, once upon a time.* His mood descended to pity.

"It means," she said, "that I am not alive. Precisely. Which is why I need you. There's . . . you cannot understand."

"I can try."

She smiled, showing teeth too even to be real. "I can't die, Lord. But I can get hungry. Hungrier. And hungrier. And only you can fill me. And only I can bring you peace."

He closed his eyes. It was truer than he liked to admit.

"And what happens when you get that hungry?" Within himself, he felt a long-ago left-behind fragment of a predator shift and awaken. A shard Mingan had left in him when they kissed.

Deep in his core, the ghost of the Grey Wolf blinked awake, and with it the ghost of the Suneater, the old mad thing the Wolf contained. The Suneater understood hunger.

Cahey cringed, feeling unclean from the inside out.

She didn't answer. *Bad things.* Mingan's knowledge, and a warning: *Take control, Cahey.* He ignored it, pushed it back, untrusting of the source.

The Imogen shifted closer. The last red light of the sun came through the window, over his shoulder. It snagged in her strange eyes and fluttered there. "You find me desirable?"

"Of course I find you desirable. That's what you're made for, isn't it? That, and to feed off my pain." Her pupils, he noticed, didn't constrict against the sunlight. "You want to barter your sexuality for your . . . meals."

"No. It is not what I am made for. I am a weapon. But I have other uses. Whatever you need, I can be."

A sharp flare of pain and longing. He tore his gaze away from hers, trained it over her shoulder at the gray stone wall with its woven hangings. "You can't be what I need," he answered. "You don't need to *pay* me, Imogen."

Silence. Waiting.

He listened to the rhythm of her breathing.

He choked on the next word. "Anything?"

"Everything."

She came toward him, shrinking, growing pale, until she was slight, fairskinned and shining. Ash-blond hair swung even with her chin. She gave him the blade of a wry smile.

Breath snagged barbed in his throat. He reached out to touch her shoulders. She looked up at him, but her eyes were golden instead of gray.

"No. Light, no." Her eyes were wrong. They should have broken the spell. But he didn't step away.

"I will give you forgetfulness," she said.

"I don't want to forget."

"I will give you peace."

A strangled sound escaped him. "This is not good for either of us. This is not what I want."

She came a step closer. "I was created to know what you want."

Silence.

"Cahey," she called him, a gently mocking nickname in the voice of a woman he had loved. Agony flared in his breast, bright as an arc-welder.

She kissed him with closed lips, and he shut his eyes, breathing in the scent of her. Her lips slid down his jawline and nestled against his throat. Her hands stayed down, laced behind her back. The only contact was her pursed mouth, wet-sealed against his skin.

His heartbeat pulsed against the pressure of her tongue. Delicately, with precision, she sucked.

He tasted salt and copper.

The pain surged, seared, ebbed.

50 A.R.
On the Twentieth Day of Summer

It took Cathmar some time to get used to the sensation of the red mare's spine jostling his ass and balls. Her hooves thumped on sand and salt grass as she cantered toward the little cottage that sat starkly shadowed by the unforgiving moon. Mardoll sat in the saddle, and Cathmar rode behind her, arms linked around her waist, watching the fast-shut wooden door and the one light on in the kitchen.

Holding tight to the girl beat getting knocked on the butt by the back of a horse. She'd twisted her hair up on her head, and her necklace glittered against the white skin of her neck. Cathmar leaned forward and kissed her right below the hairline.

She giggled and tossed her head back, tickling him with pinned hair. The necklace prickled against his lips, shimmering in a half-dozen moonlit colors as he pressed his tongue through the weave of it, against the scratch and chill of the stones. She shivered, rolling her head back, leaning against him.

The coolness of the night hung around his shoulders. "I am in so much trouble," he whispered against her skin.

Musical laughter. "Should I drop you off here? Instead of coming in?"

He sighed. "Probably. You should meet him under . . . better circumstances."

She twisted in the saddle to kiss Cathmar's lips before he slid down.

"Ow."

"It'll feel worse tomorrow. Make sure you move around. And stretch!" She drummed her heels against the mare's sides. "Elder, ha!" Her mount circled and vanished with a tattoo of hoofbeats.

Cathmar watched her go, unable to really credit how sore his inner thighs and rear end were. He turned toward the stone cottage just as the door opened, casting a wedge of light across his cheek and shoulder.

"I heard something," Cahey said, deceptively mild.

Cathmar nodded. "Hooves."

"And voices. Is your . . . girlfriend here?"

Cathmar shook his head. "No. She dropped me off." He could still hear the distant drumroll of the hoofbeats, and he knew his father could, too. "I'm sorry I'm late."

"You're lucky," Cahey answered, holding open the door, "that Borje saw you heading up the Eiledon road. Or I'd still be out looking."

Cathmar walked in, dropping his pack and hanging Nathr on the rack. His father shut the door behind him. "And you would be in even worse trouble than you are."

Cathmar nodded. "I should have told you—"

"No," Cahey interrupted. He reached out, put a scarred hand on his son's shoulder, turning him around. Cahey's voice was level and hard. "You think you're a grown-up now. I understand. I'm going to treat you like a grown-up from now on."

Cathmar looked up into his father's brighter blue eyes. "I don't—"

"If you want to stay out late, that's fine. If you want to come and go where you please, that's fine, too. You're an adult now, and I was on my own younger than you."

He's throwing me out. Of all the responses Cathmar had envisioned, this wasn't one of them.

His father's voice stayed dead level, but the long fingers squeezed convulsively on Cathmar's shoulder. "But here's the deal. If you don't tell me where you are and when to expect you, I won't be there to back you up. I'm going to assume you're just fine unless I have evidence to suggest the contrary. And I'm going to expect you to act like an adult."

Cathmar didn't answer.

"All right?"

He nodded. His mouth was dry.

This wasn't what he had expected, either.

His father's eyes held his for a moment longer, and then Cahey nodded. "Good," he said. "The water on the fire is warm if you want to wash up."

He turned away, and Cathmar peeled his boots off and tossed them toward the door. He stank of horse, and—more pleasantly—of girl.

He walked across the knotted rug and bent down to pull the kettle away from the fire, taking a rag off a hook by the mantel as he did so.

The feather almost escaped his notice. It was pinned against one of the firedogs, almost invisible in its blackness, wreathed in shining flames. Cathmar reached through the fire and picked it up.

It wasn't even scorched.

Cathmar turned around, accusing. "Dad? What's this?"

Cahey looked over his shoulder. "A feather," he said.

"Imogen was here."

Cahey, leaning back against the counter between the living room and kitchen, hesitated before he nodded. "For an hour or so."

"Aunt Selene said—"

"Aunt Selene," Cahey cut him off in a voice that sounded *wrong,* "doesn't know everything."

Cathmar came over to his father, the feather still in his left hand, the kettle forgotten in his right. He realized it, looked down, and crouched to set the kettle on the tile where it wouldn't burn anything.

His father, motionless, watched him.

Cathmar reached out with his right hand and grabbed hold of his father's shirt collar, yanking it open.

He hissed. A fresh livid welt purpled Cahey's long neck, a little well of blood still slicking the raw center of it. Two others—older, fading—showed alongside.

"Dad . . ."

Cahey shook his head. "This is not an open topic," he said. He reached up and disengaged Cathmar's hand from his collar. "Not now, not ever."

He walked past his son, opened the door, and entered the night.

Cathmar watched him go, the inviolate feather crumpling in his fist. A long moment after Cahey vanished, Cathmar turned away, walked into the kitchen, and slapped his hand down on the viscreen contact hard enough to make a thump.

He waited while it dialed.

They met him inland along the Eiledon road early the next morning. Mingan's steed relaxed beside the trail, grazing. Mingan and Selene sat on the short green grass in the stallion's shadow. They stood as Cathmar approached.

Selene walked forward to meet him, grabbed him hard around the shoulders, and pulled him into her embrace. He held himself taut for a moment before the warmth of the contact eased him. "Did he come home?" Selene asked when he stepped back, finally.

Cathmar shook his head. "I tracked him a little way. I think he walked up to the chapel. Or Borje's, maybe, but I didn't go there."

Mingan came forward, gloved thumbs hooked in his sword-belt. "He's not with Borje." The Grey Wolf stood a little apart from Cathmar and Selene, planting his boots in the grassy verge. He jerked his head back over his shoulder, a gesture that spoke to Cathmar of impatience and disgust.

Cathmar raised his eyes to the little chapel on the hilltop. "I didn't go up," he said.

Selene nodded. Her tail lashed. "Good choice," she said.

Mingan's face was expressionless, as always. "Twice in one night is too much," he said. "Selene. You and Cathmar . . . go somewhere." He looked down at Cathmar. "I'll talk to your father."

Cathmar blinked, uncertain how to describe the emotion lighting his chest. Relief. Apprehension.

And possibly something ugly.

He nodded.

The long grass tugs at the wolf's boots as he strides through it, up the little rise, past Borje's cottage and up the windward side of the bluff.

The door of the chapel lies on the lee side, the right side to anyone facing the ocean. If the wolf should glance right along the beach, he would be able to pick out the blue tile roof of Cathoair and Cathmar's cottage. He does not look that way.

He kicks sand over the flagstones as he stalks up to the door and pushes it open, spilling morning light over the interior. Until the sun comes overhead enough to cast light through the ceiling it will be dim within, although the single window will eventually frame the sunset over the ocean.

Cathoair stands before the statues. He turns, clearly expecting Cathmar, and freezes when the wolf enters. Cathoair's hand falls to the hilt of the sword he is not carrying, the one he must have left at the cottage when he stormed out.

The wolf smiles. The lines appearing around his old rival's eyes tell him that it is an unsettling one.

He glances away from Cathoair, lets his gaze flicker starlight over the inside of the little chapel. The Imogen, clothed in the form of a mortal woman, stands before the glass doors that the wolf helped Aethelred design, examining the hanging spindles of books without touching them.

"Imogen," says the wolf. He waits until she turns and catches his eye.

She meets his glance with the placid, passive expression of an herbivore, something she is manifestly not. The wolf can smell the blood on her breath, on her heart.

"It's time to return to your mountain," he says. "Your master and I require privacy."

His tone is level, a suggestion that carries a command. She still stares for a moment before she walks out past him, bootheels clicking on the pale flags. Without turning his head to watch her go, he still catches the moment when she comes parallel, turns, and inhales with her eyes half-closed—drawn like a hound scenting the breeze.

She should be able to do neither of those things—the hesitation, nor the disobedience.

"Imogen," he says, in the same tone. "Go."

She turns away and sulks out, striding stiffly. Cathoair's eyes follow.

The wolf steps inside and shuts the door between them, the morning and the departing demoness. With the closing the chapel falls still and dark, Cathoair a silhouette against the indirect brightness of the window.

"Storms blow in," the wolf says. "Off the sea, through that window. The books are never damaged."

"You . . ."

Cathoair would say more, could he find the words. The wolf holds his tongue, raises his eyebrows, lets his eyes fill up with starlight. He sees the answering gleam touch the other's gaze, recognizes in it the shadow of another presence like the stroke of a cold hand down his spine. *It was long ago,* the wolf thinks, *and the world was a very different place.*

"You had no call to speak to her like that."

The wolf rolls his shoulders in a shrug, advancing. "It is what she understands. For now. Best for her—and you, my brother— if you understand as well."

Cathoair bends his knees, settles onto the balls of his feet. Fighting stance. *He never lacked for courage.* A bark of a laugh almost slips from the wolf. *Only sense.*

"Why are you here?"

"I come here often, actually. Today, because your son asked me to. He's safe. For now, although keeping unsavory company."

A long, whip-edged silence. If Cathoair had his sword, she would be in his hand. The wolf hopes, lightly, that the experience will educate him.

"Yes," the Cathoair says at last. "You."

"And a girl who is not what she seems. But we will address that." The wolf walks toward Cathoair, brushing past him— he shudders—to take the hand of the bronze statue before the brightening window frame. The wolf bends over her out-reached hand and kisses her fingertips.

"Grace," he wishes her, then turns back to the one who had been her lover, as the wolf himself had wished to be.

"It wasn't Muire who came to you," the wolf says. Candid. Blunt.

Cathoair's reply is a river of venom: "I see you've been talking to Selene."

The wolf nods. "I do that. On occasion."

"Get out," says Cathoair.

"What happened between us was a long time ago."

The wolf steps close enough to press the other einherjar to action, already anticipating what will follow.

Cathoair spins and kicks out, an untelegraphed motion that strikes the wolf across the chest. Not a pulled blow. A true one. The wolf feels ribs snap, draws breath in pain. Does not show it. This time he does not hesitate. This time, he strikes with the strength of einherjar.

The beautiful boy may make an angel after all. He's bent, but he's not broken yet.

"Killer," Cathoair says, grounding his foot and continuing the motion of the side kick with a straight right across the body. The explosive force of the words backs his swing; his voice is lumpy with hate and fear. "Rapist."

The wolf thinks Cathoair might even be a match, with more maturity. He's fiercer than she was.

But not today. The wolf catches the crosspunch in his clawed right hand and stops it in midair. The power of the blow cracks his wrist bones: a compression fracture. It will heal.

He clenches his fist until the bones in Cathoair's hand creak, drawing Cathoair close when he gasps with pain. A chipped bone shifts in the wolf's wrist. The wolf allows a smile to brush across his face, acknowledging and dismissing the pain as he might a messenger bearing needed but unwelcome news. His other hand drops on Cathoair's shoulder, driving Cathoair down to one knee on the pale stone floor. Cathoair has the strength to resist, something the wolf never permits him to realize.

"Just like last time," the wolf murmurs. "You'll never be able to stand against me until you understand what you are."

He leans over Cathoair, his felted woolen cloak falling forward to enfold them both. Bending down, he breathes across the other's face, hand still heavy on the place where Cathoair's neck runs into his shoulder. Cathoair trembles, but raises his face to the wolf's, eyes coldly defiant and full of savage light.

The wolf sees also the way Cathoair's lips half-part at the taste of Mingan's breath, and the fury that follows that weakness. The wolf feels no mirth, but—for the effect—forces himself to chuckle. "I am leaving. As you request. We will speak again."

Striving for the appearance of ease, he hurls Cathoair back, not quite against the stone bench standing before the mosaic-glass doors. The wolf spins on his toes and stalks toward the door.

Cathoair catches himself in a crouch. He would lunge after the wolf did the wolf not glance back.

He smiles a cold, starlit smile and watches it freeze his rival. "You must learn to command the Imogen, little brother," he says. "If you do not, she will eat you."

He lets the smile fade, turns, and opens the door on the ascending sun.

Selene watched Mingan stride up the little hill to the chapel. She reached out and draped her arm around Cathmar's shoulder, turning him back toward the warhorse. The stallion raised one head from the dense grass and blew hay-scented breath across her face and Cathmar's.

"I don't want to go back home," Cathmar said, bringing her up short.

She looked over at him. He was taller than she was now, and showed promise of matching his father's height. She angled her ears forward. "I'm not an expert on human parent-child relationships," she said, "but I understand the teenage years are supposed to be like this."

His eyes slid toward her, and then he walked away from her, shrugging her arm off. "Helpful," he said. " 'Don't worry. Your dad is supposed to be a jerk.' "

She bit back a hiss. *If this is what teenagers are like, I might not blame Cahey if he took up heavy drinking.*

"Maybe it runs in the family," she muttered under her breath, striding after Cathmar. She didn't think he heard her, but it was hard to tell with human-type people. Their ears didn't flicker.

He kept walking, and she followed.

50 A.R.
On the Twenty-third Day of Summer

Aithne stretched into her pack, turning to rest it on a sandstone outcrop. "Remind me again why we're *walking?*"

Aethelred laughed at her. "Because it's hard to trip across people with problems if you fly."

She sighed and yawned, scratching under her eyepatch. Then she glanced up at the overcast and shook her head. "Might rain."

He thought it might be time to bring up a topic he'd been considering. "Aithne?" He winced when he heard his own tone.

She let her hand drop to her side. "What?" He'd set her on edge, too, which he hadn't meant to do.

"What do you think about taking a side trip. Visiting our mutual friend?" He, too, tilted his head back to study cloud formations that seethed like boiling laundry. He grinned to himself at Aithne's understatement.

She leaned back against the boulder and sucked her lip. "Fuck. Aethelred . . ." She looked over at him, uncertainty in her eyes. "If I could have stood the pity for a second longer, old man, I would have gone with him when he moved out. It's not like I was attached to the house."

Aethelred glanced down, studied her profile—the scars, a pierced earring winking in her lobe. A hard crease indented her forehead between her brows, and he realized he'd never seen her cry in all the years they'd spent tromping the countryside together. He thought about Cahey's scars, and doubted deeply that it had been his pity she was reacting to.

"It's been a long time, you know. He's not your ex-lover anymore; he's not the man who saved your life. He's just a guy you used to know. And I'm not getting any younger. I'd like to say good-bye."

She blew a puff of air out her nose. "I never told you much about that, did I?"

"I know enough. I know Cahey."

"Yeah, but . . . Hel, Priest, I never should have let him walk away like that."

"You were in love with him?"

She shook her head, but he didn't think she meant no. "I was . . . It was good he left. Or I would have started needing him, and I don't want to need people that way. He's . . . No. He *was* exactly what I needed, for about thirty seconds. Now, I don't know. We've been traveling, you know? It's not like I've had a lot of time for relationships."

"Well," Aethelred said, feeling suddenly very old. "I hear tell he's not doing so well. Selene sent me a message on 'screen. Asked me to stop by. What say we walk in that direction?"

"He needs help?" Like she didn't believe him. No, like she didn't believe Cahey would accept the help even if he needed it.

She was probably right.

The freeloading old cat peered over her shoulder. Aethelred

just nodded, keeping eye pressure on her until she turned around and met his gaze. "Selene thinks he may not make it out of whatever trouble he's into."

She grimaced and thought about it. Then, white-faced behind the freckles, she said, "Which way do we go?"

50 A.R.
On the Thirty-third Day of Summer

With a key too new to have scratches, Cathmar opened the door to Mardoll's flat. To *their* flat. It still wasn't a thought he was quite comfortable with. He glanced around, noticing that she'd rearranged the green plants on the improvised shelves again. The windows themselves were not original: she'd salvaged glass and frames from a variety of sources, using rough carpentry and layers of fabric tape to fit them to the frames. Cathmar set down a canvas bag containing six liters of indigo paint he meant to use to seal the cracks and cover the mismatches in Mardoll's handiwork. The fabric creaked slightly as the weight came off it.

They were by the quiet side of the Naglfar's sorcerously disrupted course, where it rose from its shattered bed to cross the campus of the University overhead, and morning and afternoon sun edged in under the University to paint the windows on the high floors in their building.

Cathmar picked his way around a pile of cushions that had slumped from the edge of a thick sitting mat onto the floor tiles. Dust motes hung in the slanted light that fell through the mismatched windowpanes. Mardoll was around somewhere, stirring up the air.

He called her name.

"In here," she answered. He walked across green tiles into the kitchen. It was yellow, mostly: the paint on the cabinets was peeling. The windowframes in here were freshly painted, though, in vermillion and white, layers thick enough that they made the carpentry beneath look like molded, melted plastic.

Actually, there might be some of that jammed in there, too.

Mardoll knelt down beside a bucket, washing the sun-colored walls in the sunlight, grinning with pleasure at her labor or possibly the results. She looked up at him before standing and drying her hands on her leggings. "Hey. What'd you do today?"

He shrugged. "Angel stuff." A running joke.

She pressed against him and raised her lips, offering a kiss. "Damn," she said, when he pulled back again. "How did you manage to get so tall?" He realized that he was looking down a good decimeter into her eyes.

He laughed and changed the subject. "I had an idea."

"Oh? That made you grow?" She emptied her bucket, started putting things away under the sink. A tower on the roof supplied the flat with cold running water.

He sighed and hung Nathr on the back of an old wooden chair. He pulled the seat out and swung it around, perching on it backwards. "I'm just . . . Well, I don't want you to get old, Mar."

She straightened, closing the under-sink cupboard. Turning around, she leaned back against it, kicking one foot up. "There's not much you can do about that, angel. Seeing as how I'm a mortal girl and all."

He shook his head. "There is. I just talked to Selene. She says that the Bearer of Burdens—"

"Your mother."

He tilted his head in acknowledgment. "My mother says we need more angels. And she told Selene how to make them." His mouth had gone dry, and swallowing to wet it brought no relief. He said, quietly, "You could be one of them."

"I beg your pardon?"

"You could become one of us. Waelcyrge." It's a little easier the second time.

Her frown surprised him. "Really?" she said. "What's entailed in that?"

"I kiss you. Angel-kiss. Selene does, too. We take you to my mother and she gives you your sword."

"You steal my soul."

He shook his head, watching the shadows that the sunlight made across her face. "I give you a little bit of mine."

"That's . . ."

He caught the scent of the cleaning bleach. "What?"

She turned her back on him abruptly and began running water into the sink. "That's a Hel of a commitment, Cath. That's like marriage-plus, you know? Not just a lifetime. Forever."

He pushed the chair away and strode over behind her, placing his hands on her tawny shoulders. "I don't want to push you," he lied, turning her head and tilting her chin up. He kissed her gently, tasting rose petals and moss. "Think about it. Think about everything that we could be."

Think about not dying on me in a few short years.

50 A.R.
On the Fortieth Day of Summer

Cathmar came down the steps from the flat into a mist silvering with the early-morning light. He took a deep breath, throwing his head back to feel the cool air roll down his throat into his lungs. He and Mardoll lived on a zigzag cobbled lane so narrow Cathmar could touch both stained walls with flat hands if he spread his arms. The sun hadn't yet cleared the walls of the city, or angled high enough to send fingers grasping under the edge of the University to burn the fog away, so the effect was a bit like walking through a dream.

Mardoll lay upstairs, hard asleep, and Cathmar had a mind to spend the early morning doing good deeds. *Everybody's got to have a purpose in the world,* he thought. *Mom was a street vigilante. I bet I can do that, too.*

I'd better keep my head and remember what I know about fighting, though.

His father had taught him a lot about hand-to-hand combat, as had Selene—who had also given him some weapons instruction over the years. He hadn't gotten that from his father. Cahey bore Alvitr like the victim of an arranged marriage and made it no secret that he wasn't fond of blades. Or guns.

But Mingan *did* understand swords, and he also understood the subtle art of spotting the enemy's weakness and overpowering him with his own fear. "Be absolute in attack," Mingan had told Cathmar. "Alert. Do not fear to delay for an opening, but once the opening is perceived, do not tarry in exploiting it."

"And always watch the shadows," Cathmar remarked out loud. "Come out of there, Uncle."

Mingan chuckled and stepped from an unlit doorway. The mist flowed around him, disturbed by the swing of his cloak. "Nicely observed, lad."

Cathmar smiled at the compliment, and then frowned at Mingan's next remark as the Grey Wolf fell into step beside him, boots silent on the cobbled street. "Are you going to let your hair grow? You'll be a warrior in your own right soon, you know."

Cathmar shrugged. "Mardoll likes it short. Who am I to argue?"

"Mardoll. Your lady love? The attractive blonde."

"You've been watching me."

"I watch everyone," the Wolf said. "It's as useful to know your allies as your enemies, don't you think?"

"I suppose." Cathmar knew his sullenness colored his tone, but he didn't bother to amend it. "What do you think of her?"

"That's not a question one should ask, Cathmar, unless one wishes a truthful answer." Mingan's voice, dry as gin, held habitual amusement.

Cathmar checked his stride. "What's wrong with her, then?"

Mingan turned to face him, lean body angling to the side. "She's not to be trusted. She'll use you and discard you, and she'd older than you think."

Cathmar heard a trace of some old pain in Mingan's words

and thought he knew where it came from. "This is about Mom, isn't it?"

Mingan frowned—at Cathmar's bitterness? At unpleasant memory? "Believe what you like," Mingan said softly, starlight blossoming in his eyes. "But no, I am not untrusting of women because of hurts passed between your mother and I. Rather, I know something of darkness, and I know something of your woman, in particular. And that is all I came to tell you."

"I don't want to hear it."

"Very well." Mingan smiled edgily. "I will not call on you again while you dwell with her."

"Uncle—"

"For my own safety," he said. "Also, it would be best if she never heard my name from you. Trust me in that, if in nothing else, einherjar. And trust as well, if there is need, if you are in danger, Selene will know where to find me."

Cathmar's throat felt dry. He swallowed against it. *Why is everyone abandoning me?* He nodded.

"Excellent." Mingan drew his gray cloak about his shoulders as if he were cold. It trailed into the fog that surrounded him. Cathmar knew him well enough to realize that he had planned the effect. "Oh. And you also will not mention this conversation to the lady with the red mare. If you are as wise as I think you are."

The Wolf tipped his head to Cathmar and stepped back into the mist. Cathmar, watching, thought he almost saw how his uncle vanished into the shadows.

He shivered and stepped into the fog himself, tracing the Wolf back into the dimness of the doorway he'd vanished into. Cathmar crouched to examine the pavement, though he knew what he would find: no sign of presence, no trace that anyone had stood here recently. Just the wolf-scent, musky and pungent, already dying into the dank cold of vapor and stone.

For a moment, Cathmar's thoughts pinned him there, head bowed. Then he turned and walked the few short steps to his door and back inside.

He hung Nathr on the foot of the white pine bed and lay down beside his sleeping lover. A moment, and she rolled over and cast her arm across him, the striped wool blanket sliding down the curve of her back as she snuggled close.

"Back quick," she whispered.

He chuckled and pulled her tighter with an arm around her shoulders. He wondered suddenly if he heard a little disappointment in her tone. "Decided I couldn't go out there alone in the mist and chill when you were in here."

She sighed and laid her head down on his shoulder. "You're the sweetest boy I've ever known."

It wasn't that it was a lie. But there was something inexact in the way she said it that made him wonder. *Damn you, Mingan.* "How many boys have you known? I mean, intimately." He knew he wasn't the first. It hadn't bothered him until just now.

"Cath! What a question. Besides, I don't keep a list!"

"I'm sorry." He kissed the top of her forehead. "Guy moment, I guess."

She snuggled closer, seeming to drift on the edge of sleep. But he wondered. She hadn't said *kept* a list.

Mingan, damn you.

50 A.R.
On the Sixtieth Day of Summer

T*he other problem with going on foot,* Aithne thought, her work gloves slipping on the slick wood of the beam, *is that you keep finding all those people with problems. When you're in a hurry to get somewhere.*

Aethelred grunted on the other end of the pole. Wet and charred, it was also heavy. Aithne strained at her end, determined that no man in his seventies was going to outwork her. Whether he was modified and dead fit or not.

Besides, I walk as much as he does.

"On three," he said. They swung together, counting, and tossed the burned wood down into a narrow ravine. Aithne's boot slipped in the muddy grass, but she windmilled her arms and didn't go in. She caught a glimpse of wet black earth down the side of the gully, the ever-present white fragments of bone protruding from the side of the gully like roots from a freshly dug grave.

Damn depth perception. It affected her shooting, too, but she had learned to compensate.

Aethelred turned around and surveyed the devastation. Aithne watched his face.

There was one man dead in the wreckage of the house. His partner, who had made it out, was under sedation in a neighbor's cottage. Aithne squinted against the afternoon glare and watched other neighbors moving cold burned wood and furniture. She glanced over at Aethelred, who was unconsciously scrubbing blackened hands on his trousers.

Within the past twenty days, there had been a family massacre, two other fires, and a series of lesser delays. Aithne wondered if she had been maybe a little slow on the uptake, frankly, but all the trouble was starting to feel somewhat intentional.

"If I didn't know better," she said, "I'd suspect we were being distracted on purpose. Hasn't it seemed busy lately?"

He looked up from examining the soot ground into the lines of his palms and turned his face toward her. "Yeah," after a thoughtful moment. "Since we turned back east."

"If somebody were trying to slow us down, it would take a lot of mobility. A lot of subtlety."

"And a tracing device. Or magic."

Aithne straightened up and strode abruptly back toward the house. "Come on. Let's get that body out and get back on the road. And quickly."

Aethelred swung along behind her. "And tomorrow," he added, "we replace all our gear."

50 A.R.
On the Seventh Day of Autumn

In the months that followed their argument, Cahey did not call Selene, did not return her messages. Cathmar, now living in Eiledon, stopped talking to Mingan after a conversation that neither one of them would discuss with her. Mingan continued cryptic, frequently absent, frustratingly uncommunicative.

Preserve us from sulky men, she thought, whenever playing itinerant angel—Muire's term, and Selene wondered if it would ever stop stinging each time she thought it—left her occasion for thinking. Cahey had been happiest working hard in fields and farmyards. Selene specialized in keeping the peace in larger habitations. Which was, after all, what she had been bred and built for, all those centuries ago.

Finally, worried beyond pride, she visited.

Opening the peeling blue door, he invited her in. His face was drawn, his complexion grayish-purple with weariness. Her whiskers flattened as she looked at him.

"Well," he said, "I guess you've come to tell me that I'm acting like an arrogant shit?" He shut the door behind her.

She crossed the small living room and perched on the granite counter edge that divided it from the kitchen, swinging

Solbiort to the side so the sword wouldn't stick straight out. "Have you seen Cathmar?"

He shook his head and went into the kitchen to make tea.

"And no," she said. "I've come to tell you I'm sorry, Cahey, and I want you to not be angry anymore."

He came around behind her, leaning over the counter from the kitchen side, staying a careful ten centimeters away. She felt him studying the side of her face as he leaned his cheek on the knuckles of his right hand.

Ten centimeters. Just about as close as she could usually stand to have anybody. Her ears flickered toward him. *He tries.*

"Ancient history, right?"

She was turning toward him with an answer on her lips when she glimpsed something behind the collar of his shirt. Selene reached out, turning his head with fingertips that caught on his skin like burrs. She snarled at the line of bruises flowering dark against the silken skin of his throat: some fresh, still purpling; others fading into rotten mottles.

Days' worth. Weeks'.

"Cahey," she said.

He caught her hand and squeezed it in his own. "Demon hickeys," he said with a laugh. "Don't worry; they look a *lot* worse than they are. It's actually sort of pleasant when she does it."

Selene frowned. "I think you need to talk to somebody about her." She pulled her hand free and stood, turning to face him.

" 'Talk to somebody'? What does that mean, exactly?" The tone in his voice gave her pause. She'd never heard him sound like that before. Defensive.

"Mingan. He knows things that you and I don't."

He turned his head. She saw that he was gnawing on the inside of his cheek.

"Cahey, you are . . . unreasonable . . . with regard to the Wolf."

"Unreasonable? Really? With regard to a murderer?"

She looked away from him and shook her head slowly, ears lying flat, forcing her fur down. "He has changed, Cahey. I've been spending time with him, and . . . he's just changed, is all." She couldn't meet Cahey's eyes.

She could feel him looking her over, examining the turn of her head, the line of her neck. She heard his sharp intake of breath, and her nose twitched as his scent peaked hotly.

She recognized, as well, the dead, controlled tone of his voice. *Furious.*

"You're fucking him."

"Not exactly," she answered.

"What the Hel does 'not exactly' mean, then?"

"I let him . . ." Her voice failed. "We kiss."

"The son of a bitch who turned my son against me? You're ashamed of it, at least."

"No," she said, drawing herself up and turning to face him. "Not ashamed. Unhappy to have hurt you."

"I did not ask you to leave me, Selene."

"You drove me to go! You never stopped wanting . . . needing . . . things I could never give you!"

"I never pushed you for anything," he said. "Not once."

She snarled. "I could *smell* it on you. How badly you wanted—needed—to be touched. The only time you were at

peace was when you were away from me. What could I have
done to help you, except go?"

The sound of the sea outside the window.

"I was never at peace," he said. "It had nothing to do with
you."

"I care for you. I could not bear to watch you suffer."

"Ah," he spat. "So, since you couldn't stand to have *me*
touch you, you went to *him* instead?"

She backed away a step, trying and failing to smooth the
fur along her spine. Her tail bristled. "*He* could be happy with
what I had to give. And *he* isn't hiding from his pain in the arms
of a creature without a soul."

Cahey paused. His voice was glacial when he spoke again.
"She needs me, Selene. And . . . it helps. It hurts less when she's
done."

"Because there's a little bit less of you to hurt, you stupid
bastard!" Selene wanted to hit him. She wanted to drag him in
front of a mirror and make him look at the bruises.

He shook his head slightly, covering the lower half of his
face with his hand. "It's just a little bit of peace. Cathmar . . .
everything." His voice broke. "Cathmar won't even come to see
me anymore, Selene."

"It might have something to do with the welts on your
neck, you know. I also know that Mingan tried to help you,
and you wouldn't talk to him."

"He tried to feed me some bullshit story about Muire not
being Muire." He came around the counter toward her, hands
spread wide.

She bristled. "The same bullshit story *I* tried to feed you, I
think?"

He said nothing for a long time. When he spoke again, his voice was gentle. "You should go, Selene. I don't want to ruin our friendship, and you're distraught."

"Fine," she said, picking up her pack. "But I want you to promise me you'll go down to the ocean at moonrise and summon her. Ask her yourself who it was that came to you that day."

He closed his eyes. It wasn't a promise.

She walked through the door, turned, and closed it behind her, unable to breathe until the panel edge cut off her view of his stricken face. She'd scored.

The knowledge tasted like so much rotten meat on her tongue. She wondered if she'd ever walk through that door again.

Well, Cahey thought, *my perfect record for driving people away remains intact.*

He sat down on the floor, his back against the wall, and waited for the Imogen to come.

Mingan's steed bore Selene back to the independent city of Freimarc with sorrowful beats of his wings. Neither one of them spoke.

Selene's lover, thoughtful on a faded burgundy brocade couch, looked up as she entered the room. "It did not go well," Mingan said, standing and crossing the old wooden floor to her. Her nostrils flared at the scent of bitterness that hung around him. Animal pungency tickled her with desire as she stepped into his embrace.

She hid her face against the joint of his arm and body. "It didn't," she answered. "He's far gone."

She felt Mingan nod.

"I'll go to him. Soon. When he's had time to think about what you told him," he whispered.

His body was hot and hard against hers. She leaned into his unyielding strength, shaking her head slowly, side to side, waiting for her fur to flatten and her ears to lift. *He can be gentle as well as strong, Cahey,* she thought. *I never would have known it, either. Unflinching, brutal, yes—but how different was Muire? How different are any of us?*

He stroked Selene's short mane, whispering words that didn't mean anything. At last, she stopped shivering and looked up at his face.

"There has been too much sorrow," he said.

She nodded. "Comfort me?"

The smile rearranged his careworn face into a beacon. "Lovely Selene," he said. "Your wish is my command." He bore her up in his arms, and she relaxed in his grip like a trusting cat.

That couch, it turned out, was too far away. She twined her arms around his neck, ever-so-careful of her claws, and raised her mouth to his.

He brushed her lips with his own, if she could really be said to have lips. She felt the shapes of his face outlined against her whiskers and closed her eyes, the better to read the image. She let her tongue come out against him, lightly, and relished the salt of his skin.

He sighed, and she tasted the promise of his breath like a flame.

Thee, he said inside her. Her mouth curled open in a mating snarl, a low growl rising up her throat. He breathed across her face as if across the mouthpiece of a flute; she turned her head to catch the scent of his exhalation.

Her barbed tongue left a scrape across his face: she tasted blood. He chuckled, still holding her effortlessly in arms as unyielding as a sculpture's. His right hand slid up along her spine and knotted on the scruff of her neck, drawing gently, firmly, on the loose bit of skin.

Soft as a kitten, she sagged in his arms.

Would that it could be different, my dear, he said to her.

I'd claw your eyes out and you know it, she replied, trying not to fight the sensation of her body relaxing beyond her control. She *was* first a cat, after all.

By the shape outlined against her whiskers she knew when he licked his lips, closed his eyes, and bent into the kiss.

Her mouth is slack against his, unresponsive, long teeth white and fine as bone needles pressed against his lip. He would have scars, if he scarred, from trying to kiss her without immobilizing her first, and yet still he longs for the feeling of her body striving against his. He can sense the lively mind quick within her; the fey, divided soul.

He breathes into her mouth.

A low, druggy purr starts in the bottom of her chest. He hugs her against his breast, deepening the kiss, locking his knees to hold them up as his awareness leaves his body and floods into her. She takes him in, draws him deep, leaves him dizzy and entranced.

A long, seeking, dreaming moment, and she gives him back to himself, breath forced out between the razorsharp teeth. He tastes his own blood and presses closer, drawing out the pleasure, taking as slowly as he can bear.

A long time later, he lifts his mouth from hers, eyes still closed, listening to the heavy rumble of her purr. He lets his fingers relax on the back of her neck, and she turns in his arms, cuddling like a kitten against his throat. Her whiskers tickle. "Good," she sighs, contented.

"Very good indeed."

He asked the Imogen to use the door, so she comes through the door.

He looks up at her. She tastes his pain in the room. Sweet. Sweeter than ever.

Thick as incense.

He doesn't rise. She comes to him and kneels down as he shapes her.

She shivers at the power of his sorrow, his need. She leans into him. Incense.

Her lips brush his skin beside the bruises.

"Not the throat."

"As you wish it, Lord." Clawless, human fingers are nimble on the buttons.

50 A.R.
On the Twentieth Day of Autumn

Cats excel at guilt. So Cathmar decided before he even started strategizing that whatever happened was all Selene's fault. Once he had the plan, he sprang it on Mardoll over breakfast. Her breakfast, eaten while he sat across from her at the laminate table, playing with his bowl of tea. "I'm going out to see Dad today."

She looked up from hardtack and herring and raised a pale eyebrow. "I'll come with you, if you like."

He chewed on the thought while she chewed on her crispbread. She had a little sour cream on her cheek. He handed her a napkin.

Twisting the cloth between her fingers, she waited for his answer.

"All right," he said. "I don't know how he'll be."

She shrugged. "You think he's in a bad place. Your moreau friend is working on you to help him. He's your dad. What else am I going to do?" The smile dimpled her cheek.

He gave it back. "Whenever you're ready, then."

An hour later, delayed by a side trip to the livery stable,

they rode double down to the sea. The sturdy red mare didn't mind two slender riders.

They heard the sound of the axe before they came within sight of the cabin. Cathmar, riding before—after a great deal of instruction, Mardoll was finally trusting him with the reins—glanced over his shoulder at Mardoll.

"Chopping wood?"

He was. Shirtless, sweating in the late-summer sunshine, Cahey split logs. Kindling flew from the point of impact. The axehead stuck into the stump. He straightened, releasing the handle, wiped his hair back from his eyes.

A wary expression crossed his face.

Cathmar saw one, two bruises marking his father's chest. One was faded, nearly gone. The other was darker, recent but not fresh.

Mardoll leaned forward to whisper in Cathmar's ear. "That looks better than what you described."

Cathmar nodded. He reined Elder in and waited for Mardoll to slide down before swinging his leg over the mare's haunches. He dropped her reins on the ground as Mardoll had shown him and reached up to scratch behind the ear Elder swiveled.

"Dad."

Cahey reeled out a long arm and retrieved a light-colored shirt from a nearby beach plum. "Cathmar. This must be Mardoll." Buttoning the shirt, Cahey came forward and offered the girl his hand. "A pleasure to finally meet you," he said.

She dimpled and giggled, glancing over at Cathmar, catching his eye with her smile. "Likewise," she said.

Cahey released the girl's hand and turned toward Cathmar. "Come inside," Cahey said. "Let's get out of the sun. Does your horse need water?"

Mardoll nodded. "She'd appreciate it, I'm sure. You can't have a well this close to the sea, though." Cathmar got the impression that Mardoll was watching Cahey very carefully. Assessing.

Cahey jerked his thumb over his shoulder. "There's a spring back up the road. We keep the barrels full." He paused. "I mean, I keep the barrels full."

He failed to look at Cathmar. "Bucket in the shed."

The mare watered, her saddle off and her bit slipped, they filed into the house in silence. Cahey started tea. For something to do with his hands, Cathmar thought.

The fussing in the kitchen started to annoy him. "Dad."

Cahey set down the teapot and came over to the stone slab counter, leaning over it. "Yes?"

"I'm sorry."

Cahey thought about it for a minute while the silence stretched between them. "I'm sorry, too," he said, and turned back into the kitchen. Cathmar didn't miss the darkness surging under the bright irises of his father's eyes.

That and the quietness behind everything he said scared Cathmar. *I'm glad I came,* he thought. *No bruises. But he's worse; he's not better.*

Cahey finished making tea before bringing the speckled stoneware pot out into the living room; he poured bowls for each of them and settled down on the red and blue knotted rug in front of the cold fireplace. Cathmar plunked down opposite; Mardoll sat in the chair by the door.

"To what do I owe the pleasure?" Cahey said, formally, cupping his hands around his steaming bowl.

And that was a bad sign, that formality, treating Cathmar like a guest. Maybe bringing Mardoll had been a bad idea, because Cathmar found he couldn't ask what he needed to in front of her. About the Imogen, about whether Cahey had been up to the village or seen the moreaux. About what he'd been doing with his time, and why he was still here in this cottage now that Cathmar had moved out.

He couldn't get around any of those questions, though, so instead he said, "The next time you come up to the city, let me know. You still haven't seen where I live."

Cahey glanced sidelong at Mardoll, as if checking her reaction. She stood a little behind Cathmar and he couldn't have seen her face from where he sat without craning, so he tried to read her expression in his father's reaction.

"I'd like that," Cahey said, looking down. "Give me an excuse to come into town."

50 A.R.
On the Twenty-first Day of Autumn

Cahey sat on a rock overlooking the sea. A small drum rested in the hollow of his crossed legs, and his scarred fingers tapped idly around the edges of it in rhythm to the waves. He felt her coming toward him, of course, but he didn't turn until the last moment.

"Mardoll," he said, nodding as pleasantly as he could. "I thought you would have left."

"With Cathmar? I told him I wanted to talk to you alone, as an interested stranger. I'll catch up." The wide collar of her pleated white shift slid down her shoulder. The wind scarfed it between her legs, translucent fabric gliding over her hips and thighs. She tilted her face up to him and smiled, tawny hair tangled by the wind. An elaborate necklace encircled her throat, sparkling with rainbow-hued stones.

She doesn't look sixteen or eighteen anymore. He looked away, back out to sea. *Not the sort of thought you want to have about your son's girlfriend,* he reminded himself.

His fingers ran a shimmer around the edge of the drum. Mardoll scrambled up the stone easily, settling down beside him. Her shoulder didn't brush his, but he could feel her body heat. "Why don't you come up to the chapel with me?" she said. "I'd like to hear the story in your words."

He shook his head. "Anything I could tell you, Cathmar already has." He gave her a sidelong glance, catching her sea-blue gaze with the edge of his own. She stared at him, a direct and challenging regard that ran straight down his spine. *The only way she could be plainer is if she reached down my pants and grabbed my balls.*

It annoyed him that he was tempted. He might be stuck in a young man's body, but he was growing an old man's soul.

He forced back the appalling moment of desire and frowned, looking at her directly for a long moment before glancing away, dismissively. "Does he know what you're doing here?" Cahey asked her, turning his attention back to the ocean, allowing animosity to stiffen his spine.

Out of the corner of his eye, he saw her smile blossom. "Of course not. He thinks I'm here to make you see sense. But you're much more . . . worldly . . . than your son."

"I'm also not a liar," he replied. "And I won't do anything to hurt him. Perhaps you should go."

"Oh, no," she said. "You'd never do anything to hurt any-one, would you?" There was something hypnotic about her voice. "Not on purpose. Not in malice. I'm sure of that."

Cahey shook his head, bitterness overwhelming the irrita-tion. "I see he's told you some things."

"Some. I have many means of learning." The girlish note fell out of her voice, replaced by a tone both womanly and knowing. "Do you know who I am?"

He looked back at her, the white curve of her throat bared by hair tumbling in the breeze. He allowed his head to move judiciously from side to side. "I can't say that I do."

"I am one who has already been your lover once, and who will be again."

"I think I would remember you," he answered coldly.

She chuckled. "Flattery—and a knife. Very nice, Cahey. You'll make an angel yet. Unless you change your mind."

"What do you mean?"

She passed a hand over her face.

A chill settled into his stomach when she glanced at him again. "Muire," he said. But no—the eyes were still too blue.

Raising a graceful hand, she snapped her fingers beside her face. And was Mardoll again. "Am I not powerful?" she said, with the air of one quoting something. "Am I not fair?"

"Who are you?"

"Your lover, and your son's."

"What do you want?"

She laid her hand on his shoulder. "To make you an offer, my dear. You suffer needlessly. I will speak plainly: there is history that you would change. You would take someone's place."

The realization of what she was offering hooked him through the diaphragm. His heart cramped in his breast.

"Astrid," he said quietly.

She nodded. "It can be arranged. There would be sacrifices, of course."

"Why should I believe you?"

She smiled, reached out with a slender forefinger, and brushed his forehead, between the eyes.

. . . *voices raised. Screaming, a stranger screaming his name.*

Sweat in his eyes, and Astrid, laughing, stepping toward him and ducking low for a spin kick at the side of his knee.

The resilient wet crunching sensation of bones fracturing under his heel . . .

Cahey shouted, kicked back away from her, back flat against the bluff.

He watched the tip of her finger like the eye of a snake.

"You can change that," she said, capturing his gaze.

He jerked his head to the side. His hands closed on the little drum: he felt leather and wire, the tiny glass beads detailing the rim. He seized his tongue between his teeth, breathed out slowly, brought himself under control. *One heartbeat at a time. Never get angry. Never get scared.*

"There would be no Cathmar." He didn't look at her, continuing to run his fingers over the drumskin. It made a whisper of sound that was lost in the rhythm of the sea.

"There would. But that would not be his name, perhaps, although you would have been his father. And he might have been raised by someone more suited to the job. You can't say that he wouldn't have been better off with his uncle Aethelred. Or Astrid, for that matter."

Astrid saved my life. More, she kept me from turning into my old man. He'd said it the night she died—the night he killed her—and thought it a thousand times: *She was worth ten of me. It should have been me.*

"No one to fill my place as angel." Now he did look, and met her gaze directly.

"Astrid, of course."

Hope and terror stirred in him. His breath locked in his chest. *Never get scared.* "How can you change the past?"

She touched the thing that glittered at her throat. "I will loan you my necklace. It's a road, you see. You could take Astrid's place. But there is a price."

"What's that?"

"Four days of passion." Her hand slid down across his chest, coming to rest on his thigh. So close. She smelled of growing things.

He was getting hard. He willed himself to stand and move away from her. He failed. "Four days?"

"You and I. In a bed with clean sheets. Or here on the beach. I like that idea, actually." Her hand slid ten centimeters higher, squeezed gently.

He gasped.

"Naked," she continued, "sweaty."

Light, that smile. He almost felt her tongue on his skin. "You're my son's lover."

"I am everyone's lover, einherjar. I am love. And lust, and passion. I am the irresistible goddess. And if you do this thing, you will not be his father. You will not be anything at all. And our dalliance will not have happened, although I will remember it. But your Astrid . . . will be alive."

A long, hard silence. Her hand was moving. The rhythm of his breathing made it difficult to speak. He put his hand on her shoulder to push her back, but she was immovable. It was like pushing at the living bones of the earth.

"Prove it."

Her teeth flashed ivory in the sun, necklace jewels glittering as she tilted her head. "I knew you were going to say that. Observe."

Her other hand slid into the braids behind his ear, clenched there, and turned his head by main strength. She laid her cheek to his so they both looked back down the beach, and whispered, "Watch."

The light changed, became colder and more slanted, as if the sun were lower in the sky. The wind held spring chill, not second summer.

Movement drew his attention. Someone walked there, over the sand to the edge of the waves where the beach gave way to stones. Someone he half-recognized—a tall, lean man with snake braids twisted back over his shoulders. He was walking toward someone, a woman in the water, her crimson skirts swept back and forth by the drag and surge of waves.

"No," he said, understanding that what he saw was himself. "I don't want to see this. Take me home."

A blink, and a flash of warmth, and it was again warm. The woman leaning over him continued in a challenging whisper. "If it makes it better, call me by a different name. Gullveig. I've used that one before."

She leaned farther forward, brought her mouth against his ear. Her breath, hot and wet, tickled his skin. His skin jumped, flinching away from her touch like a racehorse from a fly bite. He tried and failed to find the strength to push her away. She made him feel *owned,* and he hated it.

Hated it.

Craved it.

"All right." Rough words, caught on the nap of a long silence. "But it will be different, this time."

She tilted her head back, tossed her hair aside. "How so?"

"No more deceptions. I see your true face, no shadow put on to tempt me."

He saw her considering, saw her smile with an edge of gloating in it. A powerful smile.

"You'll do as I direct?" she asked.

"I may be a whore," he said, "but I'm an honest one."

She inclined her head and smiled. "Do you always talk to goddesses this way?"

"The ones worth talking to."

She leaned back, fingers relaxing. She didn't pull her hand back, though. He watched her sweep her glance along the beach, stop, and smile. "Oh, there," she said. "I like that."

He followed the line of her gaze and shivered more deeply. A quarter-mile down the beach lay what looked at first sight like the ruins of an ancient domed structure, bleached ivory in the sun. Cahey knew it was the rib cage of some immense sea beast, extinct since the world nearly ended almost four hundred years before.

"You want to make love in a skeleton?"

She licked her lips. "Who said a damn thing about love?"

She preceded him down the beach, sunlight shining through her pleated dress, sea breeze fluttering the colorful scarves that bound her waist. His mouth was dry. His thought—fragmentary, unreasoned—seemed to swell and fade with the pulse of the waves.

He realized he'd left the little drum on the rock. *It should be safe enough there.*

She led him down among the bones.

Sex and death, he thought. *Hand and hand. This could be the story of my life.*

He was too drained by his decision to laugh.

She turned to him. "Take off your clothes," she said. "Lie down. Unless you want to undress me with your own hands."

He shook his head and obeyed her, feeling as if he moved in a dream. The sunlight was hot on his skin. His body ached with desire and resignation and sorrow. He threw his clothes aside, revealing the hidden bruises, the ones that Cathmar had not seen.

She came toward him, naked except for that glittering necklace, pale as the bones that surrounded her. He settled down on the sand. *This isn't love,* he thought. *It isn't passion. It's not playful or holy or good business or even good fun.*

Her scarves—her belt—were in her hands, ruffled by the sea breeze. "I'm going to bind your hands. Does it matter to you how?"

"My hands?" Real fear, hurting fear, spiked through him. Grains of quartz and mica glittered on his skin. "I don't want—"

"There's still time to end the bargain," she interrupted. "You'll do as I instruct, as arranged. Four times. And then I'll grant your boon. Or you can go now, walk back up the beach, and that will be the end of it."

He bit his lip against the well of darkness that threatened to suck him down. It was moments before he could speak. "Whatever," he said, sick with remembered terror, "you desire."

He understood now why she'd chosen the skeleton for their bed. The lengths of cloth she wrapped around his wrists were silken soft, almost as blue as her eyes, and she tied the other ends to the arching ribs. The sunlight shone on his face, blinding even through closed eyelids. He turned his head to the side as she drew first one arm and then the other wide, lashing him down.

He groaned through clenched teeth, feeling the muscles in his neck and shoulders tense as he involuntarily tested the strength of his bonds. He remembered brick dust and bruising hands the scrape of concrete against his face the smell of garbage please.

please don't.

and too much pain. . . .

The scarves held.

The hands had, too.

Her voice was a teasing whisper. "You're frightened, aren't you? I like that."

He writhed away from her touch.

She stroked his hair, his face, his body, gentling him like a panicky stallion. "It will go easier on you," she said, "if you give in now. If you don't, I shall have to break you."

He couldn't answer. He struggled, and she sighed and stood and bound his feet as well. He strained like a bowstring. "Enough," she told him. "Fight until you've worn yourself out, and then what good will you be to me?"

Her hand against his neck was cold compared to the sultry sunlight. *Cold as the sea.*

The thought brought him back to himself. He remembered her dressed in the guise of his beloved.

I should hate you, he thought. He hated himself, hated the rising excitement in his body, the will to be taken. He *wanted* her mastery over him. The knowledge closed his eyes, turned his head aside.

I've never wanted anything this much in my life.

Then he lifted his head off the pillow of sand, looking

down the length of his body at her. "I should hate you," he said.

She nodded. "Yes, you should." The sound of her voice, unguarded for a moment, surprised him. There was sorrow in it, and a wild old determination.

But I don't hate her.

I hate myself.

She came up alongside him, pushed his head back, slung a thigh white as the beach sand across his face, hard feet burrowing under his painfully opened shoulders. "Hate me," she said. "Hate me, and make me scream."

And?" Cathmar said, when she caught up with him halfway up the Eiledon road.

Mardoll dismounted and handed him Elder's reins, leaning forward to brush her lips against his. "Nothing important," she said.

Still. A pity. She thought about the two of them, father and son, and despite herself she smiled. *It would be nicer to keep both of them. But one must choose.*

Cathmar was examining her face, and she wondered if he saw anything mysterious in her smile. Not that it mattered, really. One way or another.

"What did he say?" Persistent lad.

She made a show of thinking. "I suspect he'd be happy if you came to see him, once in a while," she said. "I think he wants to try to be what he's supposed to be, Cath."

Cathmar snorted. "Sure."

Mardoll ran her tongue across her teeth. "Actually," she said, "you could give him a chance."

She set out along the road and he strode along beside her, leading the red mare.

"Do you remember," Mardoll said after a little while, "when you talked about making waelcyrge? Einherjar?"

"Yes, of course." They passed under an apple tree, heavy with green fruit. Hornets buzzed around a few early windfalls.

"How would that work?"

He turned, grinned down at her, and started to explain things she already knew.

She admired the way the sun highlighted his face. Young. But there were advantages to that.

Sunset, and the Imogen comes to him as she always does, but he is not waiting for her.

He is *always* waiting for her. Where else would he be? No matter. She can find him. Anywhere.

She follows his scent—which is not his scent, exactly, but the way his passage touched the air—down across the beach, and by the verge of the water. Past the little hill with the white building on it.

Down among the bones of ancient dead things.

She think he's sleeping at first, which worries her. Which gives her pause, worry not being what she is intended for. But then she sees that his eyes are open, and his relaxation is that of despair.

The tide comes on. It rolls between the bones lower down

the beach, smoothing the furrowed sand as one might smooth a child's hair. If one had a child.

Her Lord sits watching the sea come in.

Sand cakes his clothing and his skin, his hair. And oh, his pain is sweet. Sweet, and deep.

The Imogen smells a woman on his skin, a scent so ancient she's almost forgotten it. That woman has wounded him more deeply than ever the Imogen does. There are weals on his wrists, welts on his legs, bruises on his body.

She helps him home.

The scent of blood and sorrow rouses the Imogen's appetites. The marks are the least of his suffering.

No matter.

She heals all wounds. Given time.

She is mercy. She is solace.

In her house, there is an end to pain.

Borje picked his way down the bluff from the chapel. He remembered who the pale-haired woman was, all right. She was hard to forget. Her and her sneaky questions about angels living there.

He liked Cahey. Liked the kid even more.

Knew what somebody with a ring through his nose looked like, too.

The cottage was dark, and Borje didn't bother to bring the lights up. He keyed his 'screen on and said Aethelred's name, waiting to be connected.

The link went through almost immediately. The old priest

held his small 'screen close to his face. Behind him, Borje glimpsed the figure of a woman whose hair made a halo around her in the firelight. "Borje," Aethelred said through the static on the portable. "Problem?"

"I think so," the bull replied, digging behind one ear with a bifurcated forehoof. "There's a woman here. Not here, I mean—she was with Cahey and Cathmar."

Aethelred nodded encouragement.

"And I've seen her before. I recognized her smell. But she looked different. And she was doing things . . . well. I think you should hurry. I think you should send Selene."

"All right, Borje. I'll do that."

"Right away," Borje said.

"Right away," Aethelred agreed. Behind him, the woman was already picking up her pack.

50 A.R.
On the Twenty-second Day of Autumn

𝓐 warm rain streaked the windowpane. Selene turned away from it, knuckling the corners of her eyes. "I heard from Aethelred," she said to the silver-eyed figure who had come up behind her. She had caught his scent, which wreathed him like a second cloak, but even she didn't hear him move.

She felt as if his pale eyes peeled her open.

He was already nodding when she said, "It's not good news."

"With age," he answered, "you may come to accept that it never is."

"I hope not. That seems like a hard kind of acceptance."

"We're a hard kind of creature." He tilted his head slightly and examined her face. "Tell me the bad news, then."

She sighed and arched her back, twisting. "Borje," she said, and then interrupted herself. "It's like some grown-up game of pass-the-message. Borje saw something that made him unhappy. He called Aethelred, and Aethelred . . . well."

Falling back a stride or two, Mingan fetched up against the edge of the scarred, massive cherrywood table that dominated their living space. He perched, supporting his weight on one booted foot while swinging the other idly back and forth as if his anticipation were too great to hold himself still.

Well, Selene thought, *if he's going to tell you he's going to tell you, and if he's not he's not.* "What do you know about this Mardoll person?"

One corner of his thin lips twitched upward. "Lovely, clever Selene," he said. "Not nearly so much as I want to know. But enough."

"And you won't share it with me."

"Dare not," he said. "For you are young yet, and not grown into your ruthlessness."

She came toward him, feeling her tail begin to lash. Her ears stayed up, however: although frustrated, she was also curious. "What is that supposed to mean?"

Reaching out, he let the back of a gloved hand trail down her arm, ruffling the fur and laying it flat. She shivered. "Do you trust me?" he asked her.

Enough to go limp in your arms as a kitten, she thought. But what she said was, "Not entirely."

A little purring sound as he caught his breath, looking at her. She held her gaze steady on his, one wild equal to another.

"Good." His smile trembled a little, but held. "Never entirely. Because there are things I place before you, my love, and if you are wise you will also examine your priorities."

"Things. Yourself?" His scent itched. She wrinkled her nose. Her tail stilled as she examined the thought.

"Never that," he answered. The slightest shake of his head. "Never over thee. But we serve, Selene. Never forget for a moment that we serve, and that she whom you serve must hold, always, primacy."

"I've been that road before," she said. "You may recall, I left it."

He tilted his head and smiled, a silent wolf-laugh. "Is it different when you choose it?"

She shrugged, unable to still the flicker of her tail. More evidence of her irritation. "And that's why you won't tell me what you're up to?"

One long, thoughtful breath and then another before he answered. She looked down at the narrow wooden floorboards, over at the rain falling behind the yellow and gray curtains.

"If you knew," he said at last, "you would have to do something. And what you would do—as naturally to you as breathing, what you could not prevent yourself from doing—would cost me things from which I am not prepared to be parted."

"Ah." It was easier to keep the irritation out of her tone than she expected. Especially when she stole his trick and counted breaths before she spoke, half humorous, half edged. "So it's all about you."

He chuckled and stood as she turned and drifted away. She didn't drift far, however, and then his hands were on her shoulders and he bent, rubbing his face against the fur on the back of her neck. Despite herself, a purr rumbled up her throat, although her left ear swiveled backwards in irritation.

"It's been about me all along," he said.

She leaned back against him, lulled by the murmur against her neck, although his words should have disturbed her.

"Have you ever doubted that it's about me, Selene? You know what I am. I am the hour of the wolf; I am the new moon in the old moon's arms. I am the death that makes fertile ground."

He turned her, gently, softly, and drew her into his arms. "I am a trickster and a liar, my love, and you will trust me because you must, because the other course is folly."

She stepped back away from him then. "I must do nothing, Wolf. I must do nothing, except serve the one who saved us." She raised her chin and met his gaze squarely, saw him smile that she was unafraid.

He seemed to listen to a following silence before he chuckled. "It is a lucky wolf indeed who has two such unflinching allies as yourself and my steed to treat with him."

She was distracted for a moment wondering what the valraven had said to him; before she recovered herself he bent down to kiss her throat where the fur was thin and the blood ran close, letting her feel his white, sharp teeth. She might have stepped back—but he caught her offguard, heedless when her claws curled reflexively into his shoulders, laying flesh open almost down to the bone.

"Mingan," she hissed, blood scorching her fingers, soaking her fur, showering the wooden floor.

" 'Twill heal," he answered against her skin, and it did.

50 A.R.
On the Twenty-fifth Day of Autumn

Poor boy. And such a handsome one, too. The goddess watched him, blindfolded on his own hearth-rug, trying not to fight the lengths of twisted cloth she'd bound him with. Sweat beaded his naked skin, although the fireplace was cold and she hadn't even touched him, yet. She stood, watching, fingering her necklace. He reminded her of someone she knew once. Just as beautiful. Just as doomed.

She shook her head. *Pity will not help you, Heythe.* It was necessary. This one would not surrender. He would need to be removed, even if the lies rankled. Even if she found him very brave, to face destruction, shame and old clotted terrors so selflessly, for the sake of another.

His face turned as if he sought her, despite the darkness that enfolded him. She witnessed his passion and his fear.

My enemy loved this one.

Loves this one.

Surely she will not let him continue to suffer so. Angry though he may have made her.

"I'm sorry," she whispered, too softly for him to hear. She

was a goddess. Had been, anyway, would be again if she could pay the prices she had to pay. She could look at anything.

Bitter prices, but if the cost was too dear . . . well. There were always others who *would* pay it. And so she would break this angel, force his mistress' hand. Make the Bearer of Burdens intervene on his behalf and that of his son. She saw blood on his mouth, looked away. Looked back.

She had been worshipped as a goddess. She could look at anything. And regret had never stopped her before. The Grey Wolf's sire wouldn't have cringed at rape or deception.

Heythe bent down beside him, let her breath touch his ear. He groaned and tried to pull away, but the scarves held him tight.

"Shhhhh. No whimpering." She paused, thoughtful, watching the tears leak down his cheeks, darkening the fabric of the blindfold. "Well, you can scream if you have to."

For a little while, he didn't.

He expected it to hurt. Braced for it, was ready. Pain could have been an anchor in the sea that tossed him. Cahey was accustomed to pain.

He *knew* how to take a *beating*.

He was blinded, restrained. There was nothing to concentrate on, nothing but the delicacy of her touch, languid fingers stroking and gripping and sliding. . . .

Light, if only there were pain. He strained against the ties, bruising his wrists. It wasn't enough.

It doesn't matter what she does to me. It doesn't matter, because soon none of this will have ever happened.

He bit back another little moan, and heard her chuckle. "Good boy," she murmured. "I know. It's hard, isn't it? You want to hate this, but your body *needs* it so much."

The blindfold felt wet against his face. He realized he was weeping. He wasn't really there, though—he was far away, and long ago.

I will not scream. I will not give him the fucking satisfaction of admitting he's hurt me.

Except this didn't hurt, and it wasn't *him;* it was *her.* Couldn't. Couldn't be made to feel anything but *good,* no matter how he tried. Inside, the edgy shard of Mingan's soul that rode him stirred, stretched, awakened—as it seemed to, in her presence. He felt the Wolf's presence—thoughts and emotions both wild, searing and coldly restrained—like a fist clenched in his hair.

It didn't hurt at all, and that was worse.

He gasped in tormented pleasure, reliving rapes both physical and of the soul. *It's what you've wanted all along,* the Wolf whispered inside him. *To be ravished. You liked my kiss. And you like this, too.*

No, Cahey thought, but he wasn't as certain of his answer as he wanted to be. *I want it not to hurt anymore.* But it didn't hurt at all as she pressed deeper, curled her piercing fingers into a hook, and laughed softly against his steaming skin when he chewed his mouth bloody against the forbidden outcry.

The Suneater whispered, *But you want it; you asked for it. You like the humiliation, don't you? But you can't admit it. If you could ever surrender to anything, it would make you stronger.*

Instead, your shame shows anyone who knows the way to master you.

Shut up, Mingan, you son of a bitch. He welcomed the distraction, honestly. He expected—hoped for—more mockery, and was surprised and disappointed to feel the Wolf-shard chuckle and withdraw with a smiling parting shot: *If you hate it so much, beautiful little boy, you can put a stop to it with a word.*

He mouthed the word. *No.* Almost gave it voice, and thought instead about the investment he had already made, the worth of what he was trying to buy. Felt the savaged skin on his wrists and ankles break open as he yanked once more against twisted cloth. It wasn't enough; the blood in his mouth wasn't enough to let him hold on to his fury, which was rapidly twisting into the shame the Wolf-shard spoke of—shame, and despair.

Astrid. He called her face up against the blackness of the blindfold. *I can do this for you. I can do anything for you. I've had my lifetime. Seventy years, more or less, not bad ones, and you gave me almost sixty of them.*

You deserve your lifetime, too.

"Your body betrays your will," Gullveig whispered. She leaned over him, hands still moving slowly, rhythmically. Her tongue traced spirals in liquid fire across his chest. "You like to be fucked like this. It's all right, love. I'll show you what you need." Teeth nipping the smooth skin of his chest, the smell of her sweat and heat, so close.

Light, and in my own house, too. Not that it was the first time for that, either. *I will not give her the satisfaction . . . ,* but he couldn't stop shaking, and he suddenly couldn't stop his hips from moving, either—in time to the sensual rhythm of her touch.

Her voice was breathy, controlled. "We have hours before I have to be home to your son. Plenty of time for everything."

He felt her weight shift, and her hair swept down his belly, accompanied by the heat of her breath. Again, she thrust into him. Her mouth sweltered on his skin.

It robbed the last bit of his control. From the rush of cool air down his throat he knew he cried out in torment and indulgence.

Sensation, sorrow, memory buffeted him. He foundered.

Went under.

Drowned.

50 A.R.
On the Twenty-fifth Day of Autumn

Cathmar walked through what he was coming to think of as *his* city, watching the light slide up the west walls of crumbling buildings like a counterbalance to the setting sun. He'd ranged far, through Hangman and among the broad bases of the karst-shaped arcologies, their streamlined summits casting the ways between in deep shadow. Now he joined the evening traffic, moving against the bulk of it, his companions students in threadbare robes returning to the University after a rest day spent in the city.

He smiled at his neighbors, and the ones who weren't likely to cause trouble smiled back. They were all getting to know him now, and not just the moreaux. It had taken a while, but he was finding a place in the rhythm of the city.

I'm a guardian angel, he thought, with amusement. He was getting a reputation, he supposed. He liked it. It made him feel grown-up.

I wonder what it was like when my mother did this sort of thing. His hand rested on Nathr's hilt for a moment as he rounded a corner, boot splashing into a puddle. He imagined her hand on the same hilt, her boot in the same puddle. But there had been nothing, then, but the city. And now there was a whole world beyond. *When she did it, it was probably harder.*

A crier's voice echoed in the distance, and Cathmar cocked his head to listen, smile widening. Calling the faithful. There was some little church on every street corner, and all of them disagreed.

Cathmar enjoyed knowing the real story.

And he enjoyed walking through Eiledon at nightfall. But still, it might be a good time to head home and find Mardoll. *I can try out a new recipe,* amused at himself for cooking for her. Even though he was getting pretty good at it.

He waited on the curb to let a ground-taxi go past, then headed back toward the river. It was full dark before he felt the familiar creaky stairs under his boots: he'd stopped to intervene in yet another mugging, and was still flushed with excitement as he ran up the steps.

It wasn't that long ago when I was the one being mugged. So many things have changed in the past two years.

The door to the flat was locked, but the bolt wasn't slid, so he opened it with his key. *I wonder where she is.* Concerned but not yet worried, he walked inside, the floor creaking.

The apartment was dark, but otherwise just as he'd left it, and it felt empty. Cathmar palmed the light on and walked around once, noticing that the bed needed to be made. He flipped the covers up and wandered into the kitchen to make tea.

Three hours later, when he finally heard her step on the stair, he was pacing.

He had the door open before she got her key turned in the worn brass lock. They stood eye to eye for a moment before she managed a smile. "Hi," she said.

"I was worried," he answered, stepping back so she could come inside.

She brushed past him. "I need a bath like you wouldn't believe." Some scent that hung around her caught his attention. Familiar—he was sure he would have known it at once, in context—but he couldn't quite place it. Traces of sand clung to the hems of her slacks.

"Where were you?" He shut and locked the old panel door. She stripped off her shirt as she walked farther into the flat, dimming the lights in the main room in passing.

She looked back over her shoulder, tossing her hair. "Big girl, Cath. Remember?"

He caught himself absently picking at the peeling paint on the doorframe, and forced himself to stop. "Even big girls' boyfriends worry about them." He heard his father's voice. *You think you're a grown-up now. . . .*

Yeah, Dad. I think I know what you were talking about, now.

And then he heard Mingan's voice, and a warning.

She shut the bathroom door behind her. He heard the lock click and water running, heard the sizzle of the gas stove as she started warming the kettle.

He picked her discarded shirt off the creaking tile floor and carried it toward the hamper in the bedroom. Felt grit against his fingertips. Holding it up to the light in the hall ceiling, he examined the edge of the sleeve. There was a stiff, colorless blemish along the hem, and he identified it by the scent.

Salt water and sand.

She'd been down to the sea.

50 A.R.
On the Twenty-sixth Day of Autumn

Halfway there, Cahey thought, watching the sun go down over the water. *Halfway dead,* another part of his mind remarked. He turned and glanced east, where a waxing moon was tracking across the twilight sky. *There will be moonlight tonight.*

You could say good-bye.

But then Muire would know what he was up to.

She'd never let him go through with it. But she must know. So why hadn't she done anything? If she loved him . . . no. Of course she didn't. He put a stop to that pretty quickly.

A little shard of her love, remnant of her kiss, spun at the center of his being: proof, if he cared to take it, that she had adored him out of reason. He chewed his swollen lip absently and then flinched at the pain.

Idiot. Moron. Einherjar. You never even had the guts to tell her you were in love with her.

No wonder she left you.

Who would have thought it would come to this? Random footsteps carried him down by the water. The waves rolled up on the sand, almost brushing his bare feet. He stopped and dug his toes into the cool, damp sand.

The last rim of the sun bloodied the ocean and slipped under, staining a spatter of clouds in daylily shades. The sky behind them burned orange before it faded to periwinkle and then indigo.

One by one, pinpricks opened in the night. Still Cahey stood and watched the moon slide across the sky, waiting for the Imogen to come and take the aching weight off his soul. His body hurt as if he'd gotten the worse end of a fight, and his spirit felt thin, bent and stretched.

I'm alone, he thought. *Where is she?*

A sense of presence stole over him as the gibbous moon rose higher. A few strands of his hair ruffled in the wind. The evening tide rolled in, and he took a step away from the advancing waves.

"Muire," he whispered at last.

Into a silence as loud as the whole world-girdling sea holding its breath.

A silence that begged to be filled.

He tried. "I . . ." But his voice broke on it. He cleared his throat. Saw the way the moonlight pooled on the suddenly still ocean. Closed his eyes. *Idiot.*

Yes.

"I'm sorry," he said, and turned and strode quickly away, up the beach.

He was at the top of the grassy dune when he realized that there was somebody in the cottage. The lights were on, and he could see a shape moving around inside. The door was propped open. *At least I cleaned up the living room before I left,* he thought. A wave of self-disgust curled his lip.

He walked up slowly, his hand resting on Alvitr's hilt.

Twenty yards from the door, he caught the tenor of a baritone voice singing an old marching tune.

"Aethelred?"

"Cahey!" The old priest came into the doorway, wiping his hands on a rag. "Hope you don't mind that I let myself in."

"No," Cahey answered. "No, not at all."

Aethelred took his wrist and led him inside, examined his face in the light. "You look three days dead, kid."

Cahey winced as Aethelred squeezed his bruised wrist. The priest looked down, pursed his lips, and whistled. "Bearer of Burdens," he cursed. "What the Hel?"

Cahey shook his head. "I'd rather not talk about it," he said.

"I hear tell you don't want to talk about much of anything, lately. That's a rope burn. A mean one. Who did that to you?"

Cahey tugged his wrist away gently and sat down in the chair beside the door. Without looking up, he knew when Aethelred turned away and walked into the kitchen. He came back with a pack in one hand, and two gray-glazed pottery bowls in the other.

The pack held—among other things—a bottle, from which Aethelred decanted them each a large measure of liquor. He shoved one into the einherjar's hand and clinked his own against it before dragging a straight-backed chair over. "Cahey," he said, all seriousness, "are you in some kind of trouble, kid?"

Cahey examined the brown fluid in the bowl before sipping it. He choked, downed the whole thing in a gulp, and held it back out. "I remember the last time you got me drunk," he said. The sting of the liquor took him back over fifty years, into a little bare room and the taste of sugar and alcohol and a spill of bitter words. "You did that on purpose, didn't you? You're getting me drunk enough to be honest."

Aethelred snorted as he sat down knee to knee with the young angel. After refilling Cahey's bowl he sipped from his own. "This is a wake," he said. "There are rules. We've got to kill the bottle, we've got to see the sunrise, and we've got to tell the truth. All right?"

Cahey considered. "Whose wake?"

"Mine, at the rate I'm going. Muire's. Astrid's. Maybe yours, if you keep it up. Plenty to choose from, you know. Now tell me who the Hel has been tying you up hard enough to hurt you that bad? That doesn't look like . . . fun, Cahey."

"A wicked woman," Cahey answered, after a while. It wasn't the first time he'd sold himself, after all. He'd never had to hide anything from Aethelred. "But one who maybe can give me something I want."

"What's that?" Draining his bowl, Aethelred poured himself more and topped off Cahey's drink as well.

Cahey drew a breath in slowly, tasting how the air moved over his numb tongue. "Absolution."

Aethelred toyed with his own drink. "Heh. Drink more, kid. It's gonna be a long night, and I've got a riot act to read you." He toasted Cahey with his bowl.

Cahey leaned back in his chair, let the feeling of relaxation from the liquor spread up his neck. He wanted a shower, but wasn't certain it would help any more than the last one had. Despite hot water and soap, he thought he could feel Gullveig's touch all over him, grubby handprints on his crawling skin. His stomach heaved, and it wasn't from the booze. "I think I've heard it."

"Well, unless you wanna throw me out, you're gonna hear it again."

Another sip of whisky burned his throat. "I'll listen," was all he said.

Aethelred let a low, grumbling sound collect in his throat. "Cahey, this is becoming an addiction. *Has* become an addiction, Hel. This Imogen thing."

Cahey decided not to tell him that the Imogen had nothing to do with his bruises. "Selene?"

"Kid—Selene. Cathmar. Everybody who cares about you sees it." He shook his bald head, chrome shining in the light from the kitchen.

"She . . . fuck, Aethelred. She *needs* me."

"She needs you to find a way to free her!"

Silence. "Free her?"

Aethelred nodded. "You need to be back out in the world again, doing good. Trying to make things up to Cathmar . . ."

Cahey stiffened, whisky slopping onto his hand. "Don't you dare throw Cathmar in my face."

The old priest chuckled. "That's the last thing I'd ever do, kid. I raised enough children to know." He met Cahey's eyes, and his gaze said it plainly: *You were one of them.*

Cahey took a breath. "Snakerot. How the Hel do you propose I do that, Aethelred?"

Aethelred, pouring liquor with a practiced hand, shrugged. "If I knew that, Cahey, I'd be the einherjar and you'd be the priest. And we all know I'm not cut out to do your job. Now when are you going to let go of your grieving and get started changing the world?"

The words made sense. Cahey knew they made sense. He

could feel the shape of the sense they made hanging in his mind.

The shape and the sense didn't fill up the hole, however. The hole where people had been who weren't there anymore.

"To the ones who didn't make it," he said, and raised his drink before he finished it.

There was no point in arguing. And no point in fixing what you were only going to throw away.

50 A.R.
On the Twenty-seventh Day of Autumn

Selene was waiting in Borje's already-crowded cottage early the following morning when Aethelred walked in. She had been lying on her back, studying the roof beams and the plaster between them, but when the door banged wide she rolled to her knees on the brown pile rug to examine his face. Her ears flattened when he shook his head.

"Didn't make a damn dent," he snarled, taking a red stoneware bowl of tea from Borje with a nod.

Selene rose from her place by the banked fire in the brick fireplace. Aithne, rubbing sleep out of the corner of her eye, sat up on the threadbare sofa. She was the first to reply.

"How bad is it?"

The chrome-faced priest looked as if he wanted a place to spit. "Hel, Aith, I've seen a lot of drunks. I've seen a lot of drunks with worse reasons to be drunks than Cahey has for . . . whatever it is you call what he's doing. You can't save him. I think you shouldn't see him right now. You'll . . . it's not a good time, is all."

"So who can save him?" Selene interjected.

Aethelred downed half of his tea. It must have been hot: she watched him flinch. Or maybe it was her question. "Nobody," he answered. "He's the only one who can save himself. And he doesn't want to. He's got—he didn't say, but I know Cahey, and he thinks whatever he's doing serves whatever damnfool knight-in-shining-armor purpose he's picked out for himself this week."

Aithne rolled to her feet, tugging at her tangled hair. She took a few steps to the side and fetched up against a window ledge, curling herself onto it as she dug around in her pockets. She produced a comb and a tube of conditioner and started working one though her tangles with the help of the other. "Should he have been left alone?"

Aethelred shrugged as Borje got him more tea. "We can't babysit him. All we can do is take turns yelling at him." Selene got him a chair and the old priest sat down stiffly. "And I can all but guarantee it won't work. And another thing. That girl?"

From the connecting passageway to the bedroom Mingan entered, booted feet silent on the chocolate-colored rug. He nodded to Aethelred to keep talking.

"Not the Imogen. The one Borje saw."

Borje gave a curt, mean nod that could have been a threatening toss of his horns.

Aethelred tapped the side of his fist against his chin. "She's hurting him. Whatever she's got on him, Borje, you're right. He's not doing it willingly. And . . . he's got bruises, ligature marks"—Selene heard Aithne's sudden sharp intake of breath—"and looks bad as I've ever seen him. Which is saying something. Looked like he spent a long time crying before I got there." Aethelred rolled his bowl between his fingers and sipped at the tea.

Mingan caught Selene's eye, gave her a smile so slight she thought none of the others noticed, and spoke. "Selene must go to him again," he said. "After Heythe leaves. Comfort him. Remind him that he is not forsaken. While he is in your company, the Imogen will not come to him. Lead him up to the chapel before you take your leave of him."

"Heythe? Is that the same as Mardoll? And then?" A wary glance from Aethelred, still seated near the door.

The Grey Wolf showed teeth. "I will deal with the rest."

Selene's ears swiveled at Aithne's sharp intake of breath. "Will you harm him?" the freckled woman said in a small voice.

His silver-limned eyes flicked toward her. "Nay, child. He shall come to no further hurt at my hands."

Something in his tone stood Selene's fur on end.

"Master Wolf." Aethelred's voice expressed infinite courtesy. "You understand that he's been fighting all his life. He's found an excuse to stop fighting. And an excuse is all it takes. I doubt . . . threats . . . will have any effect on him."

Mingan folded gloved hands one into the other and frowned slightly. "Master Priest," he replied, in a tone that frightened her. Not for Aethelred, or Cahey. For the Wolf. "I never . . . *threaten.* Meanwhile, may I suggest?"

Aethelred finished his second bowl of tea, nodding. "Yes. I'm heading into the city tonight, to talk to Cathmar."

The old Wolf laughed, or perhaps snarled. Selene thought none of the others caught the agony in his expression, the pinch of it around his eyes. "An excellent idea. But in the meantime, Priest: you, and the lady"—a nod to Aithne, still trying to work the wooden comb through her hair—"will you accept our kiss? Selene's, and mine?"

Confused, Aithne looked up. "I don't understand."

Aethelred sucked in air. "He wants to know if you want to be an angel, girl."

"Angel?" A long pause. "Waelcyrge, you mean?" Her green eye focused on Mingan.

He nodded, a slight inclination of his head.

"You can do that?"

Again, the incremental nod.

"What's it cost me?"

"Everything," Mingan said. "Everything. And worth it at twice the cost." There was no coaxing in his voice, no cajolery. Selene had only ever heard him sound so cold once before, and that time there had been death on his lips.

Aithne looked at Aethelred, who set his teacup aside on a small table. "I'm going to pass," he said. "I'm old. I've got plans for the next world already." A significant glance passed between him and Mingan. "And I already explained once tonight that I'm not cut out for an einherjar."

Mingan nodded. "Borje, will you join us? You've half the kiss already."

The bull put down his teapot. "I'm not all that sure I'm worthy, sir."

"I'm qualified to judge," Mingan replied, lips twitching in a little half-smile.

The bull sighed, indicating acquiescence. Mingan's intent regard traveled back to Aithne, who had not moved. Her thumbnail worried the comb. "Decision," Mingan said, gently.

She quivered. Caught a breath. "Yes," she said. "Everything I've got isn't much, so if that's all it takes . . . Yes."

BOOK THREE

Breaking

50 A.R.
On the Twenty-seventh Day of Autumn

Not too many pleasant days left, Cathmar thought, but the truth was he enjoyed the winter. He lounged against the dry stone wall of an apartment building, dark-clad in the sunlight, watching the foot traffic pass. A familiar voice in his ear jerked his head around.

"Remember me, kid?"

The speaker must have been enormous when he was younger: an old man in wheaten robes, autumn sunlight gleaming off his half-chromed head. He grinned like a scorched jack-o'-lantern.

Cathmar's lips twitched. "Uncle . . . Aethelred?"

The big man grabbed the boy around the shoulders and gave him a squeeze that belied any apparent age. "Cathmar. You look real good."

"Where have you been all this time? We got your letters. . . ."

"Been out and about, going up and down in the world. You know. Come on; let's find somewhere to talk."

Cathmar took a breath. "I'm in for a lecture, aren't I?"

Shaking his massive head, Aethelred took Cathmar's arm.

"You're too old for lectures. You're in for a conversation if you're not careful, though."

Cathmar saw that Aethelred still knew his way around the city, although a lot of it must have looked different from when he lived here, before the Rekindling. It wasn't long before the old priest was pulling him into a café he'd never entered. "Your mom used to like to come here," Aethelred said, pulling a long, wide bench out across the flagstone floor.

The serving area was in a glassed-in patio, racks of herbs growing in glass bowls against the windows. Cathmar seated himself opposite while a server brought them tea. He worried at the scars on the heavy wood table with his thumbnail. "Am I supposed to believe this is a chance meeting, Uncle?"

"Nah," Aethelred chuckled. "I've been stalking you all morning. Want something to eat?"

Cathmar shook his head. Aethelred caught the server's eye again and ordered sandwiches while the boy stared out through the big windows, watching the pedestrians go by.

"I've been talking to Selene," Aethelred said when the food got there. "And Master Wolf. You want to tell me what this spat you're having with *him* is over?"

Swallowing a mouthful of tea, Cathmar tried to find some resentment at the question. It didn't rise, and he wasn't sure why. "Why should I answer that?" he asked.

"Because I'm a priest who used to be a bartender, and I introduced your parents. So you owe me."

The level smile and dry tone provoked Cathmar into a chuckle. "Well . . . he didn't approve of my girlfriend. I didn't like it."

"And now?"

He found himself fussing with his bowl and set it aside with a sigh. "I still don't like it. But I'm starting to suspect he might be right."

"Huh. How come?" Aethelred poured more tea for both of them, into Cathmar's ivory-colored horn bowl and his own enamel one.

Cathmar frowned, warming his palm around the small container. "Little things. She always seems to want to know stuff about Dad . . . about Mom. But never talks about herself and doesn't tell me much of anything. She vanishes for hours on end and won't tell me where she's been. And every time I ask a question she doesn't feel like answering . . ." he felt himself blush ". . . she trips me into bed."

Aethelred must have caught his expression, because the old priest grinned. "Look," he said, "women—men, too—some you can trust; some you can't. It's no reflection on you, kid. You have to learn which are which the hard way."

Cathmar grunted and drank his tea. He knew the old priest was waiting him out. "Yeah," he finally said. "I've been an idiot."

"Nah," Aethelred answered. "You've been a kid. Look, why don't you go talk to Borje sometime soon? When your girlfriend isn't around. The old bull's got a level head on his shoulders. Maybe he can help you sort things out."

"Yeah," Cathmar answered, noticing the twinkle in Aethelred's eye. *I'm being set up for something.* For some reason, he didn't mind. "Oh, another thing. I just remembered."

"Yeah?"

"Well, she knew what I was right off. Recognized Nathr . . . and lately she's been pumping me for lots of information on how you make angels." Cathmar looked away, glanced up at the massive roof beams, black with age. The ceiling plaster between them had yellowed past ivory and into parchment.

"Huh." Aethelred chewed his lip. "You didn't tell her about Selene kissing the moreaux to break their bindings, did you?"

"It never came up."

The old priest smiled. "Good. You might want to keep that one to yourself, if you think you still have reason to be suspicious."

Cathmar pursed his lips and puffed his cheeks before releasing a thoughtful breath. He glanced around the room, noticing its age and the furrows worn in the flagstones by the feet of the patrons and staff. "Mom used to come here?" he asked.

Aethelred nodded. "It's been in business for—what, six, seven hundred years now. Different owners, of course."

"All right," Cathmar said, answering an earlier comment. "And how is my dad?"

"Crap," Aethelred said. "But you knew that already. We're doing everything we can for him, Cath. But I can't promise you it'll work."

"Ah." He was surprised by how much that piece of information stung. "I went to talk to him . . ."

". . . and you didn't make a dent?" The old priest poured more tea and drank it, blowing the steam out of his asparagus-colored bowl. "Sometimes you have to hit 'em in the right spot or at the right time. There's an art to it. Sometimes you can't do a damn thing but stand by and watch them go down in flames. Sometimes the going down in flames is what does it. You can't save anybody from themselves, kid."

Cathmar didn't answer, twirling the bowl in his fingers,

his gaze trained out the window—seeing, but not recording. Moreaux, humans, bicycles, a single taxi whirled past, and Aethelred's last sentence echoed in his head.

Just like nobody can save me from me.

Aethelred let the silence hang a little before he went on. "You're still mad at him, too."

Cathmar glanced back; their eyes locked. "Yeah. You're right about that."

The return question was rapid-fire. "How come?"

"Because of Mom." That wasn't an adequate answer, but he didn't know what else to say. "Because of a lot of things."

"Right. He ever hit you, Cath?"

Slowly, brow wrinkling, Cathmar shook his head. "Of course not. Why do you think he would?"

Aethelred grinned. "If I thought he would ever have been anything but gentle with you, I never would have handed you over to him, kid."

"So why are you asking?"

Aethelred finished his tea and started on his sandwich, breaking half off and setting it aside on the splotched pottery trencher. "Just think, for a second, what it took him to remember, every second, that it wasn't okay to hit you—when he had no other experience of being a dad whatsoever to go on, except being hit. You know his father's the one who cut his face up, don't you?"

It stopped his breath like a blow in the gut. "No," he said. Except yes, he did know, sort of. Whether his father had told him or he'd figured it out Cathmar couldn't remember, but he knew. He'd just never thought about what it meant, what it would be like if his own father did something like that to him.

Aethelred touched his hand, pulling him back. "Think that he did that with nobody holding his hand, with nobody showing him how to do it, with nobody to so much as trade off shifts with. Someday you'll be raising a kid and you'll understand how hard a thing that can be. And *you*"—he jabbed the forefinger of the hand not holding the sandwich at Cathmar's chest—"didn't sleep when you were a baby, either."

Thinking about that, Cathmar tapped one forefinger on the table. "Are you saying I'm selfish?"

"I'm saying you're not a kid anymore, kid. Kids get to be self-absorbed. Grown-ups have to be part of the community. And I'm saying parents are people, too, and you were lucky enough to have one who put you first. So maybe it'd be fair to re-think that anger, is all." Aethelred wiped mustard off his mouth and let the silence hang a little. "And on to other things. So tell me, Cath, what you've been doing with yourself."

50 A.R.
On the Twenty-eighth Day of Autumn

Mardoll slipped out while he was in the bathroom, and she took her riding boots. Cathmar, however, heard her sneaking down the stairs over the water splashing into the porcelain tub.

He'd been waiting for it, and his boots were still on, Nathr propped against the door.

Grabbing the sword, he shut off the water and hopped out the window onto the fire escape.

The riding boots gave him an idea where she was going. He didn't want her passing him down on the road, so he headed to Boulevard and hailed a taxi, paying the moreau behind the wheel in advance with salt and whisky. The pilot took them up while Cathmar settled himself on the ragged upholstery. "You know the chapel on the Eiledon road?"

"I do," the pilot said, nodding hard. His elegant, fringed golden ears flicked back when Cathmar talked: a canid.

Cathmar leaned forward, put a long-fingered hand on the dog-man's shoulder. "Do you remember the Angel?" he asked. He'd never quite had the courage to ask one before, other than Borje and Selene.

The driver's ears pricked as he turned around in his chair.

"Selene kissed me. Selene kissed most of us, but yeah. I remember the Angel. Who are you, to know to ask?"

"I'm the Angel's son," Cathmar answered. "And I'm going to ask you to do something crazy. You ever think you might want to be an einherjar?"

𝐴 taxi descended over Borje's cottage, and the bull came out to meet it. He was surprised when Cathmar stepped out, more surprised when the young einherjar opened the front door and held it for the driver, who powered the machine off and stood.

Borje recognized him. "Erasmus. You drive a taxi now?"

The dog chuckled, feathery yellow tail describing slow arcs in the sea air. "And I hear you clean up a church. 'Deacon Borje.' It's got a ring." He walked up to Borje, and Borje ducked his heavy head so that Erasmus could sniff his nose.

Hoofbeats reached Borje's sensitive ears from somewhere in the middle distance.

The dog pulled back then, and grinned in a disturbingly human fashion, long snout curling up over sharp yellow teeth. "The einherjar here has an idea," he said. "He wants to talk to you about something."

Borje tilted his head at Cathmar, examining the young angel's eyes. "Is it urgent, Cath?"

Cathmar shook his head. "No. It can wait until tonight." He grinned. "When the moon's up."

Borje nodded. "Good," he said. "Because we need to get inside."

"We do?"

"Yes." Borje's tail swished, driving away imaginary flies. He knew something about protecting a herd. And something about the ways of females. "Now. Erasmus, hide that taxi please. And don't take it high."

The dog scurried back to his vehicle while Borje brought Cathmar into the house, laying his hoof on the angel's shoulder and steering him to a spot behind the eyelet curtains. In bare minutes, he felt Cathmar's body tense.

Borje knew the boy heard the racing hooves a few moments before he saw the red mare and the golden-haired figure bent low over her neck.

"Yours, isn't she?"

Cathmar nodded. The girl and her mare rounded the back side of the bluff and vanished from sight.

"You need to walk around the bluff, Cath, and see what happens next."

The red mare's flaxen mane caught the sunlight like honey in a glass jar as Gullveig swung down off her back. She smiled when she saw Cahey watching her from the doorway. She wound the mare's reins around a wooden railing beside the path and turned back to him.

Sand scattering from her footsteps, Gullveig came toward him; he raised his eyes to meet hers. The shadows and the resignation around them told her everything she needed to know. Noticing the bruises, she forced herself to smile.

"I don't need to bind you this time, do I?"

His eyes spoke a word to her. The word was *defeat*.

He shook his head. He started to unbutton his shirt.

Cathmar trotted over the bluff rather than hiking around it. He wasn't sure what he was going to see, and Borje wouldn't tell him. *You have to make up your own mind,* the moreau said. *Come back and we'll talk about your idea after.*

The horse was out of sight by the time he crested the little hill, and the sick feeling in his stomach only got worse as he followed the well-worn trail to his father's house. He saw the red mare tethered by the door. Coming up beside her, he hushed her with a hand on her muzzle.

Afternoon darkness filled the house, but Cathmar caught voices clearly. Standing alongside the window by the front door, he waited for the breeze to stir the curtains, but those inside were standing near the door and he could not see them.

Cahey spoke first: "Get it over with." Cathmar shuddered at the savagery in his manner, a note like glass grating on bone.

Then Mardoll's voice, mocking. Cruel, as Cathmar had never heard it. "Such a hurry," she said. "I'd think you didn't enjoy my company, my love."

He heard his father take a breath as if in pain. Or something else.

"This isn't about *love,*" Cahey answered with a violence thick as clotted blood. "So, if you please, whatever your name is, find something else to call me."

Cathmar stuffed his fist into his mouth, stifling a gasp at the stainless hatred in that tone. The wood of the windowsill creaked in his other hand; Cathmar realized he was squeezing it with all his might.

"My pet," she answered. "Do you like that better? I think it fits, don't you?"

Cahey didn't answer, but Cathmar felt a shudder through the wall as if someone shoved somebody hard against the door.

His father's voice, when he heard it again, was a brutal gasp that made him shut his eyes and press his head back hard against the wall. *Go in there,* he thought. *Put a stop to this, whatever it is.*

He didn't move. The red mare lipped his pockets; the sun shone through his closed eyelids.

"Tell me what you want." Cahey's voice was dull, but ragged with determination.

"Pet," Mardoll replied—smug, leisurely. "This time, I think you shall decide. Just keep it interesting, or it doesn't count toward what you owe."

Cathmar shook himself—*shuddered, who are you kidding?*—shoved the mare's curious head out of the way, and bolted back toward Borje's cottage. Blistering tears smudging his vision, he fell three times. When he reached the doorway, though, the moreau was waiting.

50 A.R.
On the Twenty-eighth Day of Autumn

Selene had never marched anywhere in her life, but this was definitely marching. She didn't bother to knock. She just opened the painted wood door and strode into Cahey's cottage, not at all sure what she expected to find.

She hoped it wouldn't be the Imogen.

She didn't like the way the room smelled, or the fact that he was just sitting, curled and staring, in an armchair in the corner when she came in.

She also didn't like the lack of light in Cahey's eyes when he turned to face her as she came into the living room. He shoved himself clumsily to his feet, who had never had an awkward moment in all the years she'd known him.

"Selene," he said. The agony in his voice took her breath away.

She came to him, and he didn't resist her, thank the Light, or she would have injured him. He was strong, after all. But she was deadly.

Sheathing her claws, unspeaking, she reached up and caught him by the back of the neck, dragging him down into her embrace. He stiffened and tugged away, but she forced his face into the angle of her neck and dropped to her knees on the hard tiles beyond the hearth-rug, taking him with her. Her other arm went around his shoulders; she pulled him close and squeezed until she felt him relaxing incrementally in her arms.

She cuddled him close, stroking his head, sensing his confusion and his unwillingness to push her away, to risk her forgiveness, both at once. His arms slid around her and he cradled her to his chest as if he were doing the comforting. She crooned to him as she would have to her kittens, if she'd ever had the chance.

When she finally spoke to him her voice was ragged. "Cahey, you noble stupid fuck, what in snakerot do you think you're buying?"

He would have jerked away, but she held on to him, not caring that her claws bit. Or . . . caring. But accepting for now that she must cause him pain. He blinked at her with startled eyes, and she permitted herself a whisker-flicker of amusement. "What do you know?" he asked.

She perked her ears forward. "I know you're sleeping with your son's girlfriend, for one thing. And I know you think you have some damn good reason for doing it, and it's killing you. And she's torturing you, I know that, too. Are you going to tell me what it is so I can help you, or are you going to make me beat it out of you?"

"Gullveig," he started, and then stopped. "You haven't told Cath. . . ."

"Cahey," she said, as softly as she dared. "Brother of my heart, *he* told *me.*"

The almost lie stung her, close enough to an untruth to *hurt,* but she thought it needed to be said. Worse was the way

Cahey closed his eyes, face falling slack, head rolling back on the long neck in exhaustion. "Fuck," he whispered.

"Shhhh. He's not mad at *you*. Listen to me. He almost walked in on the two of you this morning. He . . ." She couldn't look at his face and talk at the same time. "Love, he heard. He knows. Whatever it is, he knows she made you do it."

He sighed, but he let her pull him down until he leaned back against her, sitting on the floor. "Selene," he said. "I owe you—and Cath—so many apologies. You were right. What I've been doing is . . . well. Bad for me. Stupid. To say the least."

"You'll stop?"

He considered long enough to get her hopes up before he shook his head.

She growled at the back of her throat.

"*What* do you think you're doing with . . . that woman? That creature? Whatever she is?"

He nodded helplessly. "Destroying myself." A long silence. "But what I'm buying is worth it. I think."

"All right, Cahey." Her tail twisted. "What are you buying, that's worth your soul?"

He took a deep breath and told her.

She shoved him away, far enough away to search his face, and then she pressed her face into her hands and sighed hard before looking back up at him.

"You stupid shit," she said.

It wasn't the answer he was expecting.

A rich, irritated sigh hissed from her. "Cahey, you beautiful idiot. What gives you the right to put her through the agony you had to go through? And—moreover—what makes you suppose Astrid wouldn't cheerfully have died for *you*?"

He didn't have an answer in the world. She waited for a little while in the silence before she grabbed him by the arm and stood him up. "Come on," she said. "We're going up to the chapel."

50 A.R.
On the Twenty-eighth Day of Autumn

Selene had left him there alone to think, she said.

Think. The last thing I need to do right now. Cahey pushed his gathering doubts aside. *Stick with your decision. It may have sucked, but consider the source.*

He stood in front of the central statue, Muire's statue, watching the sun grow lower over her shoulder. He'd teased her, once, about the statue's face being reversed, for she had sculpted it in a mirror. It troubled him to realize that when he pictured her now he saw this image, and not what she had truly been.

There was no sound of the door opening, no shift in the light, no sense of presence behind him. The voice made him jump.

"I've been looking for you, Cathoair."

A rough voice, familiar in its softness. He had dreamed, when he still slept, about that voice, like a hand riffling the fine hairs at the back of his neck.

Shuddering, Cahey turned away from the statue of his goddess and toward the door of the chapel.

The Grey Wolf lounged, lean and fierce, against ivory stone.

He straightened and drifted into the chapel, cloak flowing around him like a shadow. "Cahey." As he came forward. "How I have envied you all these years."

"Envied me?" He placed a hand on the hilt of his sword. He saw Mingan's smile——*satisfied,* he thought—at the gesture. *Yeah. I can learn.*

Mingan nodded, a single arrogant inclination of his head. "Envied you—the taste of her skin, of her sex, the strength of her body against yours. Envied you her love, her passion. Envied you . . . every inch of her."

Only when he felt the pain did Cahey realize that he had bitten his cheek. "I have none of those things." He detested the quaver in his own voice. His hand didn't move off Alvitr's hilt.

"But you *did* have them," the Grey Wolf answered, a step closer.

Cahey remembered an alleyway, the taste of Mingan's mouth, the sun-heat of his body. A fever and a chill crawled up his neck as he met the other's starlit regard. He did not speak.

"And you never had the slightest clue how precious a thing you let go." Mingan's voice was mocking. "I have the taste of you, you know. But *you* were nothing compared to *her*." The Wolf licked his lips with a berry-red tongue. "Draw your sword, boy, if you think you can best me. Draw your sword in hate, and I will *tell* you why you hate me."

His hand clenched on Alvitr's hilt, but Cahey didn't pull her from her sheath. He realized, seeing how the cloak hung in heavy folds around the Grey Wolf's form, that Mingan was not carrying his own blade.

"She forgave you," Cahey said.

Mingan came a step closer, sweeping across the softly colored paving stones. His voice was low, provoking. "She had no power to forgive me. My sins were beyond her compass. And you— You never did, boy. So now because of it I own your son. He's down there now, waiting for me to come back to him, to be what you have not."

"Shut up, you son of a bitch!" The sword was in his hand before he had a chance to think about it.

Mingan threw back his head and laughed. He spread his arms wide and came three steps closer before he sank down on his knees.

Laughing. As if to say, *Oh, how little you know what truth you have spoken.*

Cahey advanced, leveling Alvitr at Mingan's throat. But the Wolf only knuckled his eye and said, headshaking, "My mother was a giantess. And she spawned *monsters*. Think thou art my match?"

The Wolf reached out, catching Cahey's sword in his gloved hand. Blood smeared the edge of the blade. Mingan leveled the tip of his rival's sword at his chest.

"There," Mingan said. "Thrust. Between the second and third ribs, brushing the lung, piercing the heart. It will suffice, with a blade like that, even for such as I."

Cahey's hand knotted on the hilt of the sword. He felt his lips drawing back from his teeth.

"Thrust!" Mingan cried. He pushed the blade against his breast, a trickle of blood darkening his shirt. "An you hate me, child, claim me. Take me if you want me. I am yours!"

A shiver ran through Cahey's arm. His knuckles gleamed pale on the hilt of his blade. He groaned between his teeth and turned his face aside, feeling the slight resistance of Mingan's body before the razorfine point of his sword. *Nothing. A gesture. And he'd be dead.*

"Thrust!" Mingan screamed. "I wounded you. I took from you. I rendered you powerless and I raped you, boy. *Kill me now!* You hold my surrender!"

A gesture, and it would be over. Hate, fear, shame—all silenced. His body tensed behind a lunge.

Which did not happen. *Silenced. Yes. As they stayed so silent the last time I killed to shut them up.*

The sword fell from nerveless fingers, ringing on the stone between them. Cahey sank to his knees, and from there curled into a ball.

"I am sorry," the Grey Wolf said, standing in a charcoal-smudge swirl of cloak. "For everything I did to you, I am sorry now." He came the two steps closer and knelt down beside his brother, laid a hand on Cahey's shoulder.

Cahey coiled tighter, shaking. He was silent for a long time. "Leave me," he whispered at last.

The Wolf shook his brindled head, slanting red light casting gleams off the silver ring twisted through his ear. "I cannot do that," he said. "Cathoair. There is something you still must learn, to be truly einherjar."

Cahey drew his knees up to his face. Mingan laid a gloved, bloody hand on the other's shoulder. "Surrender," he said. "That which I have given you," he continued, "you must give as well."

Silence was his answer.

"What I did to you was wrong," he continued. "Wrong,

and meant to break you." He bent down, gathering Cahey in his arms and drawing him close. "I felt your pain when I kissed you, and I thought I could ruin you and then she would be mine."

"I don't break," Cahey said into Mingan's shoulder.

"My brother," the Grey Wolf said, smoothing his hair. "Not yet, at any rate."

"You're no different," Cahey answered, although he did not draw back from the embrace. "You're the same old monster. Brother."

"I've heard that before," said Mingan. "There's one way you can find out for certain what I am."

Cahey recoiled, shoving himself away, sprawled on the floor with his back against the dais and the statues. "Light," he said. "No!"

"Surrender," replied the Grey Wolf, still crouching. "I am not that I was. Open yourself, and I will show you what I have become. I give you my soul, little brother."

Bottomless terror surged up in him. "I want you out of me," he whispered. "I do not want you in me anymore."

The Grey Wolf laughed at him. "It's not me that you hate, Cathoair. It's what I showed you about yourself. That you *like* to be mastered, though you both desire and fear it. That you seek blame and deny responsibility. You were hurt gravely, boy, and you were too strong to let it destroy you or turn you into something vile. So you fight that hurt by choosing never to surrender, although you crave the release surrender brings."

Cahey shook his head.

"You're einherjar now, Brother. Act like it." Mingan hesitated, as if waiting for a reply. None came, and he finished his argument with a final weapon. "When have you ever said 'no,' lad, and meant it?"

Again, the silent refutation.

"Ah," said the Grey Wolf, bending razory lips in a smile, "deny. But you are in me, and I know you. You were beaten; you were taken against your will. How can it not have scarred you?"

Cahey shut his eyes against the words, but he did not stop his ears.

Mingan did not hesitate. "And to recompense, you seek control over yourself and others, never understanding that the path to healing lies in surrender, that your heart craves peace and certainty. Heythe—Gullveig—you cannot bend her, Cahey; you cannot control her. As I am older and stronger than you, she is older and wilder than I. And *never* has she done any man's will.

"And Muire . . ." Mingan gasped with bitter laughter. "If you could but surrender yourself to the sea, you could have her. But there is no trust in you, and no faith, and no healing. And thus, you are worse than useless to us. *Brother.*"

Something glittered in the Grey Wolf's eyes. Sorrow, Cahey realized. Unshed tears, unrequited love. All the loss he himself felt, and more.

Mingan spoke softly when he continued. "Because you cannot forgive yourself, and you cannot release the pain of what was done to you."

I'm glad it hurts him. Cahey started to his feet. "What do you know about rape, you bastard?" he snarled, leaning down and grasping Mingan's black, silver-shot braid in his fist. The silver band that bound it slipped and strands coiled loose. The Wolf did not resist, even when Cahey yanked on it for emphasis with every breath. "Other than dealing it out? What do you know about being eleven and pretty and having nowhere to run?"

"I know a little about being taken," Mingan interrupted. Something about his voice killed Cahey's in his throat, and that somehow doubled his rage. Cahey drew back his hand and struck Mingan across the mouth, all of his weight behind it. Blood spattered. Sickness burned in his throat. *I'm just like my father. All I know how to do is hurt things.*

Mingan closed silver eyes and tilted his head to the side, baring his throat. "Strike," he said. "Unleash at me your vengeance on all those you were unable to defend yourself from. It's deserved, Light knows."

Cahey roared. He hauled his rival to his feet by the hair and spun, throwing him across the chapel.

Mingan fell against the benches, rising again with pain. Cahey stood, panting, his hands clenching and unclenching. "Pick up your sword," Mingan said. "If my death is what it takes to heal you, *pick her up!*"

Cahey bent down and grasped her by the hilt. He took several steps forward; his rival stood unblinking. Raising the blade, he leveled her at Mingan's neck and drew her back in a slow, unwavering arc.

"I am not your father," Mingan said. "I am not a stranger in an alley. I am your brother and your ally. I wronged you, and for that I am sorry lo these many years gone by. I am deserving of thy justice."

Cahey froze, on the verge of uncoiling, his pose echoing that of the statue behind him. His face contorted in fury and agony, his hand clenched on the hilt of his sword.

"I bare my throat to thee," Mingan said on a breath. He

tilted his face away from the blade, exposing the tender curve of his neck.

A long, soft moment passed. And Cathoair looked from his blade to the arc of the Grey Wolf's neck, and let Alvitr sag until she scratched the stones.

"Stand up," he said, and let the blade ring to the floor.

Mingan stood, and as the last light of sunset bloodied the stones under their feet he reached out his hand and pulled Cathoair into his arms.

"Thus the art of surrender," he said into the other's ear.

Cahey drew his face out of the other's hair. "I don't need to know anything more about that," he said.

"It's not me you hate," Mingan repeated.

"That's an easy thing to say."

The Grey Wolf smiled. "You hate what I showed you about yourself. Need. Desire. And an ineffectual fury."

"What do you want from me?"

Mingan placed a hand under Cahey's chin and lifted it. "Surrender," he said. "Exactly what I have given you, you must give to fate. Continue fighting the history that shapes you and you will destroy us."

Cahey jerked away. "I can't."

"You must," Mingan replied. "Learn to give yourself utterly. That way lies divinity and responsibility. Is it not what *she* did, after all?"

"I accept responsibility for my actions," Cahey said.

Mingan shook his head. "You accept *blame*. Blame is a useless thing."

"I'm not about to forgive you, my father or anyone else. I'm not in a forgiving mood today, for some reason."

Silver Light flooded Mingan's eyes, gleamed painfully bright. "We're einherjar, boy. Forgiveness is not a part of our purpose. And it is foolish to offer it where it has not been earned."

Cahey wasn't quite sure what he was hearing, but he knew that it was not what he had expected to hear. "Then what?"

"Release," Mingan said. "Once vengeance is served, it is served. Let it go. Forgiveness"—he hesitated—"is not what we do. But when clinging to old bitterness cripples you, it affects that which we serve." He glanced up at the central statue. "That I will not permit."

Cahey tried to understand him, and was afraid that he did. "You don't want me to absolve you of your crimes?"

"My hands cannot be washed," Mingan said. "There is no absolution for what I have done."

"What do you want of me, then?"

The Grey Wolf stood, holding out hands to draw his brother to his feet. "Your kiss," he said, shortly. "Given and received. In trust and honor, a bond between us."

Cahey chewed his lip. Nausea swelled, coupled with longing, on the remembered scent of musk. Half a century and more, and he still remembered the abandon of that kiss.

The abandon, and the terror. He clenched his eyes.

"Say no," the Wolf whispered, breath hot on Cahey's cheek.

Cahey opened his eyes. "Quickly," he said around the thickness in his throat.

The Wolf crossed to him in a single stride and drew him close. "Breathe," he instructed, pressing his mouth over Cahey's.

They kissed.

Mingan teased him, he thought, drawing the kiss out slowly and with a tantalizing touch. It wasn't the hard rush of ecstasy-touched agony it had been the first time. It was the caress of a lover lingering over the quivering body of his beloved. He stared into the Grey Wolf's cold starlit eyes.

He doesn't love me, Cahey reminded himself.

Shhhh, the Wolf whispered, inside. *What do you know yet of who I love? For now, surrender.*

Cahey thought of Mingan and Selene. The image rose with a bitterness, a violence up his throat. He pictured them kissing, as he was now kissed. Drawing himself up, he grasped Mingan's shoulders, nearly forcing him away.

But Mingan hung slack in Cahey's grip, unresisting, and the fight went out of him. The kiss tickled the back of his throat. His eyes drifted closed, and the shove turned into an embrace.

Surrender, Cathoair.

I'm trying.

Trying will help you not. He heard the humor in the rough old voice. He braced against the anticipated wrenching of himself out of himself. That was when Mingan breathed down his throat.

Which was a shock: he'd thought the Wolf would only take, drawing the soul and courage out of him on a single ecstatic breath. Instead Mingan's life and awareness rushed into him like water to a man bedroughted, food to a starving soul. Muire had done the same to him once, but she had been awkward, uncertain.

That had not felt like this did.

Mingan *knew*. Knew things that Muire had only just begun to understand when she had left Cahey. Things about passion, and sorrow, and the salt taste of sweat in the darkness. . . .

Knew, and held nothing back. Cahey felt his brother angel helpless in his arms and realized that it would be an instant's work—an instant's pleasure—to kill him. The Wolf's hands slid down his shoulders, hanging limp at the end of widespread arms. The taut-muscled body relaxed into fluidity, and Cahey bore him up. Cahey's hand lifted, knotted in Mingan's loosening braid, pulling the Grey Wolf's mouth up against his, hard, tasting blood, tasting the slickness of the other's mouth. He groaned, felt cloth tear in his other fist.

The Wolf's collar gaped wide, baring the bone-ridged white flesh of his bosom, the hollows black with shadows under his collarbone and each rib. That was as Cahey had expected. What he had not expected was the spill of blue light.

A slender bit of ribbon spanned the other man's throat: the shirt had concealed it. Tight enough to cut into the tendons of Mingan's neck, it cast flickering sparks across their skin. Cahey forced a finger under it and tugged, expecting it to part like a thread: it was soft as butter to the touch, but it gave no more than a band of steel. At the pressure on his throat, Mingan gasped and went rigid, clutching Cahey's wrist—a shuddering terror that made Cahey jerk his hand back as if burned. "No?"

"*Say no*," the Wolf had mocked, and Cahey saw in the burning gaze Mingan turned on him that he expected the mockery returned. The stare softened, at last, when he realized that Cahey had been asking an honest question.

"Do what you must," Mingan said at length, through gritted teeth.

"Do you want this off?" Cahey asked, hesitantly tracing the narrow bright band with a forefinger. It was knotted, one end cleanly sharp, the other frayed to a fringe. Shivers chased each other across Mingan's pale skin, following the course of the touch.

"It doesn't *come* off," Mingan snapped.

Cahey could feel the Wolf trying to relax and failing utterly, but he did manage to bring his arms down, clenching his fists at his sides. Cahey, in pity, drew his hand away. "How long?"

The Wolf smiled bitterly. "Since before the beginning of the world, einherjar." He leaned close again, mouth open, the heat rolling from his body as he raised his hands to pull Cahey down again. Cahey let their mouths touch, but caught his breath around that nakedly hungry mouth, gasped clean rank air. The bitter scent of musk overrode the smell of the sea. He *wanted,* badly. And more: Mingan was reaching for him, pressing to him. All Cahey had to do was continue to breathe in the other's life, and his ancient enemy would be dead. A shattering trust.

Mingan breathed out into his mouth, and Cahey accepted it.

How like you to teach by example. Bastard.

Hard-fought, giving back the kiss. Tasting luxury, struggling with his hunger and fury, Cahey mastered himself and breathed into his enemy's wet, open mouth. Mingan twisted against him, drew him deep. Back and forth, and now Cahey had a sense for the nuance. There were threads submerged in the Wolf's presence—Mingan himself, gray and cold; the Suneater with its mad yellow stare; Muire, sad and sane . . .

and something else, a taste as transparent as water, that Cahey could not identify.

More cloth tore. His outreached hand banged the stones, cushioning a hard fall.

Surrender, he thought, as they toppled to the polished flags.

50 Æ.R.
On the Twenty-ninth Day of Autumn

Some time later, the wolf draws himself upright. Combing his unbound hair with his fingers, he tastes blood. Some of it is his own, and he finds he doesn't mind the flavor.

Cathoair sits with his back to the dais, head leaned across it, baring his unmarked throat. He'd learned to get the Imogen to leave her bruises in less obvious places. The wolf had found some of them, under shredded clothing.

A brave start, but not yet a finish. The sensation of white wings ruffled and settled. **The bone is straightened, but it is not yet set.**

The wolf's smile becomes a frown. "Brother."

Cathoair's eyes crack open, a thin glitter of color behind tear-clotted lashes. He straightens where he sits, rolling stiffness out of his neck. Lips press thin as his jaw works. "Brother."

"You need to hear about the Imogen."

"Imogen," Cathoair echoes. His fingers probe a welt on the inside of his elbow. The wolf thinks it's an unconscious gesture.

"If you do not master her," the wolf says, "she will master you. More than she already has."

The younger einherjar shakes his head. "I don't understand."

The wolf offers a hand to lift him to his feet. Cathoair frowns at it and then shrugs, as if he has moved beyond pride. He rocks unsteadily for a moment, flinching when the wolf presses the bruises on his hands from when they fell against stone.

"I'll show you how to heal those in a moment," the wolf says as Cathoair finds his balance. "As for the Imogen . . . she's a powerful tool, Cathoair, but soulless. And she feeds on pain. Soul-deep pain. And you, einherjar, are a creature on the verge of being nothing *but* soul."

"I understand that."

The wolf shakes his head. "No. Not even a little do you understand. She must have the pain of angels. Nothing else will do. The deeper, the wilder, the more textured and resonant and many-layered the pain, the sweeter and more nourishing it is to her. Best of all is pain that is both old . . . and fresh."

Cathoair falls silent for a moment, understanding flickering across his face. "Oh."

A sharp sea breeze flickers in the open window, riffling the wolf's tangled hair and furling his cloak. The scent it carries is rich and complex, redolent of green life and rot.

"Yes," the wolf says. "Oh. And in the end, if you let her have what she wants, there will be nothing left of you, but that which exists to feed her."

Cathoair stretches, biting his lip, intelligence and focus coming back into his gaze as he considers that.

Ah, Muire. Perhaps you chose well after all.

And in which of us did she choose poorly?

Hush.

Not silence so much as the impression of an irritable snort. **Would you rather have been left so alone as you feared?**

Cathoair speaks into Mingan's musing quiet. "I don't want to destroy her. She's . . . innocent. Can you say a monster is innocent?"

"Monsters are nothing but innocent. You cannot destroy the Imogen. She is undying."

"And how do you know so much about her?"

"She is my sister," says the wolf. "I shut her away, long ago, before the Last Day. I was her partner, you see." A bitter admission, even now. "She was too dangerous a weapon to use against my brothers."

"And how did she get out again?"

"I released her."

"You . . . ?" An hour or two previous, Cathoair would have been feeling for his sword. Now, the wolf sees him reminding himself of fresh lessons. "To come to me?"

"You're strong enough to bind her," says the wolf, negligently. He knows Cathoair sees through him, knows that from now on he will. Something more than brotherhood but alien to friendship had been sealed on the ice-cold alabaster stones. "And she will be needed. Soon."

"You said—*she* said she was a weapon."

"She is," the wolf says. "Heythe—the one who calls herself Mardoll, and Gullveig, and a half-hundred other names as besuits her—will be most put out with you when you refuse to destroy yourself to suit her whim."

"How did you know about that?"

The wolf smiles around his sorrow. *Pointless deaths, all of them.* "Heythe. This is not her first attempt to bend this world to her wishes. But of those that might remember the last one, only I and my mount remain. This time, at least, she has no army."

It takes a moment, but Cathoair at last looks up with wide eyes. "The Last Day. You and she—"

"There is much you need to know. And I will have to give you some history. For there is surrender, and there is capitulation, and they are not the same."

"I don't understand."

"You will. There are stories older than our world, Cathoair, and I am going to tell you one of them. Part of it, anyway." The wolf glances up around the dark chapel before leading Cathoair over to sit on one of the slab benches near the racks. He takes a breath, taking on his storyteller's voice, making his words sonorous and rich.

> *"An axe-age, a sword-age; a shattering of shields*
> *A wind-age, a wolf-age; fate is heard in the horn*
> *The wrack before; the ruin of the world."*

When the wolf hesitates, Cathoair keeps watching him, seemingly fascinated. "Muire used to quote poetry to me."

The wolf clears his throat and speaks again in normal tones. "She wrote most of it, Cathoair. She was our historian. A quiet little thing, unlovely compared to the others, overlooked: a kestrel among eagles. But the wit and the will in her—none of her sisters ever matched that." He silences himself, too late, for sudden comprehension flares blue-white Light into the other's eyes.

Cathoair opens his mouth to speak; nevertheless, a long moment passes where the wolf hears only the wind and the sound of the sea. "You never told her."

The wolf turns to the window, frowns at the sky beyond. "Her choice lay elsewhere. And I never dreamed she would have survived the Last Day. She was not so much a warrior. Compared to some. But . . . painfully bold."

"And then to find her again . . ."

The shape of his own honesty lies strange in his mouth. "I tried to kill her."

"You couldn't."

"Aye. I could not. And lost her again." The wolf tastes fresher blood. "She always preferred beautiful men," he says softly, glancing back at Cathoair, who watches intently. "And I am not that." He raises one hand and gestures vaguely in the direction of the three statues. "See for yourself who she loved."

He closes his eyes, feeling the pooled starlight itch against the backs of his eyelids, blinking back the streamers of Light that want to ribbon down his creased cheeks. Cathoair lays a hesitant hand on his arm, and the wolf resists both the urge to break it and the one to lean into the touch. *He cannot know. And you cannot have this.*

Taking a breath, he blinks his eyes open. He holds his gaze on the glass-covered walls of books, the filigree of metal decorating the doors.

"To speak briefly: There was another world before this one. Perhaps many worlds, but one that mattered. Gods and giants ruined it in a tremendous battle, and the children of the Light—the first einherjar and waelcyrge—were created out of the destruction. We made a new world. This world."

"I know most of this." Cathoair's voice remains wondering and strange. Enduring his sympathy had not been one of the prices the wolf had been prepared to pay. *But then,* he thinks, *we don't always get to choose.*

It was bravely done, and brightly.

Thank you, Kasimir.

She would be pleased with you.

To that the wolf has no answer.

"I don't think so," the wolf replies. "Muire couldn't have told you all of it. Because Muire never turned away from the Light, and didn't know what the tarnished knew."

"And you did."

"Yes." The wolf falls silent for a moment before forcing himself to speak on. "There was a survivor of the other world. She escaped, walked between worlds and times to find us. Would you know more?"

Cathoair nods, speechless.

The wolf recites again, trying not to feel how his collar tightens against his breath.

> *"Fetters burst; the wolf will rage:*
> *Much do I know; and more can see*
> *Of the fate of the gods; the mighty in fight.*
> *The sun burns black; earth shatters in the sea,*
> *And hot bright stars; from heaven are hurled.*
> *Now do I see; the earth in foam*
> *Rise green and renewed; from the waves again—*
> *Then fields unsowed; bear ripened fruit,*
> *All ills grow better; in Baldr's return.*
> *Would you know yet more?"*

He finishes with a half-smile. "That's us, of course. Until:

"Know too of Gullveig; many-named, many splendored,
Spitted on spearheads; burned in the high god's hall,
Burned thrice, born thrice; yet she lives—"

Cathoair leans forward.

The wolf pauses. "She survived the war; she fled. She came to us, changed, I think, by her torments. She must always have been seductive and ruthless and strong, but something also made her cruel. Desperation, I suspect. Or the aftermath of torture." He speaks a few more lines of poetry:

"From the depths below; a dark dragon flying
Pinions weighted; with the bodies of men,
Soars overhead; I sink now.
Would you know more?"

Shaking his head slightly, the wolf purses his lips. "Still, she was seductive. She seemed so right. So *proper* a leader. The war I walked away from, when the world was young and the stars were bright—" He closes his eyes, rolls his face up to the obscured sky. "We were fools, Cathoair. We were young and we loved her like a queen, like a goddess. We would have done anything to please her. I know—"

The wolf does not look, but he knows his brother watches carefully. "I know your wounds, for I have felt them as my own."

"You walked away," Cathoair says.

The wolf brushes the words aside. "About surrender: this is only the start."

The newer angel frowns, thoughtful.

"The true surrender, the difficult one, is to yourself. There are times to surrender to your anger—your wrath, your passion—and let it move you. Like Odhinn on the tree—which is another story from an older world—you give *yourself* up for the power that changes the world. It is not capitulation and it is not resignation of which I speak. It is ceasing to divide your strength by fighting against yourself. You're einherjar now, Cathoair. It's time to understand that Will *is* Action."

Cathoair's nod is cautious, but present. "Who is Odhinn?"

"Was," the wolf replies, licking his lips. He turns his face aside, wincing strangely. "A god. The father of the gods—many of them, anyway. Not your Heythe, though—she came from a different clan. He was a fighter who sold his eye for a drink of water, it's said, that gave him wisdom to rule. And then hung himself for nine days and nights on a sacred tree to obtain the strength and magic to fortify that wisdom." The wolf shifts on the bench, glancing again at the statues now barely visible in filtered starlight. The wolf tastes a memory of blood, and closes his eyes again.

"He paid for it," Cathoair says. "Like Muire paid for this." His gesture takes in the room, the sea, the world beyond.

"Surrender." The wolf smiles and bends closer to Cathoair, eye to eye, nose to nose. His collar cuts his throat. In him, a hungry mad thing snarls. "Now consider what it is you've paid for, Brother. Because paid you surely have, and in the dearest coin of all."

In the silence that follows, Cathoair stands, walks a few steps, and frowning intently turns back to the wolf.

Mingan stands as well and meets Cathoair's eyes. "But the

hardest surrender is the one that remains. To yourself, to the totality of what you are meant to be. And *that* last yielding—that, I cannot help you with." He closes the distance between them and, reaching up, brushes bloody lips across the other's mouth, waiting to see if there would be a flinch.

Cathoair closes his eyes but stands steady, drawing a ragged, powerful breath.

"Still not broken." The wolf steps away. He pauses. "Ah. The healing."

Cathoair opens star-filled eyes. "Yes."

"You are not flesh anymore, boy. You are spirit. Will it done, and it is done." He hesitates, mostly for effect. He can't quite help himself. "Although there is, of course, a price."

The Grey Wolf vanishes into the shadows with a smile.

50 A.R.
On the Twenty-ninth Day of Autumn

Cathmar didn't lift his head from Selene's shoulder when the door to Borje's cottage opened. Rather, he heard the intentionally crisp footsteps on the walk and turned away, wishing to see neither who came through that cedarwood portal nor what the expression on his face might be. There were four possible answers, and it was three to one that something had gone utterly wrong. He drew his knees up, pressing his face against her neck, and hid himself in her cloud-soft fur.

Selene squeezed his shoulders and stood, drawing him to his feet. "It's Mingan," she said. "I think it's okay."

Cathmar turned his head to see. The Grey Wolf looked torn and bloodied, although he must have healed himself on the way back down the hill. Cathmar licked his lips. He met the Grey Wolf's silver eyes.

Slowly, pushing his tangled mane of hair off his face, Mingan nodded. "I believe he'll live," he said carefully, "although the battle was hard-fought."

Selene gave Cathmar an extra squeeze before she walked over and touched Mingan's breast, claws catching on the nap of his rag-torn silvery shirt. "Yours?" she asked, of the blood that streaked it.

"Mostly," Mingan answered, meeting her eyes. "He is truly well, Selene. And so am I."

Finding his voice, Cathmar took a step forward. "What happened?"

"We had words," Mingan replied, pinning Cathmar in turn with that level gaze. "And then we found our peace, I believe, and a measure of understanding. Brotherhood. I used you to provoke him, which was unkind, and you should know of it. But I believe it is forgiven, now."

"So you took turns hitting each other until you both fell down?" Cathmar asked. His voice was more curious than dismissive.

"That was part of it." The Grey Wolf watched Selene's face when he said it, and not Cathmar's.

Cathmar, following the look, saw complexity of emotion in the back-flicker of her ears and the tilt of her whiskers. It resolved, after a moment, into the relaxed tail and forward-pricked ears of amusement.

"I see," Selene said, not turning to look at Cathmar. Mingan was the first to break the steady contact, glancing down.

Cathmar waited a moment to see if more was forthcoming. Mingan cocked his head at the boy and smiled. "You've watched Svanvitr for me, I trust?"

Cathmar nodded and went to get her from Borje's bedroom. The bull had gone for a walk with Aethelred, Erasmus and Aithne. They had things to discuss, apparently, relating to choices, and duty. Mingan took the sword back with a gracious thanks. And then a thoughtful breath that made Cathmar pause.

"What is it, Uncle?"

Mingan clipped Svanvitr to his belt before he spoke. "Gullveig. Your Mardoll." A wryer smile. "Heythe, as I knew her of old."

"Yes." Cathmar somehow knew exactly what the old trickster Wolf was going to ask of him: tasted it in the air somehow. He was nodding acquiescence even before the task was assigned.

Selene watched the young man and the old man lean together in conversation almost as if forgetting her presence. She listened to their soft words—soft to human ears, plain to hers—and thought about what Mingan had just nearly told her.

"You must take up a dangerous task," Mingan said. "For your father's sake. And for your mother's sake as well. Heythe must be distracted until Cahey has time to regain his strength and gain control of the Imogen. I knew Heythe, more than two thousand years hence, when her manipulation and her lovemaking divided the children of the Light and set us against one another. I would have been among them, that day—the Last Day—and she would have been triumphant. Except I hid away the weapon she meant to use to win the field. Do you understand?"

"A little," Cathmar answered. "Not much. Dad was always fuzzy on the Last Day, but I do remember what you've told me."

Selene leaned in the corner, silent, watching the two of

them, youthful and ancient, and feeling the fear for their lives like a stale smothering blanket thrown over her head.

"Excellent," Mingan replied. "She came to us from elsewhere, you understand. A world before, she said, a beautiful lost world on the other side of a gulf of time. She said she fled its destruction, and that she was a goddess. I was not alone in that I knelt to her, then. She has a way—"

"Of making you feel she understands you," Cathmar interrupted.

"I see I don't need to explain." Mingan smiled like a knife.

Cathmar grinned back, all boyish spontaneity. Selene had to restrain herself from reaching out to caution him.

"I'm about to send you into danger," Mingan said.

"You need her kept busy."

Selene saw surprise at Cathmar's quickness, and then approval. "Any way you can," the Wolf whispered. She thought he knew exactly what he was asking, and from Cathmar's quick glimmer of recognition and clenched jaw she saw that he did, too.

"Yeah," Cathmar said. His eyes glittered.

Selene felt her claws come out. "No," she said. "We can go after her all at once. Aithne, Cahey, Borje and Erasmus, too. Your steed. All of us."

Mingan turned to her. "I will explain," he began quietly. "Selene—on the Last Day. When there were rank upon rank of waelcyrge, valraven and einherjar. Then, if we had stood shoulder to shoulder against her, we might have prevailed. Possibly. Not only is she strong—powerful beyond even my ability to match—but she can flee in an instant. To another world, or forward in time as she has at least twice. And I do not wish to face her again. Do you understand?"

Selene sighed. "You've been hiding from her."

"I have moved as craftily against her as I understood how."

"All right," Cathmar said, his voice as deadly level as Cahey's could get, sometimes. "What do we do?"

"You keep her busy," Mingan said. "While your father learns how to control the Imogen. And Selene and I make a few more angels. Then we arrange a confrontation. She must not know—*must* not know—that you suspect her of anything. Do you understand?"

Selene didn't dare think of what could happen. *Too strong for all of us, and we send her one innocent boy alone.*

And then Cathmar smiled and rolled his shoulders, so like his father—in better times—that were she human, it would have brought tears to her eyes. "I think I do. I'll keep her busy, Uncle. You go talk to Dad. And . . . maybe I can get something useful out of her. Since she obviously thinks I'm stupid."

Oh, but Selene didn't like the hard, old Light in his eyes.

50 A.R.
On the Twenty-ninth Day of Autumn

Cahey watched him vanish and, this time, almost saw how it was done. He shook his head, stretching, and looked down at the healing burns on his wrists, the bruises on his hands. Not to mention Imogen's stigmata.

Will it done. . . . He pursed his lips and inspected his hands. Long narrow hands, fingers spidery between knotted knuckles. He examined the spreading bruise beneath the amber-colored skin of his palm. Quirked a smile, amused at his own presumption.

Concentrated, brow furrowing. Pictured the skin flawless and unharmed. *Begone.*

It vanished without a trace.

That raised his eyebrow. He thought the ligature marks on his wrists whole as well, and then—out of curiosity as much as anything—he turned his attention to the old, split scars across his knuckles. Scars from bare-knuckled boxing, scars from fighting for his life. Scars from a long time ago.

Gone as if they never were.

His breath caught, elation followed by a wave of tiredness. *So there is a price.*

"Ah." It was an inevitable thought. He glanced up at the statue of himself. Prowled over to it, hesitant. Placed a palm against the cool stone cheek, traced the line of an even older wound.

"Old man," he said, very quietly. "I didn't deserve that. Any of it, really."

He looked his statue in the eye. Cool, black marble eyes. A mocking smile marked by a trace of tenderness.

His own eyes narrowed. "I won't . . ." He tried again. "I won't apologize for who I am, Muire. Or the ways we were wrong for each other. But I am . . . sorry . . . that I hurt you."

He sighed and slapped his portrait lightly on the cheek. Turning, he strode to the glass-fronted bookracks and examined his own reflection in the moonlight shining through the window over his shoulder. The image was dim and murky in spotted and wavy glass, but the raw puffy line of the old un-faded scar stood out against the sepia of his cheek.

He raised his left hand and touched it, gently. Felt the dimple of the missing teeth beneath. Remembered Muire touching the same place, pressing fingers clad in armor to his cheekbone. *Do I want this?*

He'd been a child, an adolescent, but already hard by then as the braided leather on the end of a whip. Been in and out of the house, staying with Aethelred as often as not. Learning to fight. Astrid . . .

Was two years older. She had picked him up like a hunting dog adopting a straggly, starved kitten. Taught him to defend himself; taught him to fight. Taught him as well that there was more to making love than blood and fists and agony.

Astrid. Light. Did I ever thank you for saving me?

He was dragging Cahey's mom out of the bathroom. She was sick, but *he* didn't care, and so Cahey had gone over and put his hand on the old man's shoulder.

The old man had looked up when he looked at Cahey. And that was a revelation in itself. Soft and careful, Cahey told him to pack and go.

He laughed and threw Cahey across the room. He landed badly, one leg twisted under himself, and struggled to rise. The knee crunched, and it hurt so bad Cahey burned his throat on bile. Later, they would tell him that he'd only dislocated it. They would run a lot of other tests, too, and they would tell him a lot of other things he hadn't wanted to hear.

Things about genetic damage, and supersoldier flu, and why he couldn't be considered quite human, sorry, or expect to have kids.

Cahey hauled on a table edge, got up on his crunching knee, and groped for the armor-cutter he'd hidden in his trouser pocket. And then it was in his hand, and he pushed *up* when the old man came for him, and—

Everything was blood. It was in his mouth, all over his hands, stinging his eyes, and Mom was screaming, and the old man was still hauling himself forward through his own guts, groping after the cutter that had fallen out of Cahey's hand.

Cahey was trying to explain why he had to kill him, while the old man tried to kill him back. Luckily the old man didn't quite pull it off, but they were both still sitting there in the blood—one dead, one alive—when Astrid and Aethelred came to get rid of the body and take Cahey to a clinic to get stitched up.

"You said you never wanted to have to kill anybody again."

"Astrid?" He turned, unbelieving.

The image of her. Black braid and skin like honey, too-wide mouth and broken nose and shoulders broad as a plow-mare's.

Eyes dark hot gold like sunlight.

"Imogen," he whispered. He glanced down at the bruise in the crook of his arm, the one he hadn't had time to heal, yet. "Well, that wish didn't come true, either, did it?"

"My Lord," she whispered. "Is this the one you need?"

Mingan's voice in his ear. He almost felt the Wolf's breath on his neck. *Master her. Or she will master you.*

He closed his eyes and turned back to the reflection. The imperfect glass and the darkness robbed the color from her eyes, made them dark and perfectly opaque.

A long moment passed. She took a step closer.

"No," Cahey said, and she stopped in her footsteps. "Imogen."

"Aye, Lord."

"Your own shape, if you please."

"As you bid." She molded, melted, stood behind him as the winged demoness.

He turned back to her. "Come to me."

Uncertainly, she did. "I hunger, my Lord," she whispered.

"I know. It will wait," he answered. He tilted her chin up with his long unmarked fingers and looked into her eyes.

Selene. You were supposed to be as soulless as this one. As mindless and as bound to another's will. Muire's kiss freed you from that.

And then he thought, *Why is it, given everything, that Gullveig . . . Heythe . . . has never once* kissed *me? Fucked me. Raped me. Used me any way she could. Never put her mouth on mine.*

"Lord . . ." Her voice trailed off, her fingers twining nervously behind her back. Eyes focused; her mouth opened, red as a wound in the blackness of her fur. "I beg of you—"

"No," he said, and she fell silent. *No whimpering,* he heard, and fought the nausea that came with the memory. "First, my name is Cathoair, not 'my Lord.' Most of my intimates, of which you surely qualify, call me Cahey. And second . . ."

Oh, this is probably a very, very bad idea.

Her light-filled eyes grew wide as he called the starlight into his own, lifting her pointed chin with his fingertips. The Light caught on her irises, puddled there, reflected back against his face.

He offered her a tender half-smile. Eyes half-lidded, she leaned toward him, lips drawn inexorably toward his throat.

He shook his head slightly; she hesitated, glanced back startled into his eyes. Holding her gaze every moment, he let his lips drop down to hers.

Shocked, she sucked in a gasp of air.

Cahey pressed breath down her throat.

Somehow, on the inspiration, she keened: a long sustained note that tangled his senses and dragged at his soul like fingers. Black as the space between the stars and yielding as flower petals, her wings came up. She wrapped her slender arms around his neck. Lithe and animal, she softened against him.

The wings enshrouded him like a chrysalis; she sucked at his mouth like a feeding butterfly. He put his arms around her underneath her wings, cradling her against his chest.

She snuggled closer, tilting her head back, and he lost himself in the sweetness of the kiss. The tumble went on and on and on, a limitless spring into a fathomless chasm—drawing him in, sucking him down, losing himself in the darkness where no instinct for self-preservation could find him.

He hung in darkness, shining, a corona of azure Light whirlpooled away from him into the singularity of a companion that existed as appetite only, gravity and need—an essential pairing, he realized.

Waterfall, he thought, and *shooting star.*

And then, from somewhere, concern:

I'm almost gone, he understood, with an awesome lucidity. *She's . . . bottomless.* Something flickered inside him, raised a sleepy head: the wolf-shard, traces of Mingan's passage through his soul. He fed that to the Imogen, too, that, and the lingering fragment of the Suneater, and his breath, and himself, and the thing like water and . . .

A little glittering ghost spun inside him. A fragment, a trace, the thread of a presence: Muire's kiss. The proof of her love and the measure of her devotion, jealously guarded for many long years. He sensed the Imogen's hunger . . . nearly replete.

Mercy. The Imogen whispered inside his ear. *What have I done to earn your mercy?*

What have you done to be denied it? he replied.

Almost. The well filling up. He could do it, he thought. End that gnawing in her. Give her peace.

He also thought that it would cost him everything he had.

In the darkness of the chapel, her darker wings cocooned him. Demoness, trickster's daughter, child of the night with no soul of her own, only the hunger that never rested, the void that could never be filled . . .

Just when I had decided not to die after all, he thought, amused by the irony but not frightened. *Muire.* Something he had never said to her in life, not in so many words. *Lady, I love you.*

Surrender.

Imaginary fingers brushed the bright, spinning fragment, swept it, space-free, into motion . . .

. . . sailing, rushing, falling, failing into the fathomless, utter gravity of black . . .

. . . his sapphire aura flared, pulsed like a heartbeat, distended, burned crimson in fury and perfection—

—shattered into—

Gone.

A new star flared into airless silence. Cahey never saw it bloom.

50 A.R.
On the Thirty-third Day of Autumn

Cathmar smoothed the crumpled bedclothes over Mardoll's shoulders. Leaning back against the wall, he watched her dream, a crease forming between his eyebrows. He nibbled on the tip of his thumb, wondering how long to let her sleep. A fall of sunlight through cracked glass and a lace window shade patterned her shoulder and hip under the eiderdown.

Wouldn't want her getting too much rest, he thought. He watched the light move across her face and considered taking a quick bath, but decided he didn't dare leave her alone that long. She might wake up while he was in the bathroom. *I'll just find some excuse to insist on washing her hair, later.*

When he'd promised Mingan he wouldn't let Mardoll out of his sight, he hadn't realized how long it would be. He reached over to the nightstand and picked up his 'screen, checked for messages. There were several, all from Selene and Aethelred.

No improvement in his father's condition. Aethelred wasn't using the word *coma*. Selene, un-dissembling, was. *Do something,* Cathmar prayed.

Mardoll stirred in her sleep, her necklace—the only thing she wore—glittering in the afternoon light. Cathmar tried to rearrange his expression into something more pleasant than a scowl. Being gentle with her had not been easy. Although.

Although the sex part was easier to manage than you expected, wasn't it? He frowned. Not a pleasant thought.

Watching his betrayer sleep, Cathmar realized that he'd never *really* been angry before. Was shocked by the intensity of his urge to reach out and wrap his fingers around her slender neck, turned on a curve as she burrowed deeper into a plump white pillow. Almost, he felt the blood springing to the surface of his hands as he drove the wires and jewels of her necklace into the white skin of her throat.

That necklace. She never takes it off.

Never once. *And why did that never strike me as strange before?*

Very, very softly, he reached out and flicked the catch with a fingernail. Another, harder touch, and he realized that it would not open, and remembered what Selene had said about the bargain Cahey had cut with Mardoll. *Four days of love, if you can call it that. I wonder if that's what she paid for it. And if she paid, if I can pay the same. I wonder if she really can use it to walk time and place, she could use it to escape, again.*

As she did on the Last Day, when the first einherjar all died. Mardoll came—elsewhen? Now?

Heythe. Her name is Heythe. Remembering the conditions of that deal had brought back another thought: *And I would really like to wring her neck.*

He tried to dismiss the image and it returned, disquieting. The more disquieting because of the satisfaction he took at the image . . . and the passion it stirred in him. *Passion. No mistake that the word for sex and for anger is the same, is it?* His lip wanted to curl. He smoothed it.

I've never hated anybody before.

She stretched in her sleep and smiled. He recognized the signs of her awakening and left the bed softly, returning with a breakfast tray as she opened her eyes. He poured her tea, handed her the bowl, and settled down on the bed beside her again.

"Go anywhere?" she asked him after taking a sip of the tea.

He gestured down at his unclothed self. "Just here with you."

Her gaze lingered. "Mmmmmm. So what occasion breakfast in bed?"

He took her empty hand, kissing the palm so he wouldn't have to meet her eyes. "Things have been strained lately," he said. *Angels don't lie. Thanks, Mom, for the easy set of rules to follow.* "I wanted us to spend some time . . . closer together."

"You are insatiable," she said. "I had some things I wanted to do today—"

He kissed her wrist, the inside of her forearm, more with his breath than with his lips. He felt her shiver. He'd rather have twisted that arm behind her back. He stroked her tousled hair off her cheek with his other hand.

"What sort of things?" As if feigning interest to be polite. He should be bothered that he was good at this. Really good at it.

"Marketing . . . oh."

"I'll do it for you later." He stroked her throat with his fingertips, imagining . . . *No. Don't think about that.* Pausing with his fingertips brushing her necklace as if only just noticing it, he asked, "How come you never take this off?"

"Hmmmm? Why?"

"Oh. . . . I just realized I'd never seen you naked." Making it into a little joke.

She giggled. "It's magic."

"Okay." Putting just enough disbelief into the tone. "It makes you beautiful? Without it, you're an ugly . . . ," pause, "old . . . ," longer pause, "witch?"

"Mmmm. You expect me to talk while you do that?"

His silence indicated disinterest in whether she was talking or not. She caught him by the chin and lifted his face up. "It's a map," she said. "A map of the stars. I stole it from a dead goddess. With it, I can walk anywhere. Other worlds, even."

He laughed, meeting the regard of her bright blue eyes. "You think I don't believe you."

"You're right."

"Love," he said, turning away again, "why would you ever have to lie to me? It would be beneath you." And pretended that he thought the sudden tension in her body came from the touch of his hands.

50 A.R.
On the Thirty-third and
the Thirty-fourth Days of Autumn

Cahey awoke to cool, airy night—awakening itself a sensation that had become so unfamiliar it took him a moment to understand what had happened. He stretched, senses other than sight filling in the familiar smells and darknesses of his back room: the scent of the sea; of woodsmoke; and another odor, familiar enough to tickle his memory but not easily identified.

He was home. Smooth sheets slid over his skin. Someone had undressed him, bathed him, and put him to bed.

Bed? There wasn't a bed in his room. But here he was, eiderdown pulled up to his chin, soft pillows under his head. That scent: elusive. He almost remembered it.

He had not expected to wake up at all, and . . .

Somebody had also fetched a bed. He reevaluated how much time had passed. He stretched again, testing his arms and legs. Everything seemed in working order.

He started to sit up and the dizziness hit him. A moment later, it was followed by the memories. And the lack of them.

He'd rarely thought consciously of the splinter of his lover's self that he'd carried within him all this time, but it had been there. A little comforting shard of light, a taste of her that never left him.

Where it had been was an empty corner. A starless darkness.

The sensation of hollowness was followed by the pain.

He bit down against the first sob, turning it into a yelp. The one that followed came out a raw-throated howl.

Imogen, he thought, even as he knew that this time she wouldn't be coming to take the suffering away. His grief crested and washed over him like the wild, terrible sea. He thought it would rip him open like a gaffing hook: real, searing, physical pain. All the hurt he'd never given voice to, so many years ago.

Curled around his emptiness, he barely noticed when the bedroom door swung open and someone came in. A soft body in a nightshirt pressed against him, strong hands pulling him close, holding him down.

Her hair fell around him as she pushed his face into her neck. He recognized the smell of her then, but the shock of her presence wasn't enough to jar him out of his grief. Not yet.

He expected her to hush him, to bury his tears in her shoulder and rock him quiet as his mother would have. Not so.

"Good," she said in level tones, her voice reasoned rather than soothing. "Good. Scream, kick, bite. You need it." He knew her voice even before he felt the strap of her eyepatch against his cheek.

She hung on to him, inhumanly strong, and let him fight his grief out against her. Another woman had done the same thing for him once, after a death that, he was finally starting to understand, might not have been meant to be his. He'd held Aithne the same way, on more nights than one.

There was a lot of grief to batter through. Aithne clung to him, protected him with her body. At long last, he fell back, spent, and she pulled him against her and stroked his hair.

"Aithne," he said, when he was too tired to scream anymore. His voice sounded clotted.

She hummed in his ear, something wordless.

"I never thought I'd see you again."

In the darkness, a small cat jumped up on the bed, investigated his ear with ticklish whiskers, and left. *Aithne's still got that cat? It must be very old by now.* The incongruity of the thought, or perhaps the continuity of lives he no longer touched that it implied, startled him.

"You haven't seen me yet," she answered. It was too dark to detect her grin, but he heard it in her voice.

"Why did you come here?"

"Blame the kitty-cat," she said. "Blame the priest."

She drew back a little, slid under the covers, and wrapped her arms around him. She still smelled the same, but she felt different in the darkness: softer, womanly, strong. His body remembered hers brittle and angular, a grown girl's, not the lusher curve of breast and hip through cotton jersey. Soft. And muscled under that.

Her skin, though, was and always had been softer still. He tried to think about something else.

She noticed, of course. "Cahey, do you need to make love?"

He laughed, surprised to hear some genuine humor in it. "Of course I do," he said, "but why don't we put it off till morning and I'll see if I can manage 'want' instead of 'need'?"

In the silence, he heard her breathing.

"Unless . . . you'd rather not," he said belatedly.

She picked her head up off his shoulder. Something flickered in the darkness, caught like an edge of waxed paper dipped in fire. Her one eye blazed silver in the darkness. "I could find me a nice mortal boy instead," she said.

The answering ripple of Light filled his own eyes. "How?"

"Selene," she said. "And Mingan." He saw her smile by starlight. "Muire gave me my sword yesterday. Her name's Sceadhu. Selene thinks that's funny, but I don't underst—"

He laughed, and looked at her by the light of her own shining, and laughed some more until she started giggling, too, and pounding her fist on the bed. It was a long time before they fell quiet, not daring to look at each other.

Aithne broke the silence first. "It wasn't me, was it?"

Cahey thought about it for a long time before he answered. "I thought . . . you'd be better off with somebody like yourself. And if I left, I . . . ." He shook his head, feeling his hair matting against the pillowcase.

"Wouldn't have to watch me get old," she finished for him. "It's okay. I thought you pitied *me,* and it pissed me off, so I wanted you gone. Sometimes. There's only so much pity I can take, and I was filling the bill all by myself."

"Mercy, wasn't it?" The word came out before he remembered where he'd gotten it.

"Sometimes, mercy is served with a knife."

" 'In my house,' " he quoted darkly, " 'there is an end to pain.' "

"I still don't want your pity," Aithne answered. "And, even now, you don't need mine."

He shook his head. "I've been more about the self-pity. But you . . . you deserved somebody who could just love you, and not have to think about burying you someday."

She nodded. "I'm still getting used to it. The idea that . . . Here I am, and I'm going to be thirty-five forever. And everybody else is not."

"You'll be getting used to it for a long time," he said after a silence. *A long time, and it never gets easy. I hope.* Sleep was welling up over him again, his body's need for time to heal overwhelming his spirit's ability to mend itself.

She snuggled against his shoulder. He listened to her breathe until drowsiness coiled him under again.

He woke to morning light, the sea breeze stirring the green gauze curtains and a redheaded angel's smile. The freckles on her nose had faded over the years, but the eye was still green as a cat's.

"Thank you," he said.

She laughed at him. "Slender repayment. But it looks like I'll have a long time to make it up to you."

"You've changed," he said, still studying her face. "You have laugh-lines." He thought about it and decided that he liked them. They made the scars seem more like part of a tapestry and less like a vandalism. And then he thought, *I can show her how to fix those.*

Her grin rearranged both. "You've changed, too. You're not dead-set on saving me anymore."

He sat up in bed, realized that he was still naked under the covers. "Ah," he said.

The grin got wider. She rolled over and leaned on her elbows. "So, morning-breath, you wanna find out if the sex is any better when we're both halfway sane?"

He pressed his tongue against the back of his teeth. "Old times' sake?"

She snorted. "Fuck old times," she said. "Old times sucked. I'm more interested in finding out if you're capable of a halfway decent lay." She was still grinning, and her tone held mockery, but no sting.

"Halfway decent . . . ? I didn't think I was *that* bad for you."

She traced a fingertip down the center of his chest. She still bit her nails. "You . . ." She looked up at him, pressing her lips together. "A girl can tell," she said. "When she's not the place a boy wants to be."

"Ah," he said. "That was my problem, not yours, you know."

She nodded. "I do. And now that I've met her . . . well. I could never compete with that."

"It's not about competition," he said. "It's about me getting my head out of my ass." He looked her in the eye, bit his lip, and turned toward her under the patchwork eiderdown.

She said nothing, expressionless, watching his face.

"I don't know if I'll ever be over her," he continued. "But I'm not going to . . . Hel. What am I proving to anybody? That I can hurt myself worse than she did?"

He stared into space for a moment, unfocused, vaguely examining the light reflecting off the sand dune outside the window.

"Cahey."

"Yeah?"

She sat up in the bed, threw the covers off, and swung her leg over his hips, leaning forward to bite him on the nose. "Shut the fuck up."

Laughing, he tried to push her off. She bit him again, ear and throat, trying to pin his hands while he fended her away. He caught hold of her nightshirt and levered her back with it, but the cotton gave way and she was swarming over him, naked, all elbows and curly hair and freckles and little white nipping teeth.

He'd forgotten about the rest of the freckles, too.

"Ow," he said, laughing, finally catching hold of her wrist. She twisted around and hit him in the face with a pillow held in her opposite hand.

He grabbed the other pillow and hit her back. She blocked the swing with a forearm, grabbed the pillow-casing, and pulled.

An explosion ensued. Feathers hung suspended, dove-gray and white in the slanting sunlight. She laughed, hit him again, yanked her wrist back and away, red hair backlit, shining like a halo around her face.

He dropped the devastated pillow and grabbed her around the waist, enduring several smacks about the ears as he picked her up, rolling forward until he could get one knee under himself. He pushed her backwards, landing on top of her with his face buried in her midsection.

He blew.

A long raspberry resounded through the empty house. She laughed so hard she dropped the pillow, hands pounding helplessly on the disheveled bed, head lolling over the edge.

Well, he thought, *as long as I'm here . . .* He straightened the other leg and slid lower, snaking a wet tongue into her navel. She giggled again, once, then shivered and stopped laughing as his nose reached the hollow of her thigh.

He slid an arm around each thigh to steady her, lifting her

hips off the bed. A demanding strength, held in abeyance, rippled under his fingertips. She'd put on some weight and some muscle in thirteen years, and felt soft and solid in his arms instead of reminding him of another skinny girl.

Which, he thought, *is all to the good, really.*

Trout-brown speckles shivered on the buttermilk skin of her belly, soft as he remembered. He felt a different kind of tension in her now: anticipation, and a kind of fluid slackness that he recognized by Mingan's word, *surrender.*

He was flattered by her trust. "I can't remember," he whispered, feeling her poised between tautness and relaxation, his own delighted laughter still bubbling in his throat, "when I did anything that was this much *fun.*"

He realized as he said it that he did remember, and it was a very long time ago indeed. Poking halfheartedly at the empty place, he found it still there—but maybe not quite so achingly sore—and took that for an answer.

Humming to himself, he dipped his head down, seeking like a bee after salted honey, hearing Aithne's moans over the distant susurrus of the waves. She pulled his hair, then, and she bit his shoulder, eventually, and he found he didn't mind it in the slightest. A gritty, involved lover: she abandoned herself to his touch before regaining the initiative, becoming the aggressor.

And what a silly turn of phrase that is, he thought, sleepy, half-drugged with her kisses. And then, *I feel clean.*

So that was when he realized he *hadn't,* while she lazed against him and apologized for the bruise.

He laughed at her worry. "I wasn't about to be distracted just then."

"I . . . well. You *are* more fun when you're paying attention."

Her coarse, bright hair had tangled, so he combed it with his fingers. The scarred side of her face rested on one of his shoulders: not the bruised one. "It's good to be an angel," he said. "Look. It's already gone."

She touched it with a fingertip. "Selene mentioned healing fast . . . but . . ."

Cahey nodded. "I'll show you how. I have all kinds of things to show you. . . . Oh. Watch."

He raised the hand off her hip, brushed a fingertip across his cheek to draw her attention to the scar. Her eyes focused on it. She frowned.

Before he could reconsider, he focused his concentration and willed it gone.

She frowned. And then her one green eye widened and her body went from slack to quivering in a moment. "How?"

"You just . . . make it gone. Decide you don't want it anymore."

"You mean . . ." She was shaking hard now, so he pulled her close and held on to her for a little while. "Just like that?"

"Whenever you're ready."

"Ah. Ah. Okay. Hang on." She swallowed hard and closed her eye, and stayed there for a second, as scrunch-faced intent as a child wishing on a flower. "That feels funny. Cahey, did it work?"

"Take off your eyepatch and find out," he said, trying not to smile too widely.

She reached tentatively, letting her fingertips brush the flawless pale skin of her face. She hesitated. Trembled. Yanked it off like a child ripping off a bandage and sat there blinking at him, dazzled by the sudden light.

Cahey, laughing, fell back against the bed.

"What? Does it look wrong?"

He shook his head, trying to clear the unavoidable image of a splotch-faced, quizzical cat. "No, Aith. It's just that"—gasp—"there are no freckles where the patch kept the sun off your face."

"You'll pay for that, mister." She grinned.

"Plenty of time to take it out on me."

Her thoughtful expression brought him up short.

"If you're staying," he finished.

"You know how it is," she said, but her smile held promise. "We'll see how it goes. I don't expect you to give up all your other girlfriends for me."

He raised an eyebrow, hearing an echo of something someone had said to him, long ago. "With the exception of supernatural evils," he said, "I've been more or less unentangled. Since."

That silenced her. Cahey permitted himself a thoughtful smile, spending a few more moments teasing at the snarls in her hair and the tangle of emotions floating behind his breastbone. He visualized a knot: razor wire, ribbons, leather thongs and binding twine all wound through one another in confusion. *This is going to take a while,* he thought.

"How long was I out for?" he asked, after a little while.

A line drew itself between her eyes—concern or concentration. "Four days," she said. "Borje found you and brought you back. Mingan realized what you had done. I think . . ." She hesitated. "You actually flummoxed him."

They shared a long look, fraught with complexities.

"And you've been here since," he said.

She nodded, biting her lip. "A woman came by. Merry something. She wanted to know why you hadn't been to Newport in so long. And to say that the kid you sent her was working out fine." She wasn't looking at his face.

I'm an idiot.

He touched her arm.

Tossing her hair back out of her face, she examined him. "And I need to talk to you about something."

He tensed. A moment later, he drew a breath and forced himself to stillness. "I'm prepared to listen to all the lectures I deserve," he said.

She laughed. "It's not a lecture. It's just something I wonder if you've considered." She laid her head back down on his shoulder.

Over the clamor of his instincts, he listened.

"If it was me, Cahey . . . well. You may love women, but you don't always understand them very well."

He leaned forward enough to address a blank look to his redheaded lover.

She grinned at him with one corner of her mouth. Fond wryness colored her voice. "Cahey, you idiot. That goddess you've been screwing. Can't you see that she's just using you to get to Muire?"

He opened his mouth to retort. Stopped. Thought. *What do you have but her word that she can do what she promised?*

In another word. Nothing.

"What purpose? She can't touch Muire. Not without trying to provoke something like the Desolation."

Aithne shrugged, rolling her head from side to side. Her

neck crackled. "You're too nice, Cahey. I have to tell you, man: if *I* were raking some woman's ex-lover over the coals the way this witch has been doing to you, the only possible reason for it would be revenge—or to provoke the woman in question into doing something stupid."

"Ah." He thought about it for a while before he answered. "You know, Aithne. Sometimes you sound so much like a girl I used to know, it's uncanny."

"A girl?" Back up on her elbows, chin on the backs of both hands. "What kind of a girl?"

He drew a breath and took a moment, then looked her directly in the face. "A girl who meant a lot to me," he began.

50 A.R.
On the Thirty-fourth Day of Autumn

*A*ithne 'screened Cathmar in the city around noon; the message said that she was hiking over the hill to Borje's cottage, and that his father was expecting him. Cathmar had been waiting for the call. Mardoll was still sleeping.

Cathmar smiled miserably to himself, slipping down the steel escape with his boots in his hand until he reached the street. He leaned against the wall and stood on one foot at a time to pull them on.

Keeping Mardoll "busy"—and away from Cahey, while he recovered—had taxed Cathmar's guile. And his angelic endurance. And the strength of determination provided by his newly minted loathing for a girl who'd said she loved him.

Contemplating his own naïveté, he tasted bitterness and despair. He glanced back over his shoulder at the worn old building. *I'm never coming back.* He thought about things he might have learned, if he'd listened to his old man. *Yeah, Dad, you were right. You do know when it's the last time.*

I hope she doesn't think I learned nothing from our association.

Maybe Dad can explain why it's so satisfying to fuck somebody whom you'd really rather strangle.

Sick, Cathmar. Sick.

Erasmus' taxi waited. He went to see his old man.

The blue wood door stood open, sand drifting onto the tile floor. Cathmar heard his father singing in the kitchen as he walked up the crunching seashell path to the cottage, and winced. And then smiled. *When was the last time you heard him mangle a song? Right. So shut up about it.*

He called from the doorway. "Dad?"

The singing stopped. His father stepped away from the sink, shirtless, in ivory-colored trousers, drying his hands on a dish towel. "Cath," he said softly, and Cathmar hid his startle when he realized Cathoair's face was unmarked.

Their gazes met and both men spoke in unison. "Dad, I've been an—"

"I'm sorry."

"—idiot."

"Light, Cath, when the Hel did you get so tall?"

Cathmar suddenly found himself looking down into his father's eyes as the old man walked across the room to him. "You saw me just a few days ago," he said.

"Yeah, but . . ." Cahey shrugged and then smiled. "I think you've grown since then."

"I have," Cathmar conceded, after some consideration. "You're right." He stepped forward and wrapped his old man in a stiff, awkward hug. Cahey squeezed tight for an instant and then stepped back. They looked at each other, similarly expressionless, for a long minute.

"All right," Cathmar said, breaking eye contact at last. "Time for the council of war."

His father jerked his chin down in a short nod. "I'll make tea."

A little while later, they sat under the wide eaves in the shade, one sand dune away from the ocean. Cathmar sensed that his father was waiting for him to speak first.

He sipped his tea out of a blue china bowl he remembered and asked, "So what do you think Mardoll is up to?"

Cahey's lips twitched. "Mardoll-Gullveig-Heythe? Well, I've got a theory about that. Or Aithne does. Since apparently she's got all the smarts around here." He sipped his tea. "I need to ask you something first."

Cathmar twirled his bowl between the tips of his fingers. "Dad, what happened to your scar?"

Cahey coughed slightly. "Mingan showed me how to heal it."

Cathmar nodded. "Good. It looks better that way. What did you want to ask me?"

"Sticky question," Cahey warned, and then winced at his choice of words.

Cathmar frowned, answered the question he knew his father wanted to ask. "No. She hasn't . . . hurt me. Physically. Is that what you wanted to know?"

"Good." Cahey eased a white-knuckle grip on the handle of the teapot, managed to refill their bowls without spilling any, until Cathmar spoke again.

"She hurt you."

Tea slopped. Cahey wiped it up with a mild curse. He set aside teapot and napkin and looked his son in the eye. "She . . . worked on a hurt that was already there." He shook his head, ponytail bobbing. He opened his mouth to speak again and then thought better of it and drank his tea.

Cathmar let the silence rest a moment. "Your theory. Aithne's theory."

"Oh. Yeah. She said she'd met you?"

Cathmar nodded. "Briefly."

"What do you think of her?" The question was a little too carefully casual.

Cathmar drank his tea very slowly. "I think you're the biggest idiot I've ever met, Dad, where girls are concerned. But they do seem to like you, so maybe there's something to that." He watched Cahey studying his face, held on to the laugh as long as he could, and barely managed to swallow the tea without spraying it across the table.

It took a second, but Cahey started laughing, too. "Is that your way of saying I don't need your approval?"

"Well," Cathmar replied, "of course you need my approval. But that's beside the point. What you don't need is my permission, okay? I think we're kind of beyond that."

Cahey was still studying him, in a thoughtful manner that made him smile nervously. "What?"

"You turned out okay, kid."

He laughed dismissively, met his father's concentrated stare. Realized that Cahey wasn't kidding and flushed, looking down into his bowl. Ran his tongue across his teeth while he thought.

"Dad—well, you did okay." Cathmar startled himself with the realization as he said it that it wasn't just a comforting noise.

His father opened his mouth. No words came out.

Cathmar glanced away and changed the subject. "So can we get on with dealing with . . . her?"

He thought he caught relief in his father's face. "Yeah. Anyway, Aithne pointed out to me the possibility that it wasn't about us."

"What do you mean?" Cathmar rubbed the edge of his forefinger across his lips.

"Well," his father said, "we do have something in common. Other than"—a dismissive shake of his head—"Gullveig. Or whatever her name is."

"Mingan says Heythe."

"Right."

"So what do we have in common? Being einherjar. The swords . . . Oh." Cathmar felt the ill-defined betrayal and fury that had haunted him for days suddenly crystallize, a lump of basalt hardening under his solar plexus. "Mom."

"Sure. And I can't think of why else she'd be doing some of the things she has, except . . . to get to your mother. If she could do what she offered me, that would be a blow against Muire in itself. And if she can't, well, having me half-crazy and you on a string certainly weakens us."

Cathmar gritted his teeth in sudden comprehension. *How could I have been so blind?* "Yeah," he said, "by about fifty percent."

His dad must have seen the look of realization on his face. "Any idea what she wants, Cath?"

Cathmar nodded. "Hel, yes. Dad. She wants Mom's job. What else could it be?"

His father's face went very still as Cahey leaned forward the table. Cathmar thought his own must look much the same.

Cahey took a deep breath and let it out on a curse. "No, she doesn't. She doesn't want to take up the Burden. If she did, really wanted it, I think your mother would hand it over cheerfully."

"So what does she want?"

Cahey licked his lips. "Mingan said she worked to destroy the world before this one. That she brought down the children of the Light. He gave me—" He shook his head, looped-back braids falling in a mass over his shoulder. "He gave me some knowledge. Some fragments of things I remember now. She wants the Bearer dead. It was her killed the first one."

"That's *stupid*," Cathmar said, unable to restrain himself.

"She's tearing down something made by someone she hated," Cahey said. "Killing a child to punish the father. It's just revenge. That's all it is. Just revenge."

Cathmar leaned back, steepling his hands before him, and rolled his head from side to side to ease the pain in his neck before he realized that it was his father's gesture. "Now for the next question: what are we going to do about it?"

His father tapped on the table with fingertips, twice, and then the flat of his hand. "Well," he said through a smile that wasn't, "she wants me to be bait. So I guess bait is what I am."

Borje twisted his hoof against the tile, almost but not quite pawing at the slates. "I'm coming," he said, starlight gleaming in his wide brown eyes.

Aethelred leaned his staff against the wall and stood up straight. "No, you're not. You're staying here, and so is Erasmus."

Looking around his living room for support, Borje found

nothing. Selene, Cathmar, Aithne were all either stony-faced or shaking their heads. Erasmus stood in the corner, plumed tail wavering slightly. Mingan was nowhere to be found, and Borje knew Selene, at least, was frantic; he could see it in the way her tail coiled around her ankle and clung. Cahey had already chosen his vantage: a high, open place, readily visible from a long way off. "It's not safe."

"Bearer of Burdens. It's never safe, Borje."

As if the old priest had not spoken, Borje continued. "And we should wait for Master Wolf."

Selene hissed softly. "Borje. I haven't heard from him. Or his steed." Her hackles bristled, and it must have cost her to speak levelly. "I don't know where he went, and he may not be coming back."

"Why do we have to do this now?"

Aethelred sighed. "Because you're as sensible as a rock, and you and Erasmus are part of the community. And if every last damned one of us fails to come back from this little expedition, and Heythe wins . . ." The old soldier walked up to the bull, grabbed a steel-shod horn in his hand, and pulled the moreau's head down so he could stare into his eyes. "You two are our insurance policy. Our fallback position. Because every moreau within fifty miles was freed by Selene, and if we die trying, the two of you will have to turn them into an army and go after what's-her-name."

The bull took a breath to argue.

Aethelred stepped back, cuffed him on the shoulder affectionately. "Cleanup is the job nobody wants," he said. "But when you draw it, Borje, you know for sure your buddies trust you. All right?"

"Hel." He tossed his horns in irritation. "Hel. Yes. Man. But if you don't come back I'm kissing the first Black Silk I see and putting him in charge of the operation."

Selene laughed. "Damn straight, Borje," she said with a more normal flicker of her tail. "See? Aethelred said you have a good head on you."

She is sent for by name.

She remembers him now. From long before, in another world. She remembers . . . so much.

He waits for her on a green hilltop beside his steed, the steed who spoke to her and bade her come to this place, at this time. He calls her, and she does not have to go to him. But if she goes to him, there is nothing now to stop her.

Almost, she tastes his blood in advance, imagines the crack of his bones in her teeth.

Almost.

She furls her wings, plummets. The wind kisses her face, her feathers. Standing before him, she exults in the shadow of fear that touches his silver eyes.

"I hear you, Wolf, but you may not compel me."

He inclines his head. "I know that."

"You fear me. You freed me."

"I do, Imogen. I did."

"You who first chained me." *Blood and bones.* She runs her tongue over the sharp edges of her teeth. She tastes his death . . . but the anticipation sits uneasy.

She does not like that.

He nods. "I've come to bargain, not command."

Stepping closer, the Imogen smells his fear. His pain. Whetting her appetite. She traces the line of his cheekbone with her forefinger. He does not flinch. She thinks about the mark of his own ancient bondage that she know lies taut around his neck, one end frayed and torn. She is not the only one who has been chained.

She is not chained anymore.

His steed tenses behind her, but even that one cannot match a trickster's daughter. Even that one has nightmares. And his rider holds him in check: she sees it in the warning glance shot past her.

"What have you, Mingan, that I could not take?" She'd never spoken his name before. Always, he was "Lord."

But he was not cruel to me.

Whence that reminder? A voice inside: unfamiliar, not the voice she knows. The voice of the almost possible.

"You could not take my service," he says, proud eyes flashing. "I will serve you as once you served me, Imogen. I will place myself in thrall to you, if you wish it." She smells the fear on him as he makes the offer. Death he courted. This thing he offers her . . . frightens him. "But grant me first one boon."

"What gift?" She wants to shred him, assuage the old hunger with his flesh and agony. She needs . . . unbound at last, she needs what she has ever been prevented from taking. So what stops her? Her hand rests now on the side of his neck. Her fingers curl, and her claws draw blood. One skitters off the impervious surface of that collar, wrought as it is of improbable things.

He shows no pain, but she feels it in him. "Destroy the one called Heythe."

He is weaker. He is prey. Succulent. Why can she not close her hand?

Her soul.

That which frees her. Binds her.

She shoves him away, spins, spits, screams. She wants him. She could crush him, this creature whose father is her father, too. Split his skin, shatter bones, rend meat. Pulp, immortal pulp and pith and nothing more. She whirls on him. He does not try to stand. His stallion surges toward her, stops as if hauled up on invisible chains—a moment before she would be forced to address him with her claws.

"Take my life as the price for taking hers," he says, very softly.

She turns on the one called Mingan. Two steps and she mantles his prone form with her wings. Fury, hunger, wroth, nightmare . . .

. . . pity.

Pity?

What, oh what, is it that you have given me, Cahey?

"I reject your offer," she says to him. With the heavy down-draft of wings, she returns to the sky, owing service to one only.

50 A.R.
On the Thirty-fourth Day of Autumn

Cahey waited for her on the flag-paved hilltop beside the chapel, knowing she would come. By moonlight, he suspected.

He was right. She strolled across the flagstones, limned in silver. Smiling, gorgeous, cloying. "You are so very beautiful," she murmured, raising a hand toward his cheek, "but I think I liked you better with the scar, pet."

Cahey stepped back when she reached for him. "I can't do this."

"This is the final night of our bargain," she said.

"No more." *Buying time. Never get scared, Cahey.* And then, a comprehending smile. *No. Go ahead, get scared. But do what you have to do anyway.*

She raised a golden eyebrow at him, cocked her head as if considering the source of his grin. "Really," she said. "Threatened? You can tie *me* to the bed this time if it will make you feel better."

"Actually"—amused to know that she did not understand him well enough to recognize the poisonous levelness of his tone—"I've discovered I rather like that part."

She said nothing for the moment.

"What I do *not* like is feeling filthy everywhere you've touched me."

"Men don't refuse me, Cathoair."

"This one does."

"Am I not powerful?" She smiled at him, blue eyes bottomless as the sea. "Am I not fair?"

No. Not quite as bottomless as the sea. Muire did what she did for me. For all of us. Not in spite of us.

"You are those things and more," he told the goddess. He felt the hesitation leave him, and smiled. "But you are not anyone that I could have loved, and you will have nothing more from me that you do not take. You will certainly not have the place of the woman who gave her life for me."

"You condemn your Astrid to death."

He laughed behind gritted teeth. "I release myself to history. Now get off my beach, get out of my world, and take your seductions elsewhere. If you please. *Pet.*"

The expression on her face was all the warning he got. *Oh. This is going to hurt.*

She struck. A backhanded blow loosened teeth and split his cheek open. He grunted, rocked backwards.

He raised his hands, settling into a fighting crouch. *One,* he thought, the way he had learned as a child. To occupy your mind, and because sometimes he would ask how many times, and you would have to know, or he would think you hadn't been paying attention.

"Good," she taunted. "Strike me, pet. Fight me."

His nails pressed into his palms. He ached to hit her, crush her, make her hurt. To assert his power over her. *I am going to find a way to make you pay for what you did to my son.*

"I couldn't hurt you," he said, remembering the lithe capability in her body, the easy force with which she'd straight-armed him against the door of his house with her fingertips.

She smiled, eyes sparkling in the darkness like the moonlit sea. "It might be amusing if you tried."

He forced his hands open, stood straight, looked her dead in the eye. "I'm not interested in amusing you."

"How about serving me in other ways? I know you want to hit me. Wipe this smile off my face. . . ." It widened, and she curled the fingers of both hands toward herself, a beckoning gesture.

He shook his head, rearranging his face until he hoped he looked amused. *I just have to keep her here long enough for the cavalry to arrive. No fear,* he thought. *Nothing to be scared of, Cahey. It's just a little pain. . . .*

"You can't hit me," she taunted. "You're a coward."

"I won't hit you," he said, and let his hands fall limp at his sides.

Her next blow was a kick, direct to the diaphragm, and then another that was aimed at his chin but took him in the shoulder as he twisted aside. He nearly swung back at her but asserted himself, chose not to.

Two, three.

He knew how this worked. When they were that much stronger than you, fighting only made it worse. He just had to take it, and just hope she didn't get bored or he didn't get unconscious before Cath and the girls got there.

Cathmar shouldn't have to bloody his hands with this. And there wasn't a thing in the world Cahey could do about it.

He licked his lips. "Would it be easier for you to justify this if I fought back? Because I'm not going to. Pet."

Her left fist thumped just under his rib cage. He doubled over, gagging, straightened up again.

Four.

He wasn't frightened anymore. The anger rushing through him was a clear stream, a powerful, directed river. *Is this what wrath feels like?*

Despite the channeled rage, he found his voice calm, infuriatingly level. "Would you feel better if you had an excuse to hit me?"

A kick to the side of the knee. Agony coupled with an awful crunching sound.

Five.

He gasped, somehow stayed on his feet, without the concentration to will the damage gone. "It's all about the power with you, isn't it? Breaking me. Owning Cath. Taking Muire's place . . . as if you ever could."

She laughed, wiping a spatter of blood off her cheek, necklace sparkling. "I am a goddess, pet."

"No," he said, earning another blow, *six,* "you *were* a goddess. Now you're a mean old bitch with control issues."

She broke his nose. He went down on one knee, Alvitr's sheath cracking on the stones.

Seven.

"You know," he said around the blood in his mouth. "*She* never had to lie to get me in bed with her."

Oh, that might have been a mistake.

The fury in her face cleared, but what replaced it made him cold all over. She grabbed him by the queue, tilted his head back, bent over him. She spoke in a low, controlled tone. "Summon your mistress, pet. Call her up. Maybe she can save you."

"No," he said. That was what she'd been after all along. Getting Muire to come to him. To her.

"Say her name!" She doubled fist into fist, swung upward with her shoulder in it. The blow connected under his chin. He toppled backwards on the cold stone.

Eight.

Her words came in rhythm with the blows. "Call her. Damn you. Say her name."

nine

ten

eleven

twelve . . .

He lost count.

Stone chill against his face, he wondered bitterly if she'd counted on his ability to take a beating, or if she really intended to kill him with her hands.

The second time a rib snapped, he had to assume she did. He tried to roll away, and she kicked him again. "Get up, you son of a bitch," she snarled. "Get up and fight me!"

"No," he said around the taste of blood. "I'm not going to bait your trap."

Then her boot struck his temple, and it didn't hurt much anymore. *This is what Mingan intended the Imogen for,* he realized. *This fight. She told me she was a weapon, and I never listened.*

The enraged goddess stood over him. He had a clear view of her boots, blue leather smeared with his blood. He thought it was a fitting image, and would have chuckled if he could have drawn breath. Pain lanced through his right side, though, and there was more blood in his mouth than there should have been.

Punctured lung, he thought, and the moonlit sky overhead went red.

Light," Selene said, watching the struggling figures by the chapel on the bluff. No. Not struggling. One attacking. The other—unresisting. Getting hit.

"Come *on!*" Cathmar yelled, lurching forward, out from under the eaves of the little cottage with the blue tile roof. Selene's quick ears picked up what he said next, barely aloud. "Come on, angel steed; we need you now." She glanced over at Aethelred, who jerked his chin after the boy. Aithne was already running in pursuit.

Bright One, she prayed, *hear Cathmar and bring Mingan back fast.*

"Go," Aethelred said.

She didn't nod, just pelted after the other two, a long forever as they crossed the beach, an eternity scrabbling up the trail behind in a shower of small stones.

She would have run Cath over if she hadn't checked herself. As it was, she reached the top of the bluff overlooking the ocean a half-stride behind him, hitting Heythe low—claws and teeth bared—a second after Cathmar hit her high, grabbing at her throat.

For all the help that gave them. The goddess shrugged the angels aside as if they were irritable puppies. Cathmar struck the paving stones neck and shoulders first and Selene didn't see him trying to rise. Being Selene, and once Black Silk, *she* landed on her feet and came up with Solbiort in her hand, but the crystal sword stayed dark.

She had enough time to see the goddess backhand Aithne across the face, sending her sprawling, Sceadhu gouging sparks out of the flagstones. *Aithne* had had the sense to draw her blade before she piled into Heythe, not that it helped.

"That will do you no good," Heythe said calmly, her eyes meeting Selene's. "But you're welcome to try it."

Far below, the ocean tossed and hissed and tore.

"Yes," Heythe said. She turned her back on Selene and walked over to the edge of the bluff. Spreading her arms wide, she looked out at the moonlit sea. "Well," she said, "come and get me, then. Save them. Your lover, your friends, your son. All you have to do . . . is intervene."

Over the ocean, something began to shine. Light rippled, pooling as if everything else fell into shadow and all the radiance were drawn to one place, one point. What rose up from the sea, then, was enormous: serpentine but not a serpent, a fell tendriled beast wrought of Light.

Looming over the chapel and the bluff, casting a light instead of a shadow, she *hissed.*

Selene knew her by her eyes.

"Muire," she said. "Holy fuck."

Which is when a motion caught her eye, and she saw the

figure—gleaming with chrome—stagger down the beach to the sea, far below.

Aethelred scrambled across the moonlit sand, racing the stronger figures scaling the cliff trail. He was glad they had left him—glad and sorrowful, for they never would have permitted what he intended, but he would have liked to say farewell.

He saw the Wyrm come out of the water, and he cursed his slow feet. *Hurry, old man, hurry.*

"One last favor for my kids," he muttered, as he splashed into the surf, shoes and all.

The Wyrm coiled her head back, ready to strike a killing blow at the slender blond figure who taunted her with the lives of her loved ones, far overhead.

Aethelred drew breath deep and shouted her name. In midstrike, she pulled her blow. That great head slanted aside and struck only air.

"Muire!" he shouted. "Bearer of Burdens! By moonlight, earth and ocean, I summon you!"

Massive as a sledgehammer, the vast blunt nose swung down to him. SPEAK.

"I beg an intervention."

Cool mist enfolded him. Sorrowful, vast silver eyes filled up with starlight looked down into him. AETHELRED, she said. I WOULD HAVE HAD YOU SERVE ME LIVING, BRAVEST ONE.

"I'll serve you any way I can, old girl." He jerked his staff up at the slender blond figure raging on the cliff. "Her I won't serve at all."

You know the price. Aethelred thought he'd never heard anything as sad as her voice in that moment.

"The deal is made, my lady," he answered. Across the ocean, a great wave was building. He saw the swell, felt the undertow suck at his legs as it came.

He closed his eyes. He heard an enraged feline yowl—Selene screaming, somewhere very far away.

The water fell over him.

Although distracted by the figure on the beach, Selene hoped to see the Grey Wolf step out of the shadows, catch Heythe by the throat, end her life with a gesture.

Around the hope, Selene knew that this enemy was beyond even Mingan's power.

And then she understood what Aethelred was doing.

"Aethelred, *NO!*" She almost went over the cliff, as if in some bizarre supposition that she could reach him in time. Cathmar, prone on the flags, apparently conscious after all, grabbed her ankle and she fell hard, facedown on the stones.

She rolled aside in time to see what happened.

There was blood on the Wyrm's insubstantial face when she rose once more.

An intervention has been purchased. Heythe, would you still trade blows with me now?

On the sharpness of nausea Selene realized that that was what Mingan and Aethelred wouldn't tell anybody. That any of them could buy Muire's intervention with a life.

I was the price the Wolf wouldn't pay.

"All right," Heythe said, with a cold satisfaction. "Not what

I bargained to buy, and a harder battle, but I can fight this war, too."

Selene swore she saw the Serpent smile.

And Selene's heart locked hard in her chest when she saw Heythe smile in return, reach out into the silver-white Light surrounding the Wyrm, grab and twist and *pull.*

The Light shredded and stretched, settling around the goddess' shoulder like a cloak, threading her hair. Gold, darker and richer than the pure moonlit blue of the Wyrm's aura, spread creeping feelers along the Light. *Where's her necklace?* Selene squinted into the brightness, but Heythe's neck shone naked ivory in the tangled light.

Heythe faced the Wyrm, bound in unspoken struggle. Radiance surrounded both, blue-white shot through with golden threads. It pulsed like a heartbeat, and now the Wyrm's white Light predominated, and now Heythe's hard hot light like the sun.

Heythe faced the Wyrm. The wrong direction to notice the bloody figure of Cahey dragging himself to his feet. Selene, nearly taking a half step forward, saw him reach down and painfully fumble Alvitr's peace strings loose before dragging her from her broken sheath.

Selene didn't dare move, lest she catch Heythe's peripheral vision and cause her to turn her head.

Slowly, silently, blood that gleamed black in the moonlight bubbling from his mouth, Cahey came up behind the goddess. Selene held her breath.

He stalked Heythe like a cat stalking a bird. The pounce was catlike, too: in an instant, he clutched a fistful of golden hair in his left hand, laid the blade of his sword across her throat, and dragged her head back.

Selene's quick ears picked the words out of his amused whisper. "I wondered, 'pet,' why you never *would* kiss me." Blue eyes flared, starlit. He crushed his blood-slick mouth down on hers.

Freed, the Wyrm's head snapped back as if yanked on a string, moonlight a cobra's hood flaring around it.

Heythe convulsed, twisting away, breaking her throat open on Alvitr as she tore free of his grip. The wound vanished before it was more than a line of blood; she faced Cahey, panting.

"Gone," she said. "It's not in you anymore."

"Muire's soul?" He laughed and then spat blood on the stones, leaning on his sword. The point of her crystal blade bit into the rock. "No," he said. "You're safe from that. If only I'd known it could have hurt you, but . . . I gave it to a friend."

Heythe spun on her heel, reaching out again to take hold of the silvery Light.

Imogen, the Wyrm said. Attend me, trickster's daughter.

Ascending from the water, wide wings spread behind the Wyrm's head like an obsidian crown, eyes gleaming like the jewels set in it, the Imogen came.

"Lady," the Imogen said.

You see what must be done.

"I am not commanded," the Imogen answered. "And yet I obey."

Silently, those wings bore her down to Heythe, who coiled

herself for combat. Selene saw them brush Cahey, standing close, cheek and shoulder—a caress?

The Imogen smiled, eyes like lamps in the darkness of her lovely inhuman face.

"It won't avail you," Heythe said calmly. "I am a goddess, you know."

"And I am the thing in the mirror," the Imogen replied in a steady, disinterested tone. "Your greatest wish." Slow, strong wingbeats held her balanced in the ocean updraft. "Your darkest fear. I am the infinite void, filled by an infinite light, and I am beyond even you."

Heythe reached up to place a hand at her throat. Her eyes went wide when she realized what wasn't there.

It was over in less than a second.

The Imogen struck like a living knife, and the goddess never screamed. She came apart, a torn feather-pillow, consumed in an instant, bones and blood raining into the sea.

Daintily, horribly, the Imogen dabbed her lips with her fingers.

Selene looked away from her, away from the Wyrm. Crouched, reached down to help Cathmar stand, and crossed the flagstones to Cahey, sagging against the hilt of his sword.

He looked up. "Aithne," he said.

"All right," Aithne answered, picking herself up on her elbows. "Seemed like a smart time to stay down."

"Can you heal yourself?" Selene asked Cahey. She glanced around for the Imogen, breathed a sigh of relief that the demoness had silently vanished.

"Given a dull moment." He looked down along the length of his body. Selene heard the crackling of twisted bones straightening, and he stood up straight for a second and smiled before he folded, limp, exhausted, into her arms.

She cushioned his fall, sat down on the stones, and laid his bloody head in her lap.

Aithne clambered to her feet, helped by Cathmar, and limped over. The head of the great Wyrm hung over them, watching, lighting their way.

Cathmar sat down beside Selene and the unconscious Cahey and leaned his head against her shoulder. He looked up at the Wyrm, met her pale gray eyes. She felt him take a deep, slow breath.

"Mom," he said. "It's nice to finally meet you."

BELOVED, she answered. EVERY ONE OF YOU DESERVES BETTER. BUT I GIVE YOU WHAT IS MINE TO GIVE.

"Why didn't you intervene . . . before Aethelred, you know . . . ?" Cathmar's voice trailed off.

She shook her head, a great slow pendulum that sent a ripple down her fleshless neck. I'M NOT FOR INTERVENTION, MY LOVE. I'M FOR ENDURANCE, UNDERSTANDING AND REBIRTH. YOU AND YOUR SORT, YOU'RE THE HANDS AND EYES AND BRAINS AND BALLS OF THE WORLD. I'M JUST ITS HEART. IF YOU WISH ME TO INTERVENE, I MUST BE SUMMONED, AND A DEAL MUST BE STRUCK. SACRIFICES MUST BE MADE. PROPITIATION.

AND INTERVENTION OPENS ME TO ATTACK, AS WELL. IT'S THE WAY THE RULES WORK, YOU SEE.

"But . . . why didn't you summon the Imogen sooner?"

CAHEY. ONCE HE FREED HER, ANY POWER I HAD TO SUMMON HER VANISHED. AND WITHOUT WHAT HE GAVE HER, EVEN SHE COULD NOT HAVE CHALLENGED THIS ONE.

Selene looked over at the blood-slicked flagstones. She

glanced back up at Muire, a complex question in the set of her ears and whiskers. *Why did she come, then?* Except, more than that.

The thing in Selene that had been trapped in servitude herself had to know.

I SUSPECT, Muire answered, with a flicker of amusement, SHE THOUGHT SHE OWED SOMEONE A FAVOR.

Cathmar laughed. He held up his right hand in a fist, rolled the last three fingers open to let something sparkling in rainbow colors dangle free. "Mom, you want this? I paid for it, I guess it's mine to give."

Before she could answer, a thunder of wings broke the darkness, and Selene tensed, forgetting for a moment that the Imogen's made no more sound than a whisper. Selene looked up and breathed a sigh of relief. "Mingan," she said, as the white stallion bore his rider down.

KEEP IT, the Wyrm said to her son. AS YOU SAID, BELOVED— YOU'VE PAID.

Hooves clattered on the paving stones as the valraven furled his wings. He bowed his heads to the great Serpent as his rider slid down his shoulder, landing in the courtyard with a tired-sounding thump.

Mingan strode over to where Selene and Cathmar sat, Aithne standing beside them. "Does he live?" he asked, indicating Cahey with a negligent flick of gloved fingers.

"Yes," Aithne said.

"Good." He glanced around at the Wyrm, the bloodied and sword-scarred stones, the silence and peace of the night. The great Serpent nodded over him.

"Muire," he said. "All is well?"

THE THREAT IS ENDED, she answered. YOUR SERVICE . . . IS HONORED.

He drew a breath. Only Selene noticed the grief in his smile. He inclined his head, as if waiting for Muire to continue.

AND FAREWELL. The Wyrm nodded once more, writhed, and twisted into the ocean in a puddle of Light.

Mingan sighed, squared his shoulders, and turned back to Selene. Their eyes met. She gestured to the unconscious einherjar in her lap. "You did it," she said.

Mingan quirked an eyebrow and allowed his lips to arch in a cold sort of mirth. " 'Twill serve," he answered, turning away.

52 A.R.
On the First Day of Winter

Far out at sea, the wake of a jet watercraft curled phosphorescent in the darkness. Cahey turned to follow its track until it was out of sight, wondering. More than five decades since Muire gave herself to the ocean, and almost two and a half millennia since he died on a snow-covered clifftop, dragged down like a stag by a pack of dogs.

Something squirmed under his jacket. He pressed his left arm against his abdomen to keep it from sliding out the bottom of the coat, then stopped in his footsteps, nauseated by the sudden, vividly kinetic memory of his own guts spilling hot and slick over his hands. *That's why we don't remember our past lives,* he thought. *Well, one reason among thousands.*

"Shhh," he whispered to the squirming wolf-cub, "soon, soon. You're supposed to be a surprise."

His lover, his enemy, his rival, his savior—Mingan the Grey Wolf waited at the foot of the bluff upon which he raised a chapel to honor the sacrifice of a woman they had both loved, and whom neither of them could keep.

Muire, who was Muire the Historian once, and Muire the

poet and sculptress later, and Muire the Angel-who-went-into-the-Sea last of all.

And then she was a goddess, and beyond their reach.

The sea that she had sacrificed herself to hissed, moonlit, on the sand at his feet. *She can be summoned on a night like this.* Cahey steeled himself for what he meant to do.

"Brother," he said, though his voice did not carry as it should.

The Wolf turned from the ocean slowly, his eyes meeting Cahey's as Cathoair walked up to him, bare feet splashing in the borders of the breakers.

"Cathoair," he answered. There were centuries in his voice that Cahey never understood before, and a loneliness that ached like a blister on Cahey's heart. "Selene said you summoned me."

Cahey hadn't an answer, and so he stood and watched the starlight fill up the Wolf's eyes. The wind shifted slightly and his nostrils flared, tasting it. Cahey suspected it gave him only the aroma of the sea, rich and complex as the fragrance of a woman, but he noticed the resumed squirming under Cahey's clothes. One eyebrow inched up his timeworn face in a silent question.

Cahey unzipped his jacket and produced the wolf-cub. "Her eyes aren't open yet," he said, holding her out to the Wolf. "She's too young to be away from her mother, but her mother is dead, and all her siblings. Put her in your cloak before she chills."

The Wolf's mouth opened to argue. But he closed it and lifted the wolf-cub out of Cahey's hands and swaddled her close to the inhuman heat of his breast. "Where . . . ?"

"She was the only survivor of her pack," Cahey said. "Forest fire. Her mother died atop her."

"You were . . . fighting the fire?"

"It can't burn me. Useful for things like that."

"Ah." He turned away, hiding his face. "I know how to raise a wolf-cub," he said. "I'll see to her."

"It's time you had a pack again," Cahey answered. "That's what I mean to say. Beyond your steed and Selene, I mean. When are you going to come back to the rest of us?"

He turned back, startled. "You remember?"

Cahey cleared his throat, embarrassed by the intensity of the Wolf's regard. "Whether it was you, or the Imogen . . . yes. I remember. Fragments. Like childhood, or something that happened to somebody else. Just fragments."

"Then you remember why I was never welcomed among the children of the Light."

Cahey turned his gaze out to the shining sea. "You've changed and they've changed, Wolf. And the world—that has changed most of all."

The Wolf fell silent. The cub, contented by the smell or the warmth of him, stopped squirming.

"We need a Cynge, Mingan, or a war-leader, or something like it. Someone all the einherjar and waelcyrge can agree to follow, with the wit and the courage to lead us."

"That has never been my role, Cahey."

Cahey's laugh burned low in his throat. "No. It was mine, and I bitched it up. You can hardly do worse than I did."

"You do not understand. They will not follow me."

"They'll have to," he answered. "At least for a little while. I have something else to do."

He took a breath and turned away from Mingan, toward the ocean. He spoke on a rush, because that was what he must do to get the words out. "By moonlight, earth and ocean, Muire, I summon thee."

Mingan took a sharp breath.

The moonlight on the rippled water pooled, coalesced, and she came out of it—small, slight, her dirty blond hair cropped even with her shoulder and her eyes gleaming with liquid silver. "My faithful ones," she said, in a woman's voice, leaving the goddess behind for now. She smiled with what seemed simple joy. "It is . . . good . . . to see you together."

She came almost up to the strand, close enough to touch if they both reached out their hands. "I've come to deal with thee," Cahey said—words of an ancient ritual.

Muire took a single harsh breath. Cahey saw the rise and fall of her chest. "Your life, Cathoair? Are you so tired of it already, when we fought so hard to win it back for you?"

"No," Cahey answered, not thinking, just speaking. "Not tired of it. But this my brother"—and somehow, it was not quite Cahey's voice, his phrasing, anymore, but his and Strifbjorn's together—"has a need, and I beg an intervention to meet that need."

She pursed her lips. Mingan moved as if to step between them, but Cahey stopped him with a raised palm.

"I need your help, Muire," Cahey said into the silence, his voice his own again. "I want that fucking collar off him, and I'm willing to pay whatever you need paid to do it."

"Ah," she whispered, at the same moment Mingan said, "No!" and caught Cahey's wrist in the hand that was not cradling the cloak-swaddled cub. That hand, in its gray glove, was shaking.

"I will not permit it. Think of thy woman and of thy son."

Cahey raised both eyebrows. "Mingan, they know. They don't approve, precisely, but they know. And so does Selene. This isn't like the last time."

"No?"

He shook his head. "I can . . . repay you, somewhat. Give you the freedom you've never had. And I know I'll be back again. Soon, if I have anything to say about it."

"Back as someone else. It is not how we need thee."

Cahey laughed at him and reached out with the hand he was not already clutching, lacing his fingers into the Wolf's hair and pulling his mouth up to a kiss that he resisted and then leaned into. His mouth was as hot as Cahey remembered it—with his own memories and those of another, burning and wet. *How unfair, that these wars can never end in rest. Not for him. Not for me.*

"Mingan, you utter fool," Cahey said when they broke, noses almost touching. "You have the power to make me remember."

Mingan let go of Cahey's wrist, his hand rising to his throat. The cord still choked him with every breath. "It won't be you. It won't be fair, either, to whoever you become."

Cahey looked aside. "So ask him when you find him. Maybe he'll say yes."

"Nay," Mingan said, but Cahey knew him well enough to know that he meant "yes."

"Done," said the goddess. "Cahey, get that thing off of him, if you please."

Cahey took his hand from Mingan's throat and unlaced the collar of his shirt. "Do you trust me?"

He shivered when Cahey's fingers brushed his skin. "Aye. With my life."

"You will find me and give me your kiss?"

"With the last breath in my body."

Cahey's fingers were outlined against the pearlescent light of the ribbon, the collar. Slowly, they took on a silvery brilliance of their own. The knot was snarled tight. There were wolf-hairs caught in it, hairs that had endured all these centuries since he was bound. Cahey's fingers were not nimble enough to free it, so he had to bend down and use his teeth, the heat of Mingan's body like a brand against his face.

The warm metal of Mingan's earring brushed Cahey's cheek, which triggered another vivid memory—this one his own. Mingan stood shivering like a coyote in a leg trap, a little whine in the back of his throat. His breathing was a labored hiss—Cahey was strangling him, but he stood firm and did not flinch. *Hush, Brother. This will not hurt for long.*

Cahey hoped it would prove true of himself as well, but what's a little pain? *How bad can dying be?* He choked on a laugh as the knot began to slip: he knew the answer better than most.

The ribbon snaked free at last and Cahey straightened. Mingan's gaze crossed his for a moment, and then he closed his eyes.

Cahey slipped the bit of cloth into Mingan's hand and turned back to the sea.

"Ready as I'll ever be." His farewells were made, with the hope that they were farewells only and not good-byes.

"Then I claim my price," she said, and—unexpectedly—she smiled. He trusted her. He knew what she had sacrificed, and what she had endured, and if there were ever a truly incorruptible soul in all the world, then it was hers.

Her eyes were sorrowful and deep as the sea. Cahey put his hand on Alvitr's hilt, drawing comfort from the knotted pommel of the blade. "Muire, I'm ready to do it myself. I don't want you to have to . . ." *live with that.*

Cahey knew a little too much about it to wish that responsibility on anyone.

She shook her head and held out her hands to him. He took a step toward her, took her hands in his. Mingan stood silent witness behind them.

"Kiss me," she said, and Cahey ducked his head to offer her his lips. Diminutive as she ever was, although a figure wrought of Light, now, and not flesh, she strained on tiptoe to reach him. Her mouth brushed his, soft as a sea breeze, and he let his lips drift open, waiting for the soul-searing rush of his breath and his *self* out of his body.

It did not come. There was pain—the pain of a thing too holy for bearing, that kiss like a brand stroked across his mouth—and there was glory, but there was no *taking.* She let go of his hands—lover, friend, goddess, mother of his son— and stepped away into the sea. "You give me your life, child of the Light, and I give it back to you. Go and lead my angels, einherjar, the way you were always meant to."

He caught a breath in his throat. "But . . ."

"The price is a life, not a death, Cathoair, as I well have reason to know. You're grown-up and powerful now, the thing you were always meant to be. Why would I want to start over?"

"I don't want to be a general," he told her at last. "I never wanted to be that." Not in either life.

She drifted back to him then, as if tossed on the waves, and her hand burned like too-strong sunlight where she stroked his face. "Then be a father to them. But a leader they must have, and that, my dear, is who you were made to be."

Cahey took a breath to fight her on it, and the words would not quite come out. *I gave her my life.*

Her gaze held him fast. "Now go and do my will."

Mingan looked at Cahey and Cahey looked at Mingan. He glanced down at the bit of ribbon, just a shred of cloth now, soiled and dark. "Oh," Cahey said, remembering the years Mingan spent arguing this role with his former self.

He drew a deep breath full of Mingan's scent and the scent of the sea. He stepped out of the water and strolled up the few short steps across the sand to face him. He looked down at the ribbon again, examined Mingan's face, and then turned to look at the sea.

Mingan raised his hand and let the scrap slide off. It drifted out to sea—against the prevailing wind. When it had fluttered out of sight, he trained his eyes on Cahey's and smiled, ever so slightly. "You dealt," he said. "Now pay."

Cahey heard Muire laughing softly, fading away as the Light died out of the water—or perhaps it was just the murmur of the sea.

Cahey raised an eyebrow at Mingan, reaching out to flip his braid behind his shoulder, stepping close enough to taste the heat of his breath. Salt from his skin flavored Cahey's lips; Cahey recognized the slight crinkle at the corner of Mingan's eyes as his truest smile.

"Mingan."

"Aye, Cathoair?" His shirt collar lay open, and already the bruises were fading from marble-white skin.

Cathoair kissed the Grey Wolf's cheek and stepped away, there by the border of the sea. "You've made amends, you old dragon. I think perhaps that it's not that you've changed. I think the world has. You will be welcome in any hall."

The Grey Wolf's forehead wrinkled unbelievingly. "Thou hast not the power to make that happen."

"Oh, but I do," Cahey said. "Selene and I between us? No one will cross us." He grinned, and patted Mingan on the shoulder. "Time to live with just being one of the guys, old man."

Mingan shook his head, cradling the silent pup closer to his belly. "A wolf is nothing without his pack."

Cahey placed a hand on his shoulder and turned him back, back toward the cottage with the blue roof, and a light burning in the window. "See? That's what I've been trying to tell you. Come on. There's tea inside, and Selene and Aithne are waiting."